**What some early readers had to say about *Political Dirty Trick***

***Political Dirty Trick*** is tight, ... the characters are engaging, and the tension is real. It reads like a fast-paced James Patterson cliffhanger.
— Mystery and Thriller writer William Doonan

awesome suspense ...
—Author Steve Sebatka

Great characters ...
—Author John Lindermuth

Very exciting ... Callan has a
marvelous talent for dialogue ...
—Author Elaine Faber

Praise for the previous Crystal Moore Suspense book number two,
***A Silver Medallion***

*"A Silver Medallion* is a gripping, action-packed adventure from talented author James Callan. Crystal Moore is a tough and savvy heroine …"
—**New York Times Bestselling Author Bobbi Smith**

*"A Silver Medallion,* the second title in the Crystal Moore Suspense series, reads like a gold-medal thriller from page one …"
—**From BookLife Prize in Fiction, Critic's Report**

*"A Silver Medallion* … is the thrilling sequel to A Ton of Gold. ... The page-turning suspense kept me up well into the pre-morning! …"
—**Alyssa Elmore for Readers' Favorite (On Barnes & Nobel)**

**A Silver Medallion**

# Political
# Dirty Trick

# Political Dirty Trick

A Crystal Moore Suspense Novel

James R. Callan

ISBN 13:    978-1-7321227-0-3
ISBN 10:      1-7321227-0-9
LCCN: Applied for

# Dedication

This is dedicated to Earlene, without whose support, and tolerance this book would not exist.

# Political Dirty Trick

## Chapter 1

### Saturday, March 24

**She crept into** the room, a mere shadow. No sound. No trace of her presence. The small flashlight she pulled from her pocket produced only a slight glow, hardly noticeable from across the room, invisible from outside. But it revealed the major objects in the room: a desk, two chairs. And the Mondrian. She studied the painting for a moment. *Why would anyone pay big bucks for this nonsense? With a canvas, a paint pallet and a bottle of vodka, I could produce the same thing in an hour or two. Would anyone pay me three hundred thou for it? Not a chance.*

No one was in the house, yet she moved with care to lift the painting off the wall. Lighter than she expected and only about three feet square. She turned and glided out of the room. Except for the missing painting, nothing had been disturbed, not even the dust. She made her way down the short hall and into the kitchen, headed out the way she came in.

She froze.

A noise, ever so slight, came from the back door. A key slipped into a lock.

The owner, at a campaign rally, shouldn't be home for another hour. Light flooded the entry room and she heard footsteps coming toward the kitchen, toward her. The room was still dark, but her eyes had become accustomed to the low light. Her mind raced as fast as her heartbeat. She started forward, then stopped. Back toward the study would leave her exposed in the hall.

The only other exit was a door on her left. She opened it. A pantry. She slipped in, and eased it shut just as the kitchen lit up.

The person walked as if familiar with the house, confident of the surroundings. Leather soles. Heavy. Probably a man. He hesitated. She held her breath. What if he opened this door? Her flashlight was too small for a weapon. The muscles in her body tightened like a boa constrictor.

The person moved on, headed down the hall. She waited, mentally counting off the number of seconds she had taken to reach the office. *Please let him go into the living room.*

She waited ten seconds, eased open the door. Light spilled from the study. She stepped out of the pantry, painting in hand. Before she could close the pantry door, she heard leather shoes pivot on hardwood floors. Now the steps had more purpose, as the man started back. She looked at the lights and the distance to the back door and took the only safe route: back into the pantry. She had just closed the door when the man reentered the kitchen.

The bright lights had destroyed her night vision and now she could see nothing. But she could hear. The man stopped, and began punching numbers into a telephone.

# Chapter 2

**"That's why I'm** running for governor and that's what I'll try to do if elected."

A reporter for an online newspaper called out. "Mr. Drake, you said you'd *try*. Your opponent says he'll *deliver*. That makes him more decisive, doesn't it?"

Ron Drake, sixty-six years old with heaps of silver hair atop a trim body, smiled at the young woman. "I'd be more inclined to say it shows he doesn't have much experience with government. Whoever becomes governor has a bully pulpit, a lot of contacts, and a little sway - *if* he won by a landslide. He can suggest a direction. But if my opponent thinks he can push around 181 strong willed Texans, well..." He gave a soft laugh. "Well, he must not have lived in Texas very long."

The woman tried again. "Your opponent—"

Ron interrupted. "Doris, I don't want to talk about my opponent. Jim Bob is a nice guy. But I'm not going to give him any more of *my* press time. If you've got a question about the programs I'm proposing, let's hear 'em."

A man from the *Dallas Morning News* spoke up. "Mr. Drake, why do you put education ahead of law enforcement? A number of people think that's a big mistake. The Texas Rangers don't agree with you on that front."

"For one simple reason, Johnny. If we educate our children well enough, law enforcement will be a lot easier. If we teach our children the difference between right and wrong, give them a proper moral compass, then crime goes down, traffic accidents go down, even parking tickets go down. Law enforcement gets easier. And maybe we get back to the days of 'One Riot; one Ranger.'" He shifted his gaze to include all the reporters. "I'm totally for more law officers *now*. But the solution for the long range is education. A return to moral principles."

Crystal Moore couldn't help but grin. Ron Drake was one of her grandmother's best friends and had been for a long time. Crystal had known him all her life. Still, she marveled at the easy way he handled questions, never getting flustered, apparently never offended, and never without a sensible answer. She had heard him at three press conferences. Not once had he trashed his opponent, Jim Bob Wilson, and Wilson was an easy target to trash.

Within a few minutes, Drake ended the press conference and moved away from the podium. "Hi, Crystal. What are you doing here? Surely you've heard me talk enough over the years."

Crystal stepped forward and gave the slender, six foot politician a hug. "Nana wanted me to come and hear what you had to say to the locals. I can report back it was a fantastic speech. And your answers satisfied even the pickiest reporter."

He laughed. "They just want a sound bite. But why didn't Eula come herself?"

"She's got Melva and a couple of other friends over for Mexican Train. Had it planned before she knew you were making a campaign stop here. Wooden Nickel doesn't rate that attention very often. Why don't you come over for a bit. She made fried pies. First blackberries of the season."

"Mighty tempting. But I'm supposed to hang around here for another hour, in case someone wants a picture or something, though I can't imagine why anyone would."

Crystal laughed."Because you're the hot ticket, the next governor."

"Candidate. Only a candidate."

"With speeches like that, and your terrific platform, a raft of people think the governorship is in your pocket. And I agree."

He smiled at the granddaughter of one of his best friends. "Not so fast. You know what they say: 'It ain't over 'til –'"

Crystal immediately started singing. "It's a great day for shining your shoes."

He laughed. "Sorry, Crystal. But you do *not* qualify as the 'fat lady.' The election is still seven months away. A lot can happen."

"And I'm sure a lot will. But it won't change the outcome. The election is yours. But, I'll be glad to help you any way I can."

"I never turn down help. You can lend a hand out here in east Texas. My campaign office seems to think only the mega-cities count." He glanced down at Crystal's wrist. "Is that a newfangled watch or something?"

Crystal lifted her arm up. "No. This is a fitness bracelet. Tells me how far I've walked each day. I'm trying for 10,000 steps a day."

"Sounds like a lot to me. Surely you're not trying to lose weight?" Crystal, standing five feet seven inches tall and with a nice figure, tipped the scales at one hundred eighteen pounds. Her black hair reached just below her ears.

"No, no. But since I sit at a desk hunched over a computer a lot when I'm at work, I need to get in some exercise. I'm not much on going to the gym. So I try to walk a lot. You should try it."

He chuckled. "That's for you young kids, I'll —." *The Eyes of Texas* began playing, and Drake reached into his pocket and pulled out his cell phone. He tapped the screen and the music stopped. "Hello, Nat. What's up?"

* * *

The thief could hear the man talking on the phone.

"Mr. Drake. You haven't moved the Mondrian have you?" A moment of silence. "Well, it's gone." Another pause. "I mean it's not in the study where it usually is. I went in to put those papers you wanted on your desk. First thing I saw was a blank space on the wall where it usually hangs."

Her heart was pounding so hard she was afraid the man could hear it. She took a deep, silent, breath. *Calm down.* Drake was still at the rally. This man would leave. She would have plenty of time to slip out before Drake returned. *Relax. It will be okay. Deep breaths.*

"Yes sir." The man was talking again. "I'll wait right here. How long before you get home? Fifteen minutes? Okay. I'll help myself to a Dr Pepper and wait."

Drake should be at his rally for another hour. It was supposed to be two hours, and those things never ended on time anyway. Fifteen minutes meant he was leaving right now.

She heard the refrigerator door open, close, and then the fizz as a soda can popped opened. *Go back into the office*, she willed. *I'm sure you'll find a much more comfortable chair there.*

Instead, she heard the creaking of a chair as the man sat down beside the kitchen table.

## Chapter 3

***Calm down. Make*** *a plan. You're good at that.* But her heart raced in double time. If she got caught—and if she stayed here she would get caught— she'd be looking at grand theft. It wouldn't be a prank, a political dirty trick. This was an expensive painting. Of course, that's why she chose it.

She cracked the door open a quarter inch. The man sat with his back to her, relaxed, apparently not planning to move until Drake got home. She could almost sneak out without him knowing it. Except the painting would scrape on something, or the floor would squeak. Some small noise, just enough to make him turn and see her. With the Mondrian.

What if she could knock him out for a couple of minutes? She glanced around in the pantry. Even with the door open a crack, her vision wasn't good, but she could pick out bags of sugar, flour, coffee filters, canned goods, a broom. A broom! She could hit him over the head with the wooden handle. But would that knock him out? Probably only wake him up, make him mad, alert him that she had the painting. She picked up the sack of sugar. No. Too soft. She turned her attention to another shelf. She picked up a big can. It felt heavy enough. And solid.

Even as her heart raced, she moved slowly. She knew the slightest sound in the silent house would grab his attention. The door opened without a squeak. *Three steps, that's all I need.* Her soft, rubber-soled shoes did not make a sound. She raised the can. A medium tap was all she needed. Her arm started down.

At that instant, he turned his head, beginning to look around in her direction. She brought her hand down faster. His sudden movement foiled her aim and instead of hitting the back of his head, the can slammed into his right temple.

The Dr Pepper can slipped from his fingers and fell to the floor, spilling brown liquid across the clean tile. The man slumped forward, tumbled from the chair, hitting his head on the counter before landing on the floor.

The thief studied him for a few seconds. She thought about checking his pulse, but didn't want to touch him. *He's definitely out.* She stepped back into the closet. She glanced at the can as she set it back on the shelf. Stewed tomatoes. With her gloves on, there would be no fingerprints. She grabbed the Mondrian and took one last look at the man. Still out. *I didn't hit him that hard. He won't be out long and I'm sure he'll be okay.* In less than thirty seconds from the time he hit the floor, she was out the back door.

Three minutes later, the thief was in her car, slowly driving away. She smiled. She remembered the times she had sneaked up on her dad. He said she was like a shadow, passing over things without disturbing anything, not making a sound. She had been a shadow tonight. At least she was until that man came in. And then he wouldn't leave. But when he woke up, he wouldn't remember her. He didn't see her. He didn't hear her. He wouldn't have any idea why he fell over and hit his head on the counter.

Her mind wandered to her meeting with George Weeks ten days ago, the meeting that got this whole thing started.

# Chapter 4

**Wednesday, March 14**
**Ten days earlier**

**"Wow. Look at** these numbers. Old Drake really started fast out of the box," she said.

"He's going to be tough. I won't say this to any of the guys at campaign headquarters, but I don't think Jim Bob has any chance of catching him."

"Come on, George. There's over seven months to go. Things are just getting started." Ginnie Leverett wore a red jumpsuit that stopped at mid thigh, and red boots. At thirty-five and divorced, the tall, slim brunette needed something new and different to be involved in. She chose the Texas governor's race. Working for Jim Bob Wilson's campaign enlivened her ho-hum life.

George Weeks shook his head. "Drake is just better. Has the experience. Has more money. People like him."

"There must be some angle we can work to get Jim Bob in as governor."

"I don't know. Short of a really good Podirt, I'm afraid Jim Bob is going to lose. By a lot."

Ginnie cocked her head, looking puzzled. "Podirt. What's that?"

"Sorry. Forgot you're new to this. It's a Political Dirty Trick. Something that drags your opponent's numbers down like they had a cement anchor attached."

She frowned. "Like what?"

"Oh, like digging up an illegitimate child, or a problem with the IRS. Or faking some award or military service."

Ginnie was shaking her head. "Is that legal?"

"Absolutely, if it's true."

She looked down and mulled this over. "Okay. I don't want to get into something that's illegal."

"You have to look at the situation from a political point of view. It's not something you'd do to an ordinary person. But when a person runs for office, they open themselves up to lots of scrutiny. Anything in their past is fair game. Doesn't make any difference how long ago or what the circumstances. I've done plenty of those in other campaigns."

Ginnie's frown showed her disapproval.

George Weeks smiled. "Nobody got hurt, except at the polls. I know I've made a difference in some elections."

"So, you make public he didn't pay his income tax and people realize he isn't the type of leader they want in the governor's office."

"Yeah. And military service is a big one. I remember one time a guy was really rising in the polls. He began to talk about his service in the Vietnam War, how horrible it was in the jungles and the brave things he did. I found out he was in the navy, but he never left San Diego. Once it went viral, he was toast."

"Why'd he do that?"

"Just dumb, when you get right down to it. He didn't need to pump up his credentials. But he got carried away. It's easy to do in a heated campaign. I think he began to believe it." He shook his head. "Stupid, though. Cost him the race."

"And you're saying we need a Podirt on Drake if Jim Bob's going to win."

"That's the idea. The problem is, Drake's a straight shooter. I don't think we could find anything like that. We have to come up with something that will sink him in the polls, but that doesn't have too much collateral damage."

"Like, if it was an illegitimate child like you mentioned. You don't want to expose them since they didn't do anything."

George's head wobbled and his mouth drew into a straight line. "Yeah. Something like that. But as they say, 'that ain't gonna happen.' I've looked already. Nothing. Drake really is one of the good guys."

"Any ideas at all?"

George looked away, but said nothing.

"What?"

"Nothing. Forget I mentioned it."

"Come on, George. What you got?"

For nearly a minute, the broad-shouldered man looked down as if he were studying his grey sport coat. Finally, he raised his head and looked at his trainee in Jim Bob's campaign office. "Drake owns a very expensive piece of art. A Mondrian. What if we could steal it?"

"Whoa. That sounds totally illegal."

George raised his eyebrows. "Think about this. Steal it and hide it in a mini-warehouse —rented under Drake's name." Now he smiled.

"So?"

"After awhile, you unlock the warehouse."

Ginnie's puzzled look remained. "And?"

"What can happen?"

She shook her head. "I don't know. How am I supposed to know?"

"Think about it. What can happen?"

She shrugged. "Somebody opens the door and finds it."

"And then what?"

"Well, they could recognize it and turn it over to the police. Or they could sell it and keep the money."

"Bingo. Suppose they turn it over to the police. When the Mondrian is stolen, Drake will get a ton of press on a major theft.

Lots of publicity. But then it turns up in his own warehouse." George's eyebrows shot up. "Oops. What was he trying to pull? The public will react badly. His numbers will sink."

Ginnie started to speak but George held up his hand and kept talking. "Or, the person who finds it, sells it. You can be sure the art police will track it down. The trail will still lead back to Drake's own warehouse, and the media will jump all over it." He spread his hands and smiled. "And here's the best scenario. Before it's found, the insurance pays Drake for his loss. Now, the doodoo *really* hits the fan. Insurance fraud. And much more. He's a loser now. Jim Bob wins."

"But Drake didn't actually do anything."

"Exactly. That's the beauty of this plan. He didn't do it. And eventually, his high-priced lawyer will make that clear, poke holes in whatever might be brought against Drake. So, in the end, Drake will get off all charges, and get his painting back. No problems. However, by then, he's lost the race. Jim Bob is the next governor."

Ginnie frowned, still trying to process this.

George looked pleased. "Don't you see. It's a perfect Podirt. No one gets hurt. But you change the direction of a political race."

"How do you get a warehouse in Drake's name?"

George laughed. "Piece of cake. Pick the right time and place and it's a five minute job."

"But you're stealing a work of art." Ginnie was still struggling with the legality of this. She didn't want to get involved in something questionable.

"Not really. You're not going to keep it, or sell it. You're putting it somewhere for safe keeping, in storage *under his name*. Drake doesn't lose a painting. Only misplaces it for a few months."

"I don't know." Ginnie shook her head and sighed. "You think that's Jim Bob's only chance?"

George nodded

# Chapter 5

**Saturday, March 24**
**Back to the Present**

**The sign for** the Wooden Nickel Mini-Storage brought Ginnie's mind back to the present. She circled the self-storage units. *No one here. Course not. Who would be at 11:30 at night? That's why I waited to this late hour.* She continued back around and parked in front of unit number seventy-three. She had suggested this unit to George because it was not visible from the road. No one in sight. She didn't want anyone to see her doing something illegal. She'd never broken the law. George said this wasn't really a crime. Just a Podirt — a political dirty trick. Just putting *Drake's* painting in *Drake's* storage unit — for safe keeping.

She left the motor running but turned off the lights, got out and retrieved the painting. In seconds she had the lock opened and was pushing the door up. Suddenly she was seeing her own shadow in front of her. She stood very still. *Go to the next row. Go somewhere else.* Her shadow became more distinct and a car drove up and parked at the unit to her left. *Turn your damn lights off.* But she heard the door close and the lights stayed on.

"Hi, there. I thought surely I'd be the only one here this late." The man's voice had a friendly tone.

If she answered, would that make him think she wanted to visit? Maybe if she didn't answer, he'd think she was unfriendly and go away.

"I didn't mean to startle you," the man continued, and sounded closer. "My name's John Littlefellow. Looks like we're going to be storage neighbors."

She turned her head and was shocked to see how near he was. "Good to meet you, John." She turned back and struggled to push the door up, while holding the painting.

"Here, let me help. I don't think they ever put any grease on these railings."

"I've got it," Ginnie said and gave the door another push. It opened and she started into the shed.

"You're storing a painting in here? I hope you're not going to leave it very long. These places are terrible for paintings. Either too hot and humid or too cold. I've even seen rats chew into the canvas. You can ruin a good painting in no time at all."

Ginnie marched in away from the headlights and placed the painting against the wall, with only its back visible. *Is he ever going to leave?* She waited but couldn't hear him move. Was it worse to stand there or turn and face him? She couldn't decide, but it was getting awkward. She put a smile on her face, turned and walked out to face the intruder. She grabbed the door, yanked it down and snapped the lock closed.

"Don't mean to be rude, John, but my husband didn't want me to come this late, and he'll be racing in if I don't get home."

"I understand. I won't let Donna come down here this late at night. But I've seen paintings get ruined in one of these units. Or a basement. So don't leave it here too long." He paused a second. "Well, goodnight." Littlefellow walked over to his unit and opened its lock

Ginnie jumped in her car, reminding herself not to throw gravel on the man. No point in doing any more to wave a red flag in front of him. Slowly she backed up, eased around his car, and gave a friendly little wave as she drove out of the lot.

# Chapter 6

**"Well, how'd Ronnie** do tonight?" Eula Moore asked her granddaughter when Crystal walked into the kitchen.

"Very well, I'd say. He asked why you weren't there."

"And you told him Mexican Train came before a politician, I hope."

"Not exactly. But you need to hear one of his speeches, Nana. I've heard three now, and I believe he's going to be the next governor of Texas."

"Wouldn't surprise me. Smart as a whip, straight as an arrow, and likeable as a baby lamb. Want something to drink? Sweet tea's made up."

Crystal sat on a high kitchen stool. "How about a fried pie?"

"None left. Those women were like a swarm of grasshoppers, eating everything in sight. Have some tea. So, you think Ronnie's gonna win come November?"

"No doubt about it." Crystal put ice in a tall glass and filled it with tea.

"'Course, beatin' Jim Bob is hardly a fair fight. That man has the sense of a retarded mule. How on God's green earth did he get nominated?"

"He was going to be the lieutenant governor on the ticket. Then, after the filing deadline, the top man, Warren Poker, got caught with his hand in the cookie jar. He's lucky he's not in jail. But it dumped him from the ticket, and Jim Bob moved up."

"Well, he might have worked as lieutenant gov, which is about as important as teats on a boar hog. Fills a space, but don't work. Can't see him being in charge of anything. How'd he get on the ticket at all?"

Crystal shrugged. "His father's money, I guess."

"Which old Jim Bob number one probably swindled someone out of."

"Won the lottery is what I heard." Crystal took a sip of the ice tea.

"And you don't think old Jim Bob's money can buy enough votes to beat Ronnie?"

"His daddy didn't win *that* much money. When people hear both of them speak, the choice will be clear. The latest poll shows Ron with sixty percent, Jim Bob with twenty-three percent and seventeen percent undecided."

"Hope you're right. Ronnie'd make a fine governor. Texas could use a strong, honest man, or woman, running things." Eula got up. "I'm heading to bed. See you in the morning, honey."

* * *

The EMS and police screamed into the driveway within minutes after Ron Drake arrived home and found his friend on the floor unresponsive. It took even less time for the medics to pronounce Nathanael Owens, Ron's property manager, dead. Before Ron could ask any questions, the EMS people had packed up and left.

A crime scene tech took fifty photographs, then dusted every surface in the kitchen and office, and around the back door. They checked all the doors and windows, trying to determine how the intruder had gained entry. Ron heard one of them grumble that a little more dust would have helped. They asked Ron to check and make sure nothing else had been taken, or disturbed.

Even after the body was released by the Pine County justice of the peace and removed by the funeral home, Ron remained at the kitchen table, head in his hands. He answered questions from his friend, Sheriff Bill Glothe, in a monotone, often after a deep breath and without looking up. He had known Nat for ten years and considered him more of a partner than an employee.

Finally, everybody had left except Glothe. "You're sure you're gonna be all right, Ron?"

Ron's face now looked ten years older than it had at the rally earlier in the evening. "Yeah. It's so senseless. Nat was sitting in this chair. He wasn't chasing the thief. Why would he be killed?"

Glothe skipped over the question. "I hear what you're saying. 'Course we're not sure he was sittin' in the chair, although it looks that way. Once the crime scene guys finish analyzing the photos, we'll have a better idea. Don't think the autopsy will help us much. But I got to agree with you. He had a soda in his hand. Wasn't chasing anybody. And I don't think he was threatening the thief with a Dr Pepper can." The sheriff shook his head. "Makes about as much sense as diapers on a bull."

Drake eased up out of his chair. "Go on home, Bill. We can work on this tomorrow. I appreciate your staying, but I'm okay. I'm going to fall into bed, not even shower. I'll stop by your office in the morning."

# Chapter 7

**Sunday, March 25**

**The next morning**, Ginnie Leverett slid into the booth opposite her best friend, George Weeks. "Glad you came." She was grinning like a kid who found a twenty dollar bill. She checked the nearby booths, and the position of the waitresses. No one was near. Even so, she leaned close to George and whispered.

"We've changed the race. Jim Bob will win in a walk. The Mondrian is in a safe place until the time is right." Her hands were in constant motion as she bounced on the booth's faded faux leather seat.

George Weeks's expression befitted an undertaker. "Are you not at all concerned a man is dead?"

A frown replaced Ginnie's smile. "Dead? Who?" Her mouth gaped open and deep lines creased her forehead.

"The man in Drake's kitchen?"

"He's dead?"

"As a doornail."

Her face sagged, and she stared at the table, slowly shaking her head. "I just knocked him out so I could get out of there. He came in and found the painting missing and called Drake. Said he'd wait until

Drake got home. And he sat between me and the door. What was I supposed to do? I couldn't just wait until Drake came home and found me with the Mondrian hiding in the pantry." She looked up at George. "I just tapped him on the head. I didn't kill him."

"The police think you did."

Ginnie almost screamed. "Me?"

"The thief. That whoever took the painting killed the man."

"Killed ..." She looked down at the table and slowly shook her head. "I've never even gotten a parking ticket. I never cheated in school."

A waitress approached and Ginnie order coffee. The waitress went for the coffee and Ginnie stared at George. Neither said a word. Ginnie's hands were shaking and she clasped them together, trying to stop them.

After the waitress delivered the coffee and left, Ginnie grabbed the cup in both hands and took several sips "It was an accident. An unfortunate accident. I was just going to tap him, knock him out for a few seconds." She stared down into the cup, as if trying to read something in the coffee. After a minute, she looked up. "Okay. Let's not panic. I wore gloves. There's no way they can trace this to us."

"Us? *I* didn't kill anybody," George said.

His determined tone jolted Ginnie, and she realized her friend sounded very distant. "We're in this together." She tried to hide the desperation surging inside her. "We talked about stealing the painting, waiting until Drake collected the insurance money, then letting it look like he had hidden it himself."

"I didn't join up for anything violent. I didn't kill anybody. There's no *us* concerning the murder."

Ginnie was taking a small sip of her coffee and almost choked. Her eyes now turned hard. "You rented the storage unit in his name. You planned this. You talked me into being a part of it. You're in as deep as I am."

Even before she finished, George was shaking his head and moving a little farther away from her. "If this all comes tumbling down on us, I'm in trouble for falsifying the rental document. I'm in trouble for helping plan a political dirty trick." He continued shaking his head. "I've got no part in the murder. We never discussed that. The dirty trick was to steal the painting, make it look like Drake was into insurance fraud"

Ginnie looked at him with dismay, but said nothing.

The tall, heavy set man leaned his elbows on the table and lowered his voice. "I've been dabbling in politics since college. And I graduated fifteen years ago. This is not the first podirt I've been involved in. But never—*never*—did any of them involve violence, or anybody getting hurt. Physically, anyway. I'm not going down for murder."

They sat in silence for a minute, each studying the other, two friends who were no longer certain of each other. Ginnie broke the silence. "Well, it wasn't really murder. At worst, it was, ah," she thought for a few seconds. "Manslaughter. I certainly didn't intend to kill him. It's just that as I was starting to hit him on the head, he turned in my direction. So, I rushed, maybe hitting him a little harder than I intended. And because he turned, I hit him on the temple instead of the back of his head. I'm sick about it. I'm truly sorry he's dead. But it wasn't murder. It was manslaughter."

"But you did mean to hit him."

"Well, yeah."

"And you were there to commit a burglary, weren't you?"

"You know I was."

Again, George was shaking his head. "Ginnie, you don't understand. In Texas, those two acts taken together add up to a lot more than manslaughter." He put his coffee cup down and looked directly into her eyes. "That's capital. That's the needle."

# Chapter 8

**Crystal tapped the** doorbell at Drake's country house. Eula put her finger on it and held it there for ten seconds. The seventy-seven year-old Eula was short at five feet two inches, but she was long on gumption.

"Hello, hello. Glad you stopped by." Ron Drake gave Eula a big hug and Crystal a smaller one. "Come on in. Alice has made coffee and scones." He leaned in between the two women and whispered, "She's a great housekeeper. But truthfully, I don't care for scones. She thinks they're a special treat and I don't have the heart to tell her. So, anything special comes up, I get scones. Please eat several. And take some home with you."

Eula laughed. "That's a man for you. But, just wanted to come over and see the real color of your office. Crystal said you got a call at the rally that your picture was stolen. Figured whatever was behind that picture was probably the original color."

"You come on back and take a look. Actually, I don't remember the color myself," said Ron.

"I know you'll miss the picture. But I won't miss it. Always thought it was ugly," Eula said as they walked back to Ron's office.

"Nana! That's rude. Ron's lost a valuable painting and you're –"

"It's okay, Crystal," said Ron. "Truth be known, it wasn't one of my favorites either. But Ellie loved it. So I bought it, then kept it after she died. A reminder, I guess. We didn't always agree, but we seldom disagreed."

Crystal looked at Ron and for a moment, she thought his eyes misted over a little.

"Glad to hear that," said Eula. "I always thought that was a flaw in your good judgment. 'Course I'm talking about the painting. You couldn't do better than Ellie. She was as fine as they come. But that painting; I wouldn't give you two cow patties for it."

Ron smiled. "Glad you don't work for the insurance company. I think we had it covered for four hundred thousand."

"Humph," Eula snorted. "I guess the insurance company shares that flaw with you. Four hundred thou. You *are* talking dollars?"

"That's about what we paid for it." He looked up at the ceiling for a few seconds, then back at Eula. "That could have been fifteen years ago."

"You were probably under-insured," Crystal said. "It would probably cost you at least a million today. I read one of his brought fourteen million a few months ago."

"Crazy fools," muttered Eula. "Proves most people got more dollars than sense."

"When will the insurance pay you for the loss?" Crystal asked.

"Not any time soon," said Ron. "First, they'll try to track it down. Somebody tries to sell it, most likely the buyer will be an undercover insurance investigator. So, they'll see if they can catch the thief. Obviously, insurance companies don't like to part with money."

Eula laid a finger on her temple. "I'm thinking 'bout putting some bowls of paint and a canvas in the cage with my pet gerbil. See what he can come up with. Probably bring in a hundred thousand."

Ron chuckled. "Good idea, Eula."

"Except she doesn't have a gerbil," Crystal said.

"So you just twiddle your thumbs until they feel like paying you?" asked Eula.

"That's pretty much how it works," answered Ron.

"Well, I'm satisfied seeing the blank space on the wall. Let's go have some scones," said Eula and she marched out the door heading toward the breakfast room.

"I thought I saw a police car leaving as we drove up," Crystal said.

"Probably heard he had scones," Eula muttered.

"Any news on the painting?" Crystal asked.

Ron stopped, and his entire body seemed to sag, like air escaping from a balloon. "I guess you haven't heard the full story. When I got home from the rally last night, Nat was lying on the floor in the kitchen, dead. The police believe Nat came in and caught whoever stole the Mondrian, and the thief killed him."

Crystal's hand flew to her face. "Oh my God."

"I'm so sorry, Ron. I know you and Nat were close. Terrible to come in and find your friend dead. And I apologize for being so ... ." For once, Eula was at a loss for words.

Ron put his hand on Eula's shoulder. "You didn't know. Actually, it was good to be thinking about other things."

"So, the police just now left," asked Crystal.

"No. They came back this morning to check a few more things. Last night, they thought they had an idea what happened. But this morning, they're not so sure."

"What are they thinking?" asked Eula.

"Nana, Ron probably doesn't want to talk about it."

"It's okay, Crystal. I can't think about anything else. As I said, they thought Nat came in and surprised the thief and the thief hit him. But after thinking about it last night after they left, I couldn't make that work. Nat called me to tell me the Mondrian was gone. I said I'd be right there. And Nat said he'd grab a drink from the fridge and wait for me. When I found Nat, a Dr Pepper can was on the floor, open, but spilled all over the place. So, it looks like he called me, got a Dr Pepper and then got hit on the head by the thief."

"Whose prints were on the can?" asked Eula.

"Only mine and Nat's. I'd put it in the refrigerator and Nat took it out."

Eula gave a quick jerk with her head. "So old Billy Goat thinks you killed Nat."

"Well, he isn't saying that. But I'm sure someone at the police department has suggested it."

"But Nat was your friend," objected Crystal.

"Police will tell you victims are most often killed by a relative or someone they know."

Crystal nodded twice. "Is there anything we can do?"

"Have a few scones and then take a bunch with you," said Ron. "I'm going to be okay."

* * *

Ginnie sat in her red Fiesta, tapping her fingers on the steering wheel. Clearly it was an accident. No malice or forethought or whatever. Manslaughter. Maybe a year in jail. *I could do that. If I turned myself in, maybe less. And time off for good behavior.*

She'd never spent a day in jail. Not even an hour. Six months would be a long time.

George didn't think the police would call it manslaughter. He's smart, but does he really know Texas law? Maybe not. Maybe just trying to scare me. I need to check this out. But not from my computer.

She headed for the library.

Forty-five minutes later she was back in her car. The library's only computer had been available. With the help of Google, she had found the Texas statues on murder and specifically on capital murder. She had run searches from every direction she could think of. But they all came back to the same passage. The charge could be capital murder if the defendant committed a felony and in performing that felony, committed an act that was clearly dangerous to human life and this act caused the death of an individual.

Stealing, and that's the way the police would look at it - not a political prank - was a felony. Certainly stealing a painting as expensive as this one had to be a felony. Not that Ginnie knew much about paintings. But just the name, Mondrian, meant it was expensive. Could she argue hitting someone with a can of tomatoes was not dangerous? She had planned to tap him lightly, just enough to knock him out for a minute. No more.

But the man was dead.

She closed her eyes and an image of the man lying on the floor materialized in her mind. Her eyes shot open and she shook her head, trying to erase the image.

Maybe he had a heart attack. She'd have to check the news.

Her palms were sweaty and she wiped them on her pants. Capital murder. That was serious. It could mean the death penalty. Or a life sentence. That might be even worse. And the damn article said "without the possibility of parole." That could mean locked in a cell for fifty years.

She replayed last night's escapade. She had worn gloves, so her fingerprints shouldn't be on anything. She had used a bump key, so she hadn't left any marks on the lock. Not that scratches on the door or lock would give the police much help. But certainly they'd get nothing from the lock. Even her shoes were Walmart specials. Millions of them sold. No pattern on the soles. And it hadn't rained in weeks. So, the ground wasn't soft. Shouldn't be any print there.

In her mind, she retraced her steps. Through the woods, onto the grass, then the gravel drive and the cement. No place for impressions, except the woods. And why would they look there? If they did, what part of the woods would they look at? It's not like there's a path. And if they found any prints, so what? She was wearing generic shoes. One pair out of a gazillion.

Her mind went back inside the house. In the pantry, she had only touched the door knob on both sides and the can of tomatoes. But she'd had on gloves. And, she had replaced the can back on the shelf, more or less where it had been before. So what if they found the can and decided it was the murder weapon?

Her mind recoiled at the thought. She had meant to just tap him, knock him out for two minutes. One minute. *It wasn't murder. It was an accident.*

Could a strand of her hair have caught on anything? She had worn a knit hat and tucked her hair under it. Unlikely any hair was left behind. Had she leaned against anything? Could a fiber from her jacket have caught on anything? Even if it had, would her DNA be on her jacket? Probably not. The jacket would have to be burned.

She thought about the man. She hadn't touched him. The can did. How could he have died? *I didn't hit him that hard. Did I?* Maybe he was sick and anything, any shock to his system, could cause him to stop breathing.

For awhile she sat in silence, thinking about the body on the floor. *I'm sorry, mister. I didn't mean to ... hurt you.*

But her mind was certain about one thing. She refused to even think about the death penalty or life in prison. It was an accident.

She started the Fiesta and moved out of the parking lot. Whatever, she didn't leave any clues. Drake didn't have any security cameras. She was in the clear. For the first time since talking with George, Ginnie allowed herself a slight smile. *I was like a ghost, a gentle breeze. I was in and out and left no trace, no hint I was ever there.*

The smile disappeared. The painting was missing and a man was dead. She had left evidence someone was there. But nothing pointed to her.

She had stopped at a signal light when a new thought slammed into her mind.

Someone saw her put the painting in the storage unit.

# Chapter 9

**Somewhere a horn** was blaring. Then another. Ginnie blinked twice and looked in the mirror. A man in a convertible behind her was yelling at her and shaking his fist. She looked ahead, saw the light was green and accelerated through the intersection. The jerk deserved a one finger salute, but Ginnie decided she didn't want to call any more attention to herself. She pulled into Sonic and parked at one of the order stands.

"Welcome to Sonic. Can we help you?" a voice came over the speaker.

"Yes. A tall cherry limeade please."

"That will be $1.63. We'll bring it right out."

Ginnie fished in her purse for money. But her mind was on the man at the storage unit. *If he knows a valuable painting was stolen last night, he'll figure out it was me. Maybe he already knows.*

A girl on roller skates brought the drink. Ginnie handed her two dollars, said to keep the change and the girl skated off. Ginnie took a long pull on the sweet and sour drink and settled back in the seat. She shook her head, trying to understand how all this had happened. It was just a political dirty trick, a podirt. If things worked out right, it would cost Drake the election—which was a good thing. And with all his money, he'd get the charges dropped and continue on with his life. Only not as governor.

She almost choked. *But now I've killed someone.*

If George was right, and he usually was, the police would call it capital murder. The article on the Internet basically said the same thing. She took another sip and her eyes hardened. She gripped the cup so tightly it cracked and started to leak. She wrapped a napkin around it. *I can't get the death penalty, or life without parole for this, for an accident.*

She had been so careful during the robbery. If that man hadn't come in to Drake's right then, she would have been gone. *But he can't tell anybody who I am. The police will never connect me with the murder.*

Suddenly her eyes popped open wide.

Unless that man from the storage place goes to the police.

She tried to reconstruct the scene at the storage unit. He had seen a painting, but not *what* painting. If he had suspicions, wouldn't he have gone to the police already? Wouldn't the police have picked her up by now? How could he have known about it last night? In fact, how would he find out about it today? The *Wooden Nickel Gazette* didn't come out for four days. They'd probably run a full page story and picture on the theft and murder. Everybody would know then.

What about the *Tyler Press?* Would they carry the story? Probably tomorrow.

A thought materialized in her mind. George had known this morning. She rummaged in her purse and pulled out her cell phone.

"George, how did you find out about the … dead man?" She almost said murder.

"I ran into this woman I know. She's a dispatcher for the sheriff. She told me. Made me promise not to tell anybody. Of course, I thought you knew."

"Well, don't tell anybody else. I won't be in today. Maybe not tomorrow. I'll see you when I see you."

*Why didn't I run into, or run over, the guy at the storage unit.* She took another sip of her drink. It tasted only sour now. She tried to remember the scene last night. He had driven in and left his car lights on. She never got a chance to see what kind of a car it was. Dark. But it was nearly midnight. Anything other than white looked dark. He'd sounded friendly enough, even introduced himself.

She sat up a bit straighter. What was his name? John. She remembered saying "Good night, John." Not much help. She remembered his last name was a little strange. How strange? Foreign? No. Unusual. But nothing came to her mind.

*I will think of it. And when I do, I'll tie up that loose end. I'm not going down for capital murder. Get rid of that guy and no clues lead to me.*

She started the car and backed out.

*Nobody's looking for me now. John Whoever doesn't know about the theft or mur - ah, dead man - yet. I need to see he doesn't find out. Before the Gazette comes out.*

She clenched her teeth. Were two capital murders any worse than one?

* * *

It had taken two hours, but it finally happened. She was sitting in her living room, typing away on a piece she had promised out this week. No rush. But, crank these out when you can, don't wait for the deadline. She had stopped to review what she had written, copy for a long video meant to sell something nobody really needed or wanted.

Without warning the name appeared in her mind. John Littlefellow. That was it: Littlefellow. She set her laptop aside. A quick check in the telephone directory revealed only one Littlefellow. Donna. She smiled. He had said his wife's name was Donna. She noted the address and set out. The piece she was writing could wait. Littlefellow could not.

* * *

It was a modest house, well kept. The lawn was neatly mowed, and some flowers were planted and blooming. Someone cared. She breathed a sigh of relief when she saw no children's toys around.

How did she get into this? Fate? Bad karma? She didn't mean to kill the guy in Drake's house. But would any jury see it that way? She was about to be caught stealing a very valuable painting. They would see her as killing to avoid being caught. If they convicted her of capital murder, there could be capital punishment.

They wouldn't catch her if she could snip off one loose end.

But how could she do that? Kill him? The man in Drake's house had been a mistake. It had just happened. An accident. Now, she was considering a deliberate act. Her stomach roiled and for a minute she thought she might throw up. Could she do it—deliberately kill someone?

"Remember, Ginnie. Always do what's right." Her mother's voice came through as clear as if she were sitting in the car. "Stay away from bad things. If you do, you will be blessed and you'll live a long, happy life."

Ginnie shook her head. She didn't need to imagine her mother preaching to her today. She didn't need a guilt trip. She'd heard it all before, many times. Right now, she needed to think clearly.

At this point, it's him or me. If Littlefellow goes to the police, tells them what he saw, then he is effectively giving me a death sentence. That will be a deliberate action by him that will result in my death. Not an accident. He will have to work it out, plan his call, turn me in. I didn't plan to kill the man at Drake's house. But Littlefellow will plan to kill me.

She sat for several minutes, eyes closed, her mind flashing pictures of Littlefellow going to the police, the police arresting her, the jury convicting her. When her mind started toward the death chamber, she shut it down. Littlefellow would start things in motion ending in her death.

Her eyes opened.

*This is self defense. And self defense is acceptable everywhere.*

Her queasiness was fading. Now that she rationalized this was self defense, she felt better. Maybe "better" wasn't quite the right word. Maybe justified. Either way, a life would be lost. It was hers or his. She had a right to protect herself. Even her bible reading mother would accept that. Ginnie would not put it to that test.

The door to the small house opened and Littlefellow came out, got into the car and backed out. Ginnie followed at a discreet distance. *Maybe I'll get lucky. Maybe he'll drive in front of a train or an eighteen wheeler.*

He drove to the local convenience store, brightly lit, and went in. Ginnie waited half a block away, lights out. After a few minutes he came out with a bag, got in his car, and drove home.

Something needed to happen before the *Gazette* came out. Even tomorrow, the Tyler paper would carry the story.

# Chapter 10


**"Well, how was** your visit to the Piney Woods?" Brandi Brewer, Crystal's petite housemate, sat curled up on the sofa.

"Much more relaxing than here in Dallas." Crystal dropped her briefcase on the table and slumped into a pink over-stuffed chair.

"Ah, but Mark O'Malley is here, right?"

"My job is here. Mark is just my boss." Crystal tried not to sound defensive.

"Yeah, And the Milky Way is just a cloud. Can't blame you, though. That's one gorgeous hunk of man."

"My job is here," Crystal repeated. "And I like my job."

"And your boss. But, enough of your love life."

Crystal let out a loud guffaw.

Brandi ignored her. "I'd say you backed a winner this time. I mean Ron Drake, not Mark."

"I believe you're right. But how did you come to that conclusion?"

"The old-fashioned way. I listened to their speeches."

"Good for you." Crystal cocked her head to the side. "But I must say, I'm amazed."

"I'm not as smart as you, but I *am* amazing," Brandi said. "So, I decided I'd listen to them and decide which one was telling the truth and which was trying to pull the fur over my eyes."

"Wool. So, what'd you think?"

"Your friend Drake sounds like he knows what he's talking about. Made sense, even to me. And, he didn't promise me a load of stuff I know he can't deliver. Old Jim Bob, on the other hand, reminded me of the men my mama warned me about. You know, the kind who offer you candy if you'll come with them. "

Crystal laughed. "I think you've nailed both of them."

"I didn't go to college, but I'm a graduate of street U. I can spot a phony day or night. How do you know Drake?"

"He's been a good friend of Nana's forever and I've known him probably twenty years."

"Since you were ten?"

"That's about right. Just a couple of years after my parents were killed."

"You gonna work on his campaign?"

Crystal shook her head. "No. He's got a P.R. firm here in Dallas. I've just gone to several of his speeches because he's been a friend for a long time. I'd like to see him be our governor. I'd certainly help if I could be of any use, but I doubt he'll need me."

"Even as smart as you are, I don't think he's gonna need you. It would take something drastic for Jim Bob to beat him. Course, this is Texas. And there's a lot more Jim Bobs and Billy Joes than Ronalds."

Crystal kicked her shoes off. "What shall we have for dinner?"

"Pizza's on the way."

"How'd you know?"

"I'm psycho."

"Psychic."

"Whatever. But, since we've polished off the election and dinner is on the way, let's get back to your love life."

"Once again, I don't have a love life."

Now it was Brandi's turn to let out a loud guffaw. "I see you after you've been out with Mark. Boy, do you have a glow, like you've been irradiated or something. I don't know about Mark, but I know about you. No use denying it. You've got a thing for Mark."

For more than a minute, neither woman said anything. Brandi watched Crystal who just stared at the painting on the opposite wall.

She looked back at Brandi. "We get along well. We really enjoy each other's company. He's funny and thoughtful, kind and supportive."

"And sexy."

Crystal smiled. "Well, there is that. But I've been out with a lot of sexy guys. Mark is so much more. And we can talk about all sorts of things. A lot of guys can talk about football, their job, their favorite bar or beer, maybe the crazy things they did in college. Mark and I have some really interesting conversations on a wide variety of topics."

"I'll bet he's a good kisser, too."

"He is very good." Crystal held up her hand. "But, you'll have to take my word on that. I'm not letting you check it out."

"So, you've claimed him for yourself."

Crystal didn't answer, but a little smile caressed her face.

Brandi let out a whoop. "See. There it is. You're getting that glow just talking about him."

Now the smile was full blown. "He does make me feel like I'm glowing."

# Chapter 11

**Monday, March 26**

**Ginnie spent much** of the day waiting a short distance from Littlefellow's house, then following him. He went to the high school, parked and went in. Ginnie waited half a block away. Fortunately, it was a cool day. Cumulus clouds kept the bright sun from raising the temperature to a normal March day in Texas.

After it was clear he was in there for the day, Ginnie drove to the Sonic and had lunch, but nothing tasted good to her. She threw away half of her fries and returned to her vigil. Several hours later, Littlefellow came out and drove home. The trip offered no chance for Ginnie to make a move.

It was just after dusk when he once again came out of his house and drove away. Ginnie almost ignored him, imagining another trip to the brightly lit convenience store. But, her time was running out. She didn't own a gun. Her options were limited. Her hands shook as she turned the key and started her car. She followed John's car, trying to ignore the churning in her stomach.

But instead of the convenience store, he pulled into the post office, parked across the lot and went in. A mud-covered extended cab dually had pulled in cross wise, taking up most of the space close to the door.

Great. Just what I need. A witness.

But even as she spoke, a petite young woman came out of the post office, climbed up into the big truck and drove out of the parking lot.

Ginnie watched the truck turn at the next street and quickly disappear from view. She checked in all directions. No one in sight. The post office had been closed for hours. This late, no one would be working inside. Her head swiveled continuously, checking to see if any other car turned onto the street.

Littlefellow came out and started across the pavement to his car.

She started slowly, lights out. When he was in the middle of the drive, she pressed the gas pedal to the floor. The Fiesta's spunky engine took hold and the car jumped forward.

Littlefellow turned his head at the sound. He paused, peering into the dimly lit parking lot. Then his lanky body leaned forward and he started to run.

Too late.

The red Fiesta, still accelerating, hit him with its right front fender, crushing bones. Littlefellow's body flew through the air, thumping down on the unforgiving concrete some twenty feet away. The third-class mail he had been holding was still fluttering in the air as the Fiesta exited the parking lot.

Ginnie did not look back. She did not check to see if he was really dead. She did not stop down the block to see if anybody found him. She kept driving and didn't stop until she was inside her garage.

Then, she broke down. She put her head on the steering wheel and started to sob.

She had deliberately taken a life. She had killed a man simply because he had seen her put a painting in a storage unit.

She remembered a case in Florida where a man was acquitted of killing a person because he felt threatened. Ginnie had felt threatened by Littlefellow.

Not anymore.

* * *

Twenty minutes later, she sat at the kitchen table, drinking a cup of coffee. Self defense, she told herself. Finally, the knot in her stomach began to relax and she was able to think. Her mind started to access all aspects of her situation.

Her biggest problem was the car. Soon the police would be looking for a car with a damaged front end. She could not drive around town until they pulled her over. She got up, went to her bedroom and threw a few things in a small suitcase. She wouldn't be gone long. But she couldn't have the car repaired here. Or any place close. She picked up the telephone and dialed.

"Hi, Sara. Ready for some company?" She listened for a moment. "In a few hours. I'm leaving now. I know it'll be late, but I wanted to come see you." *And I need to get away right now.*

She tossed the overnight bag in the car and drove slowly and carefully out of town.

* * *

Ginnie had crossed into Louisiana an hour ago and was nearly two hundred miles from home when she had her plan worked out. Her mind had been on the accident most of the trip, when it was not focused on the man in Drake's house. She would have the car repaired in Rayville. But trying to cover every possible loophole, she needed to disguise the source of the damage to her car.

As she pulled off the highway, she saw her opportunity. Just a few feet to the right of the exit ramp was a tree. She pulled off the road, stopped and got out. She needed to do this right. She walked over to the tree. Nothing in the way. Nothing to present a problem. She got back into the Fiesta and slowly drove into the tree, catching it squarely with her right fender. She jerked forward, her body pulling at

38

the seatbelt. She could hear the metal crumpling, glass breaking. But, the airbags did not deploy.

She got out and inspected the damage. The headlight, broken when she hit Littlefellow, now hung by two wires. She studied the car in the dim light provided for the intersection of the exit ramp and state road. To her, it looked perfect. She had hit the tree with the right front fender, exactly where she had hit Littlefellow. All the damage could have been caused by the tree.

She could hear the body repair shop macho guys: "Dumb woman driver hit a defenseless tree. That'll cost her." That caused another thought to pop into her mind. She probably didn't want to claim this on her insurance. Might be okay, but she was taking no chances. And no check or credit card. Better to pay for the repairs with cash than to have any trail.

Satisfied that evidence of the earlier collision with a man had been obliterated, she got back in the car and made her way to her friend's house.

* * *

The next day, *The Wooden Nickel Gazette* carried two stories on the front page. One article above the fold covered an art theft and murder, the other a hit and run accident that resulted in a vehicular homicide. The lead story said the art, a $700,000 Mondrian, was taken from the home of Ron Drake, currently the leading contender in the gubernatorial election. Dead was Nathanael Owens, a fifty-three-year-old employee of Drake. Police theorize Owens came in during the robbery and was killed by the thief.

The story continued with more information on the painting, a little history on Mondrian, and a good section on the gubernatorial race and Drake's widening lead.

The second story, near the bottom of the page, said thirty-four-year-old John Littlefellow, a social studies teacher at the Wooden Nickel High School, was the victim of a hit and run accident.

Littlefellow's body was thrown sixteen feet by the collision. The police found no skid marks.

Each story contained a critical bit of information: "At this time, the police have no suspects or leads on the crime."

## Chapter 12

**Monday, October 1**
**Six Months Later**

**"Thanks for coming** by, Will."

"When my boss calls, I jump."

Jason Dustin, department head at the National Fine Art Insurance Company, picked up the note on his desk. "When it suits you. You're recommending paying the insurance claim on the Mondrian now. Why so soon?"

Will Timson sat down, relaxed. "Well, two reasons come to mind. First, we haven't heard a single word about the Mondrian. Not a whisper. Usually there would be rumors floating around. On a painting of this type, we should have found it months ago and be watching the trial of the thief. The claim was filed on March 27. Today is October first. That's over six months and not a peep."

"You've worked all your sources?"

"You bet. I've offered a pretty good chunk of money for a lead. Nothing."

Dustin nodded a few times. "You said first. What's second?"

Now, Timson scooted forward on his chair. His eyes sparkled and a sly grin spread across his face. "This piece was grossly underinsured. Probably about right when he first bought it and got the policy. But, he hasn't updated the coverage in ten years. And old Piet Mondrian has really gotten pricey lately. One of Mondrian's rectangular paintings brought over four million at auction last year. Stupid people. Of course, Drake's is not one of those that's just colored rectangles."

"Your point is?"

"My point is, he's got this one insured for $400,000.

"Again, your point is?"

Timson spread his hands. "We pay him, and the painting is ours. Ours for $400,000. And it's worth probably twice that. We make four big ones clear, if we ever recover it." He smiled and moved to the very edge of his chair. "I say, let's pay him before we find it and have to give it back."

Dustin laid his hands on his desk and sat back in his chair. "Doesn't sound quite kosher to me."

"Perfectly legal. And the document the insured signs when we make the payment says that should it be recovered, it's ours."

"You're talking about the subrogation clause."

"Yeah. It's all there in black and white. We have specific clauses setting forth the subrogation rights of our company. And of course, it is clearly laid out in the document the insured signs when payment is made."

Jason focused on his desk but said nothing.

"We've been diligently looking for it for six months," Will continued. "We didn't just dog it. I've covered every angle I can think of. I've offered big bounties to anyone who could give me a lead. And I've got nothing. Let's just close this out. Clear the files." Again, a big grin split his face. "And if we happen to recover it, that's our good fortune."

"I don't know."

"Give it some thought. If we were dealing with a case where a New York Court would decide, then I'd have to rethink it. But in Texas, I believe the courts will say, we acted in good faith and upheld the conditions and intent of the insurance contract. A San Antonio Court of Appeals ruled the insurer acquires its subrogation rights once it pays the loss."

"And if a different court rules against us?"

"Should it ever come to a court battle and we lose, we're not out anything. We just don't get a bonus."

Timson went on, "Looks like a win-win situation to me. Drake gets his money. If it's never found, we are out that much, but that's the insurance business. Plus we get brownie points for paying off quickly. Good for business. But, if we do later find it, we can be big winners."

"You're sure you've put in due diligence?" Dustin cocked his head slightly and gave Timson a hard, piercing look. "You're not playing games here, are you, Will?"

"Absolutely not. I have all my efforts documented. Duke Bentley's been on the case, and you know what a bulldog he is. Feel free to check with any of my sources. They'll all tell you I've never offered so much bounty." Timson was very serious now. "You know me, Jason. I like to catch the bad guys. This time, I don't think we're going to. Not any time soon, anyway. This was just not done in the usual way. No known MO. We've done all we can. We can just sit and wait, and get a bad rap for not paying off in a timely fashion. Or we can pay off now." Again, a big smile. "And hope we find it later."

# Chapter 13

## Saturday, October 6

**"You're sure he's** collected the insurance money?" Ginnie Leverett asked.

"Absolutely. On that front. But are we sure we want to continue this? I mean, it's already caused one death." George Weeks locked his eyes on Ginnie's. "Is one the right number?"

Ginnie ignored his question. "Time to start phase two. It might take a week or two to hit the fan. But that will be just right. Maybe two weeks before the election, old Drake will be on his knees and fading fast."

"I don't know."

"What's not to know? You helped develop this strategy. We've waited six months for things to come together. I wasn't sure the damn insurance company would come through in time. Of course, we'd still have the painting in his warehouse. But with the insurance company paying him, we're in great shape. One thing I *am* sure of. If we don't pull this off, Jim Bob is toast. He'll finish third in a two man race."

"Be careful."

"Relax, George. Nothing ties this to us. Nothing. No links." She got up and looked down at her friend. "Let the game begin."

* * *

It was well past midnight. She couldn't afford a mistake this time. She had watched for an hour. No one had come near the storage units. No police had driven by. No kids looking for a place to park and make out. It was as quiet and dark as a grave. She smiled. *Drake's political grave.* She slid out of her car, decked in black from head to foot, plus black gloves. Though no one was around, she tiptoed down the drive, and around the back until she found unit number seventy-three.

She fished the key out of her pocket and unlocked the padlock. Carefully, she slipped the lock and key in her pocket. She patted her pocket, checking the key really got in there. No links. No clue she had ever been here. *Should I check to see that the painting is still there?* She stood there for nearly a minute, trying to decide. Finally, she retrieved her small penlight, pulled the door up just a foot, bent down and shinned her light inside. She swept the light along the side wall. Her grin gave the answer. *There it is. Waiting like a good puppy. Time for you to move on little puppy. Find a new home.*

# Chapter 14

**"Four months ago**, when the polls showed you leading Jim Bob sixty to twenty-three, I thought you were invincible." Crystal Moore stood at a worktable in what had been a large TV room in Ron Drake's house. Now, it held all sorts of campaign paraphernalia. While the lighting had been perfect for watching television, Crystal found it poor for dealing with artwork. She studied a poster board. Ron Drake stood on the other side of the table, making notes on a yellow pad. "Now, October sixth, you're past sixty-five and poor old Jim Bob has dropped a point."

"He's still out there, campaigning hard as ever," said Drake.

"A waste of his time and effort. But then, I guess this ad is too. You've got it locked up. If you didn't run another ad, or hold another rally, you'll still be elected come November."

"Let me give you Drake's maxim. Overconfidence is the prologue to failure."

"Thank you, Mr. Drake. I'll inscribe that and put it up beside *mine*: There are no five minute jobs."

"I like that. May I borrow it? I can't tell you how many times people ask me to do something and say it will only take five minutes. Half an hour later, I'm half way through."

"I'll make you a beautiful sign, put it in an ornate frame, so you can hang it over your governor's desk. You'll really need it there."

She studied the ad layout one last time, then pushed it aside. "Looks a little subdued to me."

"The P.R. guys said with the lead I had, this approach would be best for the last month."

Crystal sat and put her elbow on the table. She rested her chin in her hand and looked very serious. "I never asked why you wanted to take this on. Certainly you don't have anything left to prove. You started your own company and grew it into a large, successful corporation. You've served on the board of education, on the police civilian board, and then mayor of Dallas. Why governor?"

Drake looked at the floor for a moment, as if deciding what to say, then looked at Crystal. "You're right. I've had a successful life. When I was young, I never dreamed of being this successful, having this much money. Growing up, we were lucky to have a decent car. No thought of having two cars in the family. Very few of our friends had two cars. The thought of having two houses was not even on the radar." He stopped and looked down, eyes half-closed. After a few seconds, a small smile crept over his face and he looked up. "Now, as the cliché goes, it's time to give something back.

"Looking at the condition our state now finds itself in, I said, instead of grumbling about it, complaining it isn't better, maybe I should get in the fray and try to *make* it better. I've learned a lot running a corporation, making it fiscally responsible, ensuring it treated employees and customers right, and maintaining a steady, moral compass. I think I made a difference in Dallas when I was mayor. Maybe I can transfer some of that to state government. At least, that's my hope."

Crystal studied the man in front of her and decided he was actually embarrassed over his statement. She thought it was great. "Can I use some of that in a press release?"

He grinned. "Maybe not. I don't want to sound like goody-two-shoes. But you can use the moral compass part. People have told me

I'm crazy, but I believe most people really want to do what is right, don't want to cheat the system or violate the laws. We just need to expand that to everybody. And that starts at home and in the schools. If we can teach our kids, the next generation, to choose properly, we'll make our life, and theirs, so much better. We'll stop white collar crime, welfare fraud. People will be willing to help the police. And everybody, top to bottom, will be better off."

"Where is my recorder when I need it?"

They both laughed.

"Well, I'd better get moving," said Drake. "Surprise, surprise, I've got a campaign rally to attend. The real question is, can I stay on my feet for the final four weeks?"

"You could slow down. The election's in the bag."

Drake's frowned. "You've already forgotten."

"What?" She looked confused. "What have I forgotten?"

"Drake's maxim: overconfidence is the prologue to failure."

"Okay. I won't forget again. But before we leave, I've been meaning to ask. I know they haven't found the painting. Did the insurance company ever pay off?"

"As a matter of fact, yes. Two days ago. They said on these kinds of theft, they usually recover them within a month or so. It goes on the market and the insurance detectives get wind of it. They said they haven't heard a single word. Nothing for six months. So, they went ahead and paid off. $400,000." He pursed his lips and looked down for a moment, a dark cloud covering his eyes. "I don't think I'll replace it. Ellie picked it out. She isn't here to select its replacement."

* * *

"Hi, Nana, Brandi." Crystal sank into a rocking chair on Eula's veranda. "Ron says hello."

"He got you working on something?" asked Eula.

"Oh, just a few press releases geared for east Texas. He feels like this region is being overlooked by his agency. I'm happy to be able to do something for him, though I think the election's in the bag. He doesn't."

"Ron's a smart guy. I'd listen to him."

"Oh, I do. You and Brandi have a good visit?"

Brandi said, "Fine as seven dollar wine."

"We had a great time," said Eula. "Fact is, Brandi is more fun than you are."

"Nana!"

"I love you more than anything, Crystal. But you *are* pretty serious. Got that from your mother, I reckon. Brandi can be pretty zany at times. When was the last time you acted crazy?"

"You thought I was crazy going to Mexico to rescue those two little girls."

"That was dumb crazy," Eula clarified. "Brandi is funny crazy."

Brandi jumped in, trying to save her housemate. "Your grandmother told me about your tree house. I want to see it. The only tree we had when I was growing up was as big around as a pickle and tall as a basketball player. Only a skinny squirrel would try to climb it. Let's go."

"Granddad built it when I was a little girl. I spent a lot of hours in it."

Eula snorted. "Yeah. And you used it until you went to college. Truth be told, and my eyes didn't lie to me, you were up there a few times after you got back from Stanford."

Crystal took a deep breath. She did not want to get into a discussion of her departure from Stanford. Best way to avoid that was to leave. "Okay. Off to the tree house." She got up and started toward the stairs off the veranda.

"Hey," called Brandi. "Do I need shoes?"

"Shoes are optional in the tree house."

Brandi caught up with Crystal. They wandered through the woods for five or six minutes and came to a stop before a large white oak tree. Wood steps climbed the side for about twenty feet, stopping at the bottom of a large platform.

"Wow. That's some tree. What is it?" asked Brandi.

"An oak tree."

"We've got oak trees in Dallas but they don't look like this. I couldn't reach around this one."

"It's a white oak. Mostly, Dallas has live oaks, which don't grow very tall or big around."

Brandi gazed up into the branches. "Pretty cool of your granddad to build it for you. How'd he happen to build it?"

"Nana asked him to."

"Why?"

"She told me it would be my very private place. No one would bother me there, not even her. It was my safe place to work out whatever was bothering me."

"Interesting. My mother said if I had a problem, just suck it up and keep moving forward."

"I thought it was silly when he built it. But, was I wrong. Remember, my parents were killed in an auto accident when I was just seven. I was pretty mad at the world. I didn't like anything. But I did find it peaceful to sit up in my personal tree house. And Nana was true to her word. Neither she nor my Granddad ever came up. It was mine." She began to climb the steps.

Brandi poked her head through the opening and looked around. "Wow. This is bigger than my bedroom. Nice."

She pulled herself up into the room. It was indeed a house with sides and a roof. "And look. You've even got a beanbag chair here. How long has that been up here?"

"Not too long. Nana was right. I was up here a few times between Stanford and IRS. In fact, I spent some time here after I was offered the job at IRS. I was so uncertain of myself then. I sat up here, first trying to talk myself out of taking the job, then trying to convince myself to give it a try."

"I can see that. This is a great place. No noise. No TV. Even I could think up here."

Crystal laughed. "Brandi, you'd last ten minutes. You'd have to have something going on."

"But if it were this quiet, I might could hear my thoughts. Then I'd know I was thinking. Maybe even know what I was thinking about." For a moment, neither spoke, then Brandi said, "Can we stay here a little longer?"

"Sure," said Crystal. "But I get the beanbag."

# Chapter 15

**Tuesday, October 9**

**Ginnie looked at** her watch. I've been here most of two days and no one has noticed it was unlocked. Maybe I need to open it tonight, leave it open. Maybe put up a sign: "Valuable Painting Inside."

She knew storage unit seventy-two was rented. It had a lock on it. Three months ago, it didn't. What she didn't know was if and when the owner was going to come visit it. And would he or she notice the unit to the right was not locked? And would they look in it? And would they take the painting if they did? And would the info get back to the insurance company and the police?

She swore under her breath. People were so undependable. So much was left up to fate. If the miserly insurance hadn't taken so long to pay Drake, the plan wouldn't be on such a tight schedule.

I'm not fussy. Anybody driving into the lot can notice it. Somebody driving back to unit 100. Okay by me. Just stop, open the door, see the painting, take it, and sell it, take it to the police, the insurance company. I'm not at all picky. But, unit seventy-two will most likely park at an angle, with unit seventy-three right in front of them. The lock is right there. She laughed. Only there won't be any lock.

She slumped down in the seat, as a car entered the storage lot. Unconsciously she held her breath, then released it in a sigh of disappointment when the car turned and went to the other side. No chance to see the unlocked unit.

She took a deep breath. *Not to worry. If no one takes it out within a week, I'll call the police and tell them I saw a painting in a mini-warehouse.* But right now, her stomach was growling. She reached for her Dairy Queen drink cup and took a sip. Empty.

She started her car and headed for the Dairy Queen. Once again she reminded herself she did not need to be there, to see who took the painting. But she couldn't resist. She wanted to see someone find it, maybe take it to the police. Or better yet, call the insurance company. Just the thought sent her adrenaline pumping.

Forty minutes later, she came back to resume her vigil. To her surprise, a car sat in front of unit seventy-two. She let out a small gasp when she saw the door to unit seventy-three was open. She parked and slumped down in the seat. She was barely visible from outside. But she could see the door to the storage unit. She had to wait only a minute until a man came out. His stomach hung over his belt a few inches and his jeans were a few inches too long, but he looked like a rock star to Ginnie. He had the painting in his hands. *Go man, go. Valuable painting. Call the insurance company and get a reward.*

The man looked around three hundred and sixty degrees. *He wants to know if anybody is seeing him take the painting.* He opened the back door of his faded Malibu and slid the painting behind the front seat. He shuffled over to unit seventy-three, pulled the door down, went back to his car, and drove out of the lot.

Ginnie followed the man to a house near the edge of Wooden Nickel and watched as he took the painting into his house. As she drove slowly by, she could see a garage crammed with junk. *Great. Was the painting just going to end up hidden in a different garage?* But, he'd taken it inside, not to the garage. Maybe he liked it, wanted to keep it for himself. Or maybe he planned to give it to his mother for her birthday. *No. He's going to try and sell it. He's not going to let it sit in the barn. And he's not going to give it away.* Their whole plan depended on it.

* * *

By sunup the next morning, Ginnie sat down the road from the junk collector's house. At five minutes to seven, he came out, without the painting. She followed him to the local supermarket where he parked far out and walked in.

With all those open spaces close to the door, Ginnie decided he must be an employee. She waited. When the store opened the doors to the public, she was the first one in. She picked up a flyer and pretended to look at it while she studied the management pictures posted on the wall. To her amazement, there was the collector: Bert Monday, assistant produce manager. He looked like a Monday to Ginnie: a slow, unfriendly, unwelcome sight. She started toward the produce section. In mid-stride, she shifted directions. She did not want him to see her. She would have to follow old Bert, maybe several times, and see what he did with the painting. If he saw her, he might remember her. She couldn't have that.

She almost missed it. There, taped to the door of the office was a work schedule. There was Monday, scheduled for the seven to three shift today. But tomorrow, he shifted to the three to eleven evening shift for the rest of the week. She headed for the door, dropping the flyer in the trash as she exited.

She needed to do some work herself. This game was exciting, scary, and certainly managed to produce adrenalin rushes. But it did not pay the rent.

* * *

Shortly after three that afternoon, Bert Monday pulled into his driveway, parked and entered his house. Ginnie watched from her car, parked under a nice shade tree five hundred feet down the road.

She had her laptop powered up and was working on copy for an infomercial assignment which was due in a week. In truth, she could send it off tomorrow, but wouldn't. For what she charged, she didn't want it to look too easy or too fast.

Monday puttered around in his junky garage for awhile, went back in the house, and didn't come out. At a little after eleven, all his lights went out and Ginnie went home.

* * *

The next morning, Ginnie arrived on Monday's street early. His car was still in the drive, exactly where it had been when she left last night. She had brought work with her again and quickly powered up her laptop and began to pound on the keys.

She had rewritten the same paragraph three times. It still didn't convey the emotion she wanted. The message was okay, but it just didn't engage the reader. She let out a frustrated moan, shook her head and stared out the window. At that moment, Monday stepped off his porch and headed for his twelve-year-old blue Malibu.

The painting was in his hand.

# Chapter 16


**Crystal had given** Mark a progress report on her project at Intelligent Retrieval Systems. She gathered her papers, ready to leave.

"How is Ron and his campaign doing?" asked Mark.

"Great. I'd say he's got it wrapped up." She got up.

"Have a seat. I want to talk to you a little, as your boss."

Crystal's eyebrows came together and crowded down over her eyes. She sat back on the edge of the chair.

"Your project seems to be ahead of schedule. And it looks like you have been giving JT a lot of responsibility. She can keep the project moving and you can give her the direction she needs. But I think you should spend some time over the next couple of weeks helping Ron with the rush to the finish line."

Crystal's face relaxed into a smile and her tense muscles relaxed. "Thanks, Mark. I have been doing a few press releases for him. Frankly, I think it's a waste. He's running away from Jim Bob."

"Seems like he is. But having ridden bulls to put myself through undergraduate school, I know the last little bit before the finish is often the hardest. Frankly, I think Jim Bob would be a disaster for Texas. Take a little time and help ensure Ron's win. Texas needs him."

"Thank you. And I know Ron will be grateful, too. I'll see what I can do."

"My only objection to this is, if you're in east Texas I won't get to see you as much. It's tough enough not hugging you here in the office."

"Yes. But I know the company policy. No romance in the office."

"When I put that in, I hadn't met you."

"I'll pop back often for some romancing, outside of office hours."

"Okay. Go make sure we elect a great governor. But before you leave ..."

Mark came around his desk as Crystal stood up. He wrapped his arms around her and touched his lips lightly to hers.

"Mark, I need to talk ..." JT stood in the doorway. "Ah, excuse me, I'll ... ah, go away." She turned and fled.

"Wouldn't you know it. You see why we don't do this in the office." Mark backed off two steps. "How long will it take this to spread through the office?"

"JT doesn't gossip much. But I'll talk to her."

"Call me tonight. And plan on a few days, and nights, in Dallas."

"Oh, I will."

# Chapter 17

**Wednesday, October 10**

**Monday headed out** of town. Ginnie, lagging far behind him, checked her fuel gauge. Half a tank. Unless he was going to Houston, she had enough gas.

Twenty-five minutes later, they were in Tyler. Twice, both times due to a stupid driver and a red light, Ginnie thought she might lose him. She didn't. He pulled into the parking lot of a small store. *He's going into a pawnshop? Doesn't the fat jerk know what he's got?* She scrunched her mouth in disgust. *Fool.*

She pulled in and parked next to Monday's Malibu. According to the sign, the AAA Pawn was owned by Emil Rohrbak. Ginnie had a good view inside the pawnshop. Monday had carried the painting inside and was showing it to the man behind the wire mesh. Monday had his back to Ginnie, so she couldn't see his face. Emil—Ginnie assumed it was the owner— looked at the painting and Ginnie imagined a slight jerk of his head. He pursed his lips and shook his head a few times. Monday's head bobbed up and down as he gestured at the painting.

Emil looked around, then stepped over to the metal door, and opened it a crack and motioned for Monday to bring the painting to him. He grabbed the painting and held it up near his eyes, turned a bit, perhaps to get better light on it. He made a couple of short jerks with his head and held it back toward Monday.

Negotiations.

Whatever the offer, Monday did not take it. He waved his hands, punctuating with short chops in the air.. The man said something else. Monday shook his head and reached for the painting.

Damn, I wish I had a directional mike.

Emil pulled the painting back, took a deep breath and appeared to be reluctantly giving in to something. He spoke two words, but Ginnie couldn't read his lips. Monday's body seemed to relax. He nodded.

Emil closed the door and walked back over to the window. He handed Monday a paper. Monday filled in several blanks and handed it back to Emil. He read the entries, and rolled his eyes toward the ceiling before slipping the paper into a folder on the desk. He reached into a drawer and pulled out some bills. Slowly, he counted out five bills into Monday's eager hands.

I don't think we have thousand dollar bills in circulation anymore. So, Monday boy got five hundred bucks, max. How stupid can you be? Okay, it's stolen. But on a three hundred grand painting, five hundred? I'll bet the insurance company would have given thirty thousand.

She watched as Monday came out, almost skipping, smiling at the world. *Idiot.* He drove off and Ginnie sat there trying to figure things out. Maybe Monday had no idea what he had. Or maybe this guy was a fence and Monday would get a cut when it's sold. *Yeah. Like that's gonna happen.* She thought about Emil's reaction. He knows. He may not know the whole story, but he knows he's got a valuable painting. And maybe he knows *exactly* what he's got.

* * *

Ginnie drove to a nearby café and ordered lunch. The man behind the counter seemed to be the owner, so she engaged him in conversation after several customers left. She asked him if he knew of a good pawnshop. The man thought about it for a moment, then recommended AAA Pawn. She asked if it was dependable because she would want to come back later in the year and retrieve her broach, when she got back on her feet. The owner said the pawnshop had been there a long time, with the same owner. He felt she had no worries about it being there a year from now.

Half an hour later, she walked into the pawnshop and asked the man if he had any paintings. He had a couple, both worth less than fifty dollars. She asked if he ever got any in, that maybe would be available after the waiting period ended, maybe some more expensive ones. He looked at her very carefully before he gave her a firm no and walked away from the window.

* * *

When Emil closed the shop at six, Ginnie noted he carried a large package to his car, a package about the size of a famous painting recently stolen. She followed him.

After eight or nine blocks, Emil parked and walked across the street to a metal building with a weathered sign which read: Art Treasures, and in smaller letters: To the Right Person. From the looks of the building Ginnie doubted she'd find any art treasures. Was Emil bringing the painting here to get an opinion on its value? Or was this a front for a well financed fence?

She parked just a little bit down the block from Emil's car, but where she had a better view inside Art Treasures. She trained her binoculars on the sign. Down at the left bottom it read: Winston Brown, Proprietor. The window in the front of the building was dirty, but she could see Emil clearly. He was talking to another man, probably Winston Brown.

Just then, another person walked into the store. Ginnie had been focused so intently on the inside of the store she hadn't noticed a car had pulled up in front. Winston casually turned the painting so the front was not visible to the new customer. Winston smiled, directed the client toward the back of the store, and watched the man until he was out of Ginnie's vision.

Winston Brown wobbled his head back and forth and said something else to Emil. Once more, Emil nodded, this time more decisively. Now, Winston smiled. He propped the painting against what Ginnie could only think was an old church pew and turned back.

*I think he's bought it, or at least agreed to fence it.*

Winston disappeared into the back, out of Ginnie's view. After several minutes he came back with an envelope and handed it to Emil. The pawnbroker opened the envelope, riffled the contents with his thumb, and then pocketed the envelope as he left the store.

She watched Emil get in his car, and drive off. She sat there for a few minutes, trying to see what Winston would do. He picked up the painting and withdrew to the back of the store, again out of view.

For a moment, she considered going into the store, looking around, asking some innocent questions about any real art treasures, particularly paintings. Quickly she dismissed that. She was working to cut any ties between the art theft and herself. No point in introducing any new strands, even small ones. It was a mistake to have gone into the pawnshop. She wouldn't repeat that.

She put the binoculars away and closed her eyes. What happened now? Would the police or insurance investigators track it down? *Do I need to give them a little nudge in the right direction?*

She started the Fiesta and swung out into traffic. *Right now, I'm in the clear.* She turned left at the next corner and headed back toward Wooden Nickel. *Of course, I hope I didn't go through all this—burglary and two murders—and still let Drake win. I just have to be careful. Very careful. Job one is to stay in the clear.*

# Chapter 18

**Friday, October 12**

**Try as she** might, Ginnie couldn't leave it alone. Two days had gone by and no mention of the painting being found. Time to take action, give this a little nudge. She chose a time when she was sure only the night dispatcher was on duty.

She had about decided there were no pay phones left in Texas when she finally thought of the airport. She sat in her car outside the terminal at the Tyler Pounds Regional Airport for forty minutes before a Boeing 727 finally landed. She slipped on beige colored gloves and walked into the terminal just as the passengers were coming in from the other side. She walked to the pay phone, placed her call, and did as much as she could to disguise her voice. She changed the pitch on every word, growled and slurred, but made certain every word was clear. If that didn't get things moving, nothing would.

"Interested in Drake's lost painting. Try Art Treasures in Tyler." She hung up the phone, and walked out of the terminal with the last of the passengers. No one, particularly none of the employees, seemed to notice her.

Back in her car, she slowly began to breathe normally. She removed her large, horn-rimmed glasses and tossed them into a bag. Five ninety-five at Walmart. She pulled off the black wig and shook out her brown hair. Even if one of the employees saw her, their description would lead the police after someone else. The passengers were only interested in getting out of airport purgatory and on to their destinations. Her fingerprints would not be found anywhere. And there was no way in hell the police could get any help from a voice recording of her message.

But, they could now find the missing painting. *Not a bad night's work.*

# Chapter 19

**Bill Glothe poked** around among the dusty "treasures" haphazardly displayed in Art Treasures. He ran his hand over an old chair, priced at four hundred ninety-five dollars. That chair could have been the same one he had thrown out years ago, tired of it taking up space in his attic. Could have been, except he had eventually burned it that winter in his fireplace.

Twice the owner, Winston Brown according to the sign, came over to Glothe and asked if he could help. Each time, Glothe asked a question, which the man answered and then left. *Obviously he doesn't think I'm a good prospect. When is Duke gonna get here?*

Just then, a middle aged man sauntered in. He wore a plaid sport jacket, maroon pants, alligator skin boots, string tie and had a long, skinny cigar stuck in his mouth. He carried a worn brown leather briefcase. He glanced around the place and then headed straight for Winston.

Glothe glanced at his watch. Nearly ten. *'Bout time.*

Glothe reached up pretending to scratch his ear, but was in fact checking the position of his earpiece. He reached into his cargo pants pocket and flipped on a switch.

"Hi Winston. My name's Duke." His voice came through to Glothe's ear speaker quite clearly. "Rumor going around you might have a real art treasure. True?"

Winston stuck out his hand and Duke shook it. "I got a lot of real treasures here. What kind of art you like?" Winston was amiable, if cautious.

Duke said, "I like good expensive art, at a bargain price, of course. Got any post-modern work by a name artist?"

"If I did, it would be expensive. But still a bargain."

Come on, Duke. Cut to the chase.

"So, what have you got? I can tell you what I've got. Cash."

Winston's smile broadened. "Cash and art go hand in hand. I got a new acquisition that might meet your desires. Does your cash extend up to a hundred thousand?"

"It does," said Duke. "But it would have to be an exceptional piece. My clients want a bargain. I want to make a profit on the transaction. And my clients would want verification of authenticity. I once bought a piece from a dealer and it turned out to be a fake." Duke let the words hang in the air as his gaze bore into Winston. He pulled the side of his coat slightly. Glothe grinned. Duke was letting Winston see his revolver.

Winston looked concerned. "Unfortunately, there are unscrupulous dealers. Who's the dealer? So's I can avoid him."

At the front of the store, Glothe ambled out the door.

"Not to worry. He no longer deals in art." Duke blew out a long plume of smoke, then tapped the ashes from his cigar onto the floor. "What have you got?"

Winston looked at the pile of ash, then back up at Duke. "Would you be interested in a Mondrian?"

"I'm interested in anything authentic, if the price's right."

"Follow me."

"No."

Winston had stepped out. He stopped and turned back to look at Duke. "No?"

"No. First, I don't follow. Second, I don't go into back rooms. You can bring it out here or I can walk out the door. Your choice."

Winston Brown just stared at Duke.

Good work, Duke. Head back there, I lose the video for sure and probably the audio, too.

Finally, Winston exhaled loud enough to be captured on Glothe's digital recorder. "Fine. Wait here." He hurried off to a back room.

"You getting all this?" said Duke. He put the briefcase down on the floor.

Glothe sat in his car, the video recorder focused on Duke. "Loud and clear, good buddy. Got a good view of you two. And either both of you are pretty dirty, or the window is. But the picture is coming through good enough."

"Take a look at this masterpiece," Winston said as he returned with a painting.

Glothe reached in his pocket and pulled out the micro-recorder just to check. Now was not the time to find it had clicked off, or a battery had run dry. The tiny device appeared to be working perfectly. He could *see* the video working. As he looked back up, a movement caught his eye. A man had parked a few spaces over and was getting out of his car.

Glothe jumped out and intercepted the man before he had moved five feet from his car. "Sorry, sir. The store is not open for business this morning."

The man furrowed his eyebrows and cocked his head. "But I can see people in there." He started toward the door again.

Glothe moved in front of him. "The store is closed. It'd be easier on both of us if I don't have to put you in handcuffs." He pulled his jacket back a little to expose the pistol riding on his hip. His badge was clipped beside the holster. "Come back another day."

The man's gaze stayed on the pistol a moment. "What—"

"Be best if you just mosey on. You can come back tomorrow."

The man took one last look at the pistol and badge, glanced inside the store, then turned and left.

Glothe slipped back in his car. He reached in his shirt pocket and pulled out a toothpick and stuck it in his mouth. He'd quit smoking, and now he chewed on a toothpick. Wasn't the same.

Duke studied the painting, ran a finger carefully over one small corner of the painting. "And you can guarantee its authenticity?" He fixed the dealer with a steely look. "Where did it come from? I don't want a mafia don coming to claim it. I always hate to fight them."

Winston licked his lips and a small tic started in his left eye. "Well, ah, no sir. I bought this from an out-of-town contact. He assures me it will pass any test you want to apply. No mafia involved." His eyes jumped from place to place, unable to focus on one spot for more than a second.

"And how much are you going to try and rip me off for this ugly painting?"

Glothe grinned as he saw Winston's mouth fall open and his eyebrows come together.

"Rip you off? No sir. You came with a good recommendation. You get the bargain-basement price. At least twenty-five percent less than somebody coming in off the street with no recommendation. In fact, I wouldn't even show this to you without a good, and I mean good, recommendation. I saved this for a special client."

"Yeah, yeah. Don't try to hustle me. My recommendation is a big bankroll." Duke studied the piece, walking around and checking the back. He pulled a powerful magnifying lens out of his pocket, held it in front of several places on the canvas. He moved back to the front and resumed his study. He scrutinized the signature at length.

After several more minutes, Duke put the glass away and turned his gaze on Winston. "Okay. Name a figure. Too high and I walk. No negotiating. So think before you open your yap."

Winston took Duke's words to heart apparently. He looked down at the floor and Glothe could tell the dealer was working on the age old question: What will the traffic bear?

Duke lowered his voice. "While you're thinking, think about this. If I find it's a fake—and if it is, I *will* find out—I won't come back to see you."

Winston opened his mouth to reply, as Duke continued. "But, *someone* will come visit."

Duke's head jerked to the side. "Who is coming in the back door?" His tone was so intense, Glothe sat up straighter and tried to focus his camera on the rear of the store.

Winston spun around. "Jake, go clean the storeroom. Right now." His voice held some authority, but Jake didn't move.

"It's locked, Mr. Brown," the young man answered.

"Then clean the bathroom. I'm busy and I don't want you up here right now."

Jake turned and disappeared. Glothe couldn't get a decent picture of the young man, but he doubted Jake had any bearing on or knowledge of what was going on. He refocused on Winston.

Winston turned back to Duke. "This is crazy. But I like you. Like doing business with you."

"We haven't done any business," snarled Duke.

"Okay. How about eighty-five?" Winston was trying to look in control, but the tic in his eye was increasing and his tongue flickered across his lips again.

"How 'bout seventy-five and I forget you tried to sucker me?"

"Eighty's a good price. I got other people interested in it." His tongue made another trip around his lips. "But I, ah, I can live with eighty."

Duke took a little step back and stared at Winston. "Did I stutter? I'll say it slower for you. Seventy-five. Cash. Right now, or I'm out the door." He picked up the old briefcase.

Good grief, Duke. Make the buy. Don't lose it because you're enjoying the theater.

Even from the car, Glothe could tell Winston was going to do it. But he wanted to make Duke think this was a tough decision. "Just give me a damn minute. I'm just trying to calculate if I'm losing money." He scratched his head, studied his shoes, then shook his head. "I shouldn't do this. But like I said, I like you. Figure you'll be a return customer. Okay. You got the money, you got the painting."

Duke dialed in the combination to the locks on the briefcase and opened the lid. A little. Winston got a look at the money and Glothe could hear him gasp involuntarily. "Now, go get some brown paper for me to put around this. We'll count the money and the deal's done."

Without a word, Winston disappeared.

Duke said quietly, "Get out of the car and be ready. Then, as I start counting out the money, come in with the video going. Get the money in his hand. But don't wait too long. There's not much real cash here."

"I'll be there," said Glothe. "Slim's out back, just in case he tries to run."

Winston came back, nearly running. He wrapped the painting up and propped it against an old desk. "Painting's wrapped. Let's see some money." Duke flipped open the briefcase. "Think we ought to do this in my office?" asked Winston.

"Didn't you hear me? I don't go into back rooms. Not then, not now, not later. Got it?"

"Yes sir. We'll count it here."

"Or, I could just give you a credit card. You take American Express?"

Winston screwed his face into a question mark. "Credit card? Are you crazy? No, I don't take credit cards."

"Just a thought. Be a lot faster." Duke positioned himself so Winston was three-quarters facing the door, and nothing to block Glothe's line of sight. Winston held out his hands, ready to receive his money.

Duke put several hundred dollar bills in Winston's hands. "Too bad they don't have the big ones anymore. Think how easy it would be with thousand-dollar bills."

"Just count. How many in each bundle there?"

Duke put two more hundreds in Winston's hand. "Five thousand."

"Just give me fifteen bundles. I trust you."

Duke laughed. "You shouldn't. You made me lose count. How much have I given you so far?"

Winston splayed out the bills. "Five hundred. Let's move or we'll never get to seventy-five K."

"Hold it right there," said Glothe as he entered the door, video camera whirring. "You're on Candid Camera."

Winston eyes went wide and he stood there like a deer caught in headlights. As Glothe approached, he said, "Would you two men tell me what you are doing?"

Winston's head wobbled slightly. Duke said, "Winston Brown has just sold me a Mondrian for seventy-five thousand dollars. The money in his hand is part of the payment for what I believe is stolen property."

The color had drained from Winston's face. He managed to stuff the money into his pocket. His breathing had accelerated. Once again he wet his lips with his tongue. "Ah, what's going on? This man and I are having a private business deal. I don't know who you are, but you are in my store and I am ordering you to leave at once." He tried to straighten up a bit taller, but his knees were shaking and it didn't work. "Or I'll call the police."

Duke answered. "My name is Duke Bentley. I am an insurance investigator, specifically tasked to track down stolen art. The man with the video camera is Sheriff Bill Glothe. That's pronounced 'gloth', 'e'. I think he's supposed to arrest and jail those who deal in stolen art."

Now Winston did manage to straighten up and look utterly confused. "Stolen? This painting was stolen?" He shook his head. "Well, I didn't steal it. I bought it fair and square. Paid a good price for it. I had no idea it was hot."

"And who did you buy it from?" asked Glothe.

"Ah, well, that's confidential. I can't reveal stuff about my clients. The Privacy Act and all that. Not that I agree with it. But the law's the law."

Duke smiled. "Okay. Just show us the receipt where you purchased it."

"Receipt?" The beads of sweat on Winston's face were joining and several rivulets ran down and dripped off his chin. "It was just a handshake deal. You know, in Texas a handshake can seal a deal." He gave a small, nervous laugh.

"I don't think he bought it, Bill. I think he stole it himself. No middle man."

"No. No." Winston was almost shouting. "I didn't steal it. I bought it. I swear."

Glothe handed the video camera to Duke and pulled a pair of handcuffs from his belt. The sheriff started reciting the Miranda.

"Hold it," said Duke. "Before you cuff him, I want my five hundred back."

"Come on, Duke," said Glothe. "You know that's got to remain as evidence till we convict this guy." His mouth shot open. "Oh, I almost forgot." He looked directly at Winston. "A man was killed during the course of the theft. So you're going up for grand theft *and* capital murder."

A uniformed officer walked in from the back of the store.

"Slim, get up here and help out. Were you able to hear everything?"

"Yes, sir. I heard it all. And I slipped in and saw Mr. Brown accepting money from Mr. Bentley."

"Good man."

"Wait," gasped Winston. "I bought it. I didn't steal it. And I certainly didn't murder anyone."

"But you don't know who you bought it from. Too bad. I hope it was a good handshake."

"I got his car license plate number. You can find who it was."

Duke and Glothe looked at one another. "What happened to the good old Texas handshake that seals the deal?" Duke asked.

Winston was whining now. "Some people you can't trust."

Glothe stared at the man. "He just parked out front and sauntered in with a seven hundred thousand dollar painting?"

"No. He parked across the street. When he left, I grabbed my binoculars and got his plate number. I've got it in the office."

Glothe nodded twice. "Slim, take him back there and get the number. Then, let's get this dangerous criminal into a jail so the good people of Texas will be safer."

The sheriff didn't think Winston was innocent, but he did believe he hadn't stolen the painting. He didn't have the nerves for it. Or the skill. If he had gotten the license plate correct, then they could take the next step. And each step would take them closer to the person who had stolen the painting and killed Nat Owens.

# Chapter 20

**Saturday, October 13**

**With less than** a month to go before election, Ron Drake was rarely in Wooden Nickel. Sometimes, he visited four different cities in a day. Crystal had heard several interviewers asked about his health. He always remarked that if a person could live through the final month of campaigning, that meant they were in good health.

Crystal was not his campaign manager, but she was working just as hard. She put out a number of press releases, each tailored to the small town newspaper that received it. She arranged for the printing of posters, banners and giveaways, several of which the paid agency copped off and circulated as well. She didn't mind. It was all to help her friend Ron Drake. She helped energize local party leaders, and acted as a go-between when they needed something from the candidate.

And it was all working. Drake's numbers in the polls inched up little by little. When Crystal was disappointed in the progress, she had to remind herself that once you approached seventy percent of the voters on your side, it was tough to move ahead rapidly. A point here, a point there was all one could expect.

Jim Bob's core group held fairly steady. The gains Drake made were taken from the shrinking undecided voter pool.

It made sense to Crystal. If you listened to Ron, really listened, then you would vote for him. By the same token, if you really listened to Jim Bob, you were *not* going to vote for him.

She was glad the incident with the painting was over, at least somewhat. Perhaps it would no longer be a distraction for Ron. Or the voters. Unfortunately, the police still had no clues to the murderer of Nat Owens. He had been a friend of Ron's for many years and Ron felt some responsibility for his death. Even as Crystal and many others told Ron he should feel no guilt, still he did. More than once, he had said to Crystal, "If I hadn't asked for those papers. If someone hadn't been stealing my painting. If I had had a better security system." He had lost a friend and he felt responsible.

* * *

It didn't take long to track down the auto from the license number Brown had provided. It belonged to Emil Rohrbak, owner of a small pawnshop not far from the Art Treasures. Before noon, Glothe and Bentley confronted Rohrbak. At first, he denied knowing anything about the painting. But a mention of capital murder charges, in addition to theft, jogged his memory.. Rohrbak produced the sheet Bert Monday had filled out. Rohrbak said he had checked the man's driver's license, and his notations showed he had paid Monday five hundred dollars for the painting, not knowing it was stolen. Glothe pointed out that was a difficult position to claim since Rohrbak sold it for ten thousand just hours later.

"Don't spend the money, and don't leave town," Bentley said. "Representatives from my company will be coming to retrieve the money. You can't make money selling stolen property."

* * *

Bert Monday's mouth fell open and he simply stared at the two men. "Worth how much?"

"In the neighborhood of seven hundred thousand."

Monday sank down onto his worn couch and put his head in his hands. Glothe and Bentley stood just inside the door to the living room of the small house. To the right of the couch was a well-used recliner facing an old style, thirty-two inch TV. An end-table, covered with circles etched into its top by many a beer can filled the space between couch and recliner. A rug, badly in need of cleaning, covered most of the living room floor.

"Seven hundred thousand dollars. Just sitting in an unlocked mini-warehouse." He jerked his head up. "Was that the picture somebody stole from that politician?"

Glothe nodded.

"Wow." For a minute he just shook his head back and forth. Then he jumped up. "You don't think I stole it, do you? I found it. That mini was unlocked. People all the time go off, leave stuff they don't want. Easier than taking it to the dump. That unit's right next to mine, so's it must be number seventy-three. Or seventy-one." He thought for a moment. "No, seventy-three's right. Always been locked since I rented seventy-two. Until Tuesday. It was unlocked. The people had given it up or something. And the picture was just there. I didn't steal it. They left it. Abandoned it. I ain't stole nothing."

Monday sank back into his chair. His breathing was rapid and perspiration covered his forehead. He was shaking his head, looking down, his hands gripping one another.

Glothe believed Monday was telling the truth, more or less. Still, they needed information. "So, who rented seventy-three?"

Monday looked up and hunched his shoulders. "No idea. Never saw nobody there."

"How much did you get for the painting when you sold it at the pawnshop?"

Monday looked down at his feet. "Five hundred."

Glothe thought the man was embarrassed to tell he got so little for a seven hundred thousand dollar painting. At least his figure matched what Rohrbak had told them. "You planning to include that on your income tax return?"

Monday was still looking down. "Ah, well, ah, I don't know; I ain't thought about it." Apparently he realized what he'd said and looked up at the sheriff. "Yeah. 'Course I will."

Bentley said, "Probably not. I imagine my company will insist on retrieving that money."

Monday didn't say anything, but it was clear this was just another bit of the bad news that had started since the two men knocked at his door.

$$* * *$$

Glothe and Bentley stood at the small counter of the Wooden Nickel Mini-storage office as a woman searched through a stack of cards.

"Gotta be here somewhere," she said as she pushed her glasses back up on her nose and started over at the top of the stack. "We don't let a unit without them filling out a card."

The two men said nothing, just shifted their weight from one foot to the other and waited. The tiny office had a single, cracked plastic chair against the front window. Glothe looked out. He couldn't see unit seventy-three from here. In fact, all he could see were the very small units, maybe four by six, easily big enough for the painting, but more exposed to a view from the office or the road. He and Bentley had already visited unit seventy-three, put crime scene tape around it, as if that would do any good. It had been months since the painting was stolen. Chances of finding any usable prints or other evidence hovered between zero and none.

Finally, the woman let out an exasperated breath. "Ain't here. Gotta be, but it ain't."

"Any other place it might be? Any other place you might have that information?" asked Glothe.

"Well, yeah. We got all the stuff on the computer. No signature, of course. But all the information ought a be there." She stood there looking at the men.

"Could you get that for us, please?" asked Bentley.

She shrugged and turned her attention to a computer terminal. She typed in a few letters and hit the return key. Almost immediately she let out a low curse and typed again. This time, she got something that pleased her. "Here it is. Rented on March 18."

"Whose name was it rented under?" asked Glothe in a tone with more patience than he felt.

"Name? Let me see." She adjusted her glasses. "Ron Drake."

## Chapter 21

**Both men had** been trained not to show surprise or shock at answers to questions they ask. Their faces remained passive even as they cut their eyes to each other to exchange a look.

Glothe pulled out a small notebook and pen and said, "Spell that name, please."

She frowned at Glothe as if he were retarded. "How else? R. O. N. Space. D. R. A. K. E." She looked at the sheriff. "You get that?"

Glothe nodded. "What other information have you got on it?"

"Paid in advance for eight months." She raised her eyebrows. "That's a strange amount of time. But it says cash, so I guess whatever time worked."

"Address?"

The woman read off the address. Bentley looked at Glothe, who nodded ever so slightly.

Bentley leaned on the counter, getting closer to the woman. "You've been very helpful. But, we really need to see the original card, with the signature." He smiled his brightest and most engaging smile. "Is there someplace you could check on that card? Maybe a place for the cards that are out of date--the rental period over."

She looked back at the computer screen. "Rental period ain't over yet. Guy's still got control of it. Card ought a be here."

Glothe didn't smile. "Would you please look at the other cards anyway, ma'am." It didn't come out as a question. She hesitated a moment, then turned and opened a cabinet behind her and pulled out a box overflowing with cards.

For nearly ten minutes she thumbed through cards, occasionally pulling one up and studying it before putting it back and continuing. Finally, she replaced the box and turned back to her tormentors. "Satisfied? No card for Drake. And no card for unit seventy-three this year."

"And there's no other place that card might be?" asked Glothe.

"Not that I know of."

Glothe pulled out a business card and handed it to the woman. "This is important. If you think of anything connected with unit seventy-three, please call me."

"Does the computer entry show which of your employees took the rental?" asked Bentley.

"Yeah. Should," she said and turned back to the computer screen, letting her glasses slide down to the end of her nose. She peered over them. "J J. That would be Julie Johnson."

"Do you have an address for Julie Johnson, or a telephone number?" asked Glothe.

"No. She's gone back to college." Glothe opened his mouth to ask a question, but the woman added, "In Dallas. Don't remember what school. But in Dallas."

"Her parents live in Wooden Nickel?"

"I guess so. Pretty sure she graduated from Nickel High."

"You have her employment form, an address where you send her W2 tax form?"

"Nah. Accountant's got that stuff. Why don't you just try the phone book? I mean, how many Johnsons in Nickel anyway?"

"Good idea. Now, how 'bout you write down the name and phone number of the accountant."

* * *

The accountant's office provided the address and phone number of Julie's parents, and after a bit of prodding, Julie's mother provided a cell phone number for Julie at the University of Dallas. "Mostly, she responds to text messages," Julie's mother advised.

*I don't do texts.* "Thank you, Ms. Johnson," Glothe said before disconnecting.

It was after six that evening when Julie finally answered her phone.

"March 18? That was just after basketball finished, you know. Yeah, I guess I was working then. But I don't remember specific customers."

Ron Drake's name got no response. Finally, Glothe reminded her he had paid cash in advance for eight months.

"Oh yeah. Didn't get much cash. Mostly credit cards or checks. And only one guy paid for eight months. If I got cash, like it was usually just for one month. But, yeah, one guy did pay for eight months."

"What do you remember about the man? Was it a man?"

"Ron Drake. It's a man's name. Let me think."

Glothe waited patiently for several long minutes.

"Drake. I remember something. But I don't remember what."

Glothe was about to comment on that last statement when she continued.

"Yeah. Yeah. He couldn't fill out the card. Had a broken hand or something. Like his right hand was all bandaged up. I said he had to sign, you know, that's the rule. He just smiled and said he'd hurt his hand and couldn't even hold a pen, much less sign anything. He just stood there and smiled sweetly. Nice man. So, what was I to do? I said I hoped I didn't get into any trouble for not getting his signature."

"What happened to the card? They couldn't find it in the file?"

"I don't know about that. I put it in the box, you know, just like always."

"Can you describe the man?"

Julie hesitated. "Ah, like he smiled a lot."

"How tall was he? What color were his eyes? His hair? Long, short? How was it cut?"

"Tall? Yeah, I guess he was tall. I guess as tall as my boy friend, and he's over six feet. I don't remember the color of his eyes. I mean, like, I don't really … I don't know. He had brown hair, I think. Maybe." She paused for a minute. "He was a little overweight. I noticed that, 'cause like I said, he was about as tall as my boyfriend, but this guy was fatter. I mean, not real fat, but, well, not skinny. You know, maybe a little fat."

"Anything else you can tell me about him? How did he act? Was he nervous, for instance?"

"I don't think so. He smiled a lot. I don't think he was nervous. I was. I never took a rental without a signature before. But, the boss likes cash. Says the credit card companies charge him to process it. So, I thought, you know, maybe he wouldn't be too mad. And I didn't get into any trouble over it."

"Did you see any identification?"

"Ah, I don't remember. I mean, I usually did. But this was so different. I mean, cash, no signature. I did put it in the computer. I remember that."

Glothe left his name and telephone number and asked Julie to call if she thought of anything else.

* * *

Glothe leaned back and stretched, then rubbed his neck and shoulders. He and Bentley had dined on Hungerbuster Hamburgers and Blizzards at the local Dairy Queen. For the past two hours they had been sitting in Glothe's stuffy office, hashing over the details.

"What're you going to do with Monday, and the pawn store owner and Winston?" asked Bentley.

"Monday didn't have any idea what he had. I think he really believed someone just went off and left it. Now Rohrbak's a different story. He bought it for $500 and sold it for ten grand. He knew it was stolen. So he's clearly dealing in stolen property. And Winston's guilty as sin. So, I'll just scare Monday a bit.Get him back on the straight and narrow, even though there's not much we can do to him. As for Rohrbak and Winston, I'll turn them over to the Tyler police. Won't be my problem. 'Course, those are pretty much slam-dunks."

"And then, there's Drake."

"Yeah, then there's Drake." The sheriff just shook his head slowly back and forth for several seconds."It's just so strange. Ron Drake has been an upstanding citizen of this community for a bunch of years. And now, he's a shoo-in for governor. Hard to imagine him resorting to insurance fraud." Glothe drew his lips into a long thin line. "Just doesn't make sense. And I know he and Nat Owens were friends for a long time."

Bentley put his elbows on the table and leaned forward. "Didn't Owens do accounting for Drake? Could there have been problems with the books, something that caused a disagreement?"

Glothe shook his head. "I can't see it." He reached in his shirt pocket, pulled out a toothpick and stuck it in his mouth. "Owens was Ron's property manager. I don't know whether he did his books or not. But, Ron has homes here and in Dallas, plus other properties out here. And money, lots of it. He's retired. And he's paying for most of his campaign himself. Doesn't want to owe any favors if elected."

"Maybe the campaign's draining his bank account. That could account for the art theft. Maybe, he didn't really want to lose the painting. So he collects the insurance money to beef up his coffers and gets to keep his Mondrian."

"You're sounding like the district attorney."

"No. Like an insurance investigator. I've seen this sort of thing more than once. Doesn't help that he has no serious security system on the house."

"His house is on a twenty-acre plot just outside Nickel. I've never known him to have any kind of security problem in all the years he's lived there. This isn't Dallas. We don't have that much theft out here. Now, if he'd had a new tractor parked out front, he might have to worry. Or a chainsaw. In all my years in law enforcement here in east Texas, we've never had an art theft. Had an antique tractor stolen a couple of years back. Hundred years old and still running. The owner drove it to the Wooden Nickel tractor show each year."

"Well, a painting was stolen, not a tractor. Home office complained, threatened to fight the payment. But I pointed out to them we had a man check out the house before issuing the policy. We didn't really have a leg to stand on over that."

Again, neither said anything for a minute. "What are you going to do?" Bentley asked.

"What are *you* going to do?" Glothe shot back, almost losing the toothpick.

"Well, we've paid Drake, so the painting is ours. First thing I'm going to do is see what it's really worth on the market. Most people have art underinsured. Company might actually make money on it. But, it's possible we'll want to file a civil suit. Don't know."

"I got to collect a few more facts. Then, I guess I'll turn it all over to the district attorney. Problem is, she's running for reelection. If she could win a good case like this..." He cocked his head to one side. "Buy her a lot of votes."

"That's Joan Abbott?"

"Yeah."

"She know Drake?"

"Not really. He did not back her in the last election."

"When're you going to talk to her?"

"I'll pull things together tomorrow and turn it all over to her." Glothe shook his head. "Glad it's not my decision."

"Did the girl's description sound like Drake?"

At this, the sheriff looked down, his eyebrows knitted. "The prosecutor could say it does. Drake is not fat at all. But then she did equivocate on that. Height's right for Drake." He looked up. "Only good thing is the hair. Ron's is definitely silver. Not close to brown. But, I imagine that won't help much. The problem is his name in the rental records."

"And the painting was in the storage unit."

## Chapter 22

**Monday, October 15**

**Glothe sat in** a comfortable blue leather chair and watched the District Attorney reading the file he had presented to her. He watched the hungry wolf eyeing a fat chicken. Occasionally a slight smile crossed her face. Then, she would glance at Glothe and the smile would be replaced with a serious but neutral look.

"Doesn't look good for our gubernatorial candidate, does it?" Joan Abbott asked.

"We do have records of a call from the Drake house to Ron Drake's cell phone about twenty minutes before the call to 9-1-1. Ron said Nat Owens called him to say the painting was gone."

The small smile again. "So Drake says."

"We have witnesses who say Drake got a call at the rally, and immediately left."

"Anybody hear what he said? Ask him why he had to leave?" Abbott was not smiling now.

"No."

"What's he saying now?"

"I haven't talked to him since we found the painting," said Glothe.

"Why the hell not?"

"He's not in town. I certainly expect to sit down and have a talk with him as soon as he returns to Nickel."

Joan Abbott jerked up a bit straighter. "Get on the phone and track him down. Tell him to get back here."

"I don't think --"

"I don't care what you think. "If you don't want to do that, I can put out a BOLO to have him picked up and brought in." She fixed Glothe with a hostile stare. "What's it gonna be, Sheriff?"

## Chapter 23

**"No. I did** not steal my own painting." Ron Drake sat facing Joan Abbott. She was behind a walnut desk, her pen poised over a green legal pad. The Assistant District Attorney Fran Summers sat in a straight backed chair to the side, hands in her lap, her small mouth in a slight smile.

"Whatever you call it isn't important. Did you collect $400,000 from an insurance company for that stolen painting?"

"I did. The painting was stolen. After approximately six months, the insurance company decided they had not recovered it in a timely fashion and sent me a check for that amount. I deposited it in my bank. The payment and the timing were their decisions."

"Did you rent a storage unit at Wooden Nickel Mini-Storage?"

"I did not."

"We have unit number seventy-three with your name on it. Would you think about that for a minute and reconsider your answer?"

Ron sat and looked at Abbott for a minute, his eyes never wavering. "I have never rented or used anything at Wooden Nickel Mini-Storage, or at any other storage facility in this county."

"And yet, they have records showing unit seventy-three rented to you with a cash payment for eight months, starting on March 18 of this year. Oddly, that is just a few days before your painting was removed from your house."

"Stolen from my house. Did the card have my signature on it? If so, I'd like to see it."

"No signature. The woman who took it said your hand was hurt and you could not hold a pen."

"No. That is not what she said." This caused Summers' mouth to gape slightly. Abbott did not react. Drake continued. "She said the person renting the unit—not me— had a bad hand. Did she get or even see any identification?"

Now, Abbott looked down, for the first time in this meeting looking a bit uneasy. "No."

"Isn't that required?"

"Yes. But she was a young woman."

"In point of fact," said Fran Summers, sitting a bit taller, "she was a high school student. So she probably forgot to ask for any. Or perhaps she knew you. Or at least knew you were an important person and didn't want to challenge you."

Ron didn't say anything, just watched the young district attorney. Finally, the DA straightened the papers on her desk, then looked up at Drake. "Don't leave the area."

Ron stood up and looked down at Abbott. "I'm in the final month of a political campaign. I expect to be out of town for the next few weeks." He pulled out a business card and dropped it on her desk. "Here's my cell phone number. If you need me here, I can come back. Will that meet your requirements?"

* * *

Crystal pushed the doorbell and waited.

Ron Drake opened the door. "Hi Crystal. Come on in."

Drake had hired Texas Public Relations, a P.R. firm with offices in Houston and Dallas, to handle the campaign. But Crystal helped Ron with many details related to the northeast Texas area, giving it special coverage as the home base of the candidate but also of his opponent.

As they walked back to his office, Crystal said, "I heard they found your painting."

"Yes. At an art dealer in Tyler. Man was willing to sell it for $75,000."

"Wow. What a bargain. Not a very smart art dealer. You should have bought it."

Ron laughed. "Probably should have. But now I'm in trouble." He sat down at a large table with campaign literature organized in neat piles.

She placed a folder on the table. A frown creased her face. "Trouble? What kind of trouble? Someone stole your painting. How does that put *you* in trouble?" Crystal took another chair, but ignored the literature.

"It's a long story. But it seems the painting first went to a storage unit here in Wooden Nickel. And the paperwork said I had rented it. So the DA thinks I stole it to collect the insurance money. Said maybe my campaign was running me low on cash."

Crystal let out a laugh. " How ridiculous can that be? The painting's worth a lot more than you had it insured for. If you needed money, you should have sold it."

"As she sees it, I collected four hundred grand and still have the painting."

"Well, that's just stupid. And you don't have the painting; the insurance company does. How'd it get to Tyler?"

"They traced it back to a man who said he found it in an unlocked storage unit at the Wooden Nickel Mini-Storage, the same unit their records show I rented."

Crystal just looked at him with her mouth open.

"Clearly I should have locked the place," Ron said with a grin. "But, let's get on with our plans for the final three weeks. This campaigning is wearing me out. I need to turn in early tonight."

Crystal pulled a paper out of the folder. "Is Abbott serious?"

"Serious as cancer. But let's don't waste any more time on that. Let's see what you have."

She handed him a sheet.

He studied the information for a minute, then looked up at Crystal. "You're going to get all this done in three weeks?"

"Most of that will happen next week. The rest, in the last two weeks."

He looked over the sheet again. "I don't know why I hired Texas Public Relations. I think you're getting more done than they are." He handed the paper back to Crystal.

"You're okay with all of that?"

"Sure. But I don't want you to lose your job, or land in the hospital."

"Not to worry. Mark is behind me on this. He told me to take as much time as we need to get you elected. Plus, I'm enjoying it and I'm doing something to help Texas."

"The *Great* State of Texas," Ron said with a laugh. "You and Mark about to get married?"

Crystal put the paper back in her folder, a slight blush creeping up her neck. "No comment. Isn't that a good political answer?" She got up to leave. "This isn't going to be in the paper is it? I mean, just the mention of it, even if later retracted, will cost us votes."

"She said she'd not let it out to the press." He paused. "Unless she was ready to charge me."

* * *

Shortly after ten, Crystal walked into the Dallas house she shared with Brandi. "Hey, I stopped on the way in and brought us some ice cream. Ready for some Moo-llennium?

Brandi sat on the couch with her feet tucked under her small, five-foot-five frame. As usual, her auburn hair was perfect. But her aqua eyes were unusually dark.

"You better get yourself a big bowl. You've got trouble. But you've only got a minute before the commercial is over."

"What on earth are you talking about?"

"Better yet, take a seat. We'll get the ice cream later. You're going to need it."

"What is this—"

"Shush. Here it comes."

Crystal looked at the TV. The commercial ended and the newsman began.

"We've just learned from a reliable source that Ron Drake, the current leader in the race for the governor's office, has been brought in for questioning on the subject of insurance fraud. We reported back in March on a high-priced Mondrian painting that was stolen from the home of Mr. Drake. We don't have the exact details, but approximately a week ago, the insurance company paid Mr. Drake for his loss, reportedly $400,000. Two days ago, the painting was recovered at a dealer in Tyler. As the police traced it back it appears the painting had been stored in a mini-warehouse in Wooden Nickel. The name on the rental papers for that particular unit was ... Ron Drake.

"No formal charges have been filed. But the local district attorney has questioned Mr. Drake. That's all we have at this time. But we will stay on top of this story, as it involves a man running for the office of governor of Texas, a man who is currently well in the lead according to polls."

Brandi punched the mute button. "They ran a teaser just before you came in which said something like possible fraud in the governor's race."

Crystal jumped up and started for the phone. "That two-faced ... liar. She said she would not release anything to the media. I've got to call Ron."

She stopped. It was late. Ron said he was tired and was going to bed early. And what could he do tonight. Let him get some sleep. "I'll call in the morning."

"You want some ice cream?"
"Yes. A big bowl."

# Chapter 24

**Tuesday, October 16**

**"It appears you** chose to share your suspicions with the media." Drake threw the comment out as an accusation.

"I did not." The District Attorney raised her chin defiantly and looked Drake in the eye. "I don't know how they got the information."

Ron nodded a few times. "I was under the impression only you, your assistant and I were privy to our conversation. I certainly did not alert the media. How do you suppose they got that information?"

"My office does not leak information. You probably told someone and perhaps another person was listening."

"Or *you* did just that."

" Did you kill Nathanael Owens?"

Ron's head jerked and his eyes opened wide. "Are you crazy? Nat was my friend, my property manager. Why would you even ask such a question?"

Fran Summers jumped in. "You called it in to 9-1-1. There was no evidence of forced entry. Your Mondrian was missing and later turned up in your storage unit, you ——"

"It was *not* my storage unit." Drake's focus remained on the District Attorney.

Abbott silenced her assistant with a glance, then faced Drake. "In a storage unit with your name on the contract. You received $400,000 for the missing painting. The only fingerprints we found belonged to you or Mr. Owens." She paused a second. "Was Mr. Owens also your accountant?"

"He was not. He did some basic book-keeping for me as my property manager, but that was it. Those records were always turned over to my accountant."

Abbott shuffled through some papers, then scribbled something on a green legal pad. "Let me remind you, Mr. Drake, you are not to leave this jurisdiction."

"Are you planning to arrest me?"

"Not at this time."

"Then I will continue with my campaign, which will take me outside your jurisdiction, but will keep me in the state of Texas. I have given you my cell phone number so you can reach me if you need to."

"Under the circumstances, I'll allow it."

Drake stood up. "And I'd like to request that you do not release this conversation to the media unless you are ready to charge me with some crime. I was rather surprised to hear the information we discussed yesterday — in private, in your office — reported on last night's ten o'clock news." Without waiting for a response, he turned and left the office.

* * *

The rally in Dallas had gone well. The large hall was filled to overflowing and the enthusiastic crowd cheered its approval as Drake outlined the programs he would initiate. When he opened it up to questions, dozens of hands went up. Drake tried to answer each one, treading that line between being thorough, yet succinct enough to move to the next person.

The questions had been good, allowing Drake to highlight some of his plans to improve life in "The Great State of Texas", as he always called it.

After forty-five minutes, no more hands were waving. He answered what appeared to be the last question and began giving his closing thanks.

From her perch backstage, Crystal could identify a number of representatives from various media outlets. Of course *The Dallas Morning News* had a photographer and a reporter present. But there were also people from *The Houston Chronicle*, *The San Antonio Express-News*, the *Waco Tribune Herald*. Even the *Amarillo Globe-News* had a representative Crystal recognized. As she searched the crowd, she could pick out a number of TV stations represented. Dallas had three stations in attendance. San Antonio's KTSA had a crew here, as did Houston's KHOU and KTRK. Several other camera crews that Crystal did not recognize had filmed a good portion of the rally. Most had started to shut down their operations and pack up gear. She would ask TPR, Drake's P.R. firm, how many requests for media credentials they received.

At the back of the hall, a man crashed through the door waving his hand and yelling to get Drake's attention. He appeared to have a recording device in one hand.

"Mr. Drake, Mr. Drake." Ron acknowledged him. "What can you tell us about your visit this morning with the district attorney in Wooden Nickel? My sources tell me she accused you of murdering William Owens."

For a few seconds, the hall was as quiet as a tomb. All heads turned to look at the man asking the question. Then, the whispering began as people returned their focus to Drake.

A man near the front called out, "Yeah, Drake. What's he talking about?" Crystal thought she recognized him as a Jim Bob Wilson supporter.

Ron held his hand up to quiet the crowd. It took nearly a minute for the noise level to subside. When it was quiet, Ron spoke directly into the microphone. "She asked me if I killed Nat Owens. His name was Nathanael Owens, not William Owens. He was an employee and my friend. I told her I did not. That's about it. Our conversation was maybe three minutes long."

Several people were yelling questions. Crystal pushed Ron aside and took the microphone. "That's all the questions for tonight, guys. Regarding the meeting this morning, there's really nothing else to say. Mr. Drake is not a suspect." A murmur went through the crowd. "Let me repeat that. Mr. Drake is *not* a suspect. Mr. Owens worked for Mr. Drake for ten years. The DA was just doing her job, asking a routine question that would always be asked in a situation like this. Nothing more." She paused for a second. "Let me ask you a question. Would Mr. Drake be here if the DA really thought he was in any way connected with the death of Mr. Owens?"

# Chapter 25

**Every news outlet** carried the information at its next possible opportunity, either the late night news, or the early morning paper. The headlines were more sensational than the meeting with the DA deserved.

The public reaction was quick. Drake's poll number dropped overnight by five points.

Crystal arrived at work early and immediately went to Mark's office and slumped into a chair. "Have you seen the latest news on the election?"

"Heard it on the late news last night. And the morning papers have been—what can I say?—sensational."

"It's criminal the way they are reporting it."

"I agree. But you can't blame them. It's been a pretty dull campaign so far. Drake was running away with it. It was like a horse race with only one horse. A yawner."

"Well, this certainly took it out of the dull class. But it's so unfair. Drake hasn't even done anything, but to read the papers, he's almost in Huntsville already."

Mark's face conveyed the concern he felt. "The real question is, how is the information getting to the media?"

Crystal shook her head but said nothing. For a minute Mark focused his attention on his desktop. When he looked up, wrinkles creased his forehead. "I'm concerned about this turn of events. And frankly, if it isn't stopped, it could cost Drake the election."

The statement brought Crystal to the edge of the chair. "You really think it will come to that? Ron's down a few points this morning, but he still has a healthy lead."

"Most people haven't gotten the news yet. I'm afraid the slide will only increase as word spreads. A few more leaks from that DA's office and Drake's lead will vanish."

"But —"

Mark held his hand up. "I want you to go to Wooden Nickel and see what you can do to help stop this. The other day, I told you to help him when you could. Today, I'm saying take off the next three weeks and see what you can do to help Ron. If you can stop this slide in a week, great. I wouldn't count on it." Mark ran a hand through his chestnut hair. "Jim Bob Wilson would be a disaster for the state. Go. Do what you can. Keep me posted."

He got up, walked over and closed the door. "But I want an unhurried, and uninterrupted kiss before you leave."

"I'll need it to get me through this."

Mark wrapped his arms around her and pulled her in for a slow, deep kiss. For a minute, Crystal forgot all about the election, or leaks to the media. The tingling running through her had only to do with the man in her arms.

* * *

Mark's glum prediction was right. Drake's numbers kept falling. Within two days, his lead of almost seventy percent dropped to barely sixty.

Crystal picked at the brisket Eula had fixed. "He's still got a comfortable lead, but it just galls me the media are painting this much darker than it is. Surely they know Ron would not be stupid enough

98

to steal his own painting and then hide it in a storage locker - one with his name on the contract. And you don't leave a fine, expensive painting in a location subject to extreme temperatures and humidity, rats, and who knows what else. It's worth probably six or seven hundred thousand, and Ron knows that. Why on earth would he put it in a forty-dollar storage locker? He wouldn't. And how was it left unlocked?"

"Just sells papers. They used to say a good multi-car accident could double sales of the *Gazette*. So they write the wildest headline they can get away with. Same thing's true for TV."

"But it isn't fair."

Eula laughed. "Fair is when it rains and the crop comes in good. You're talking 'bout politics. Nothing fair there."

The two women started to clear the table. "Since all the TV stations ran the same thing, not much advantage there. And nowadays you only got one newspaper in a town." Eula paused and looked at Crystal. "So, who really profits from spouting such a story?"

"Wilson."

"Exactamento. Old Jim Bob couldn't have asked for a better helping hand. I think he's crooked enough to do it himself, only he ain't got the smarts to do it."

"Then how did he even know about it? Or his campaign people?"

"That, my young granddaughter, is what you need to find out. And quick. It's always easier and faster to slip down than to climb up."

Eula had challenged her granddaughter. Now she worried. Crystal was so involved she might do something foolish—and dangerous. *Dear Lord, keep Your Arm around her shoulder. And Your hand over her mouth.*

# Chapter 26

**Friday, October 19**

**In spite of** Crystal's efforts and a push by the public relations firm handling Drake's campaign, his numbers in the polls continued to slip, little by little. His lead was down to nine points.

Two-and-a-half weeks before the election, Joan Abbott called Ron and demanded he return to Wooden Nickel immediately. He was forced to cancel two appearances and the news media jumped on the story. Headlines and teasers on radio and TV all gave the same message:

"Drake forced to return to face the District Attorney on charges of insurance fraud and possibly murder."

TPR contacted a number of the media that released these headlines, demanding they retract the statement. No charges had been filed. The headline and the message were misleading. A few of them changed the headline to:

"Drake forced to return to face the District Attorney on questions about insurance fraud and possibly murder."

* * *

Meanwhile, Jim Bob Wilson did not miss an opportunity to call attention to information leaked from the district attorney's office.

"Well, that pretty, young DA had to call Ron Drake back into her office. This time, it was questions about insurance fraud. Y'all know he just pocketed a nifty four hundred thou? Guess the expense of his massive campaign put a hurt on his bank account. 'Course, most of us wouldn't be able to pour out that kind of money for some painting in the first place. And I'm told it just looks like some grade school kid splattered paint on the canvas."

The large crowd assembled in the ballroom of the San Antonio Riverwalk Hilton roared its approval. Jim Bob encouraged the throng waving his hands over his head.

When they quieted down, he continued. "'Course, that's just small potatoes lined up beside a murder charge. And finding the painting in Drake's own storage locker makes his assistant's death look even more suspicious. You know, we might not even need to vote if the lovely DA moves a little faster. Ole Drake might be sittin' in the county jail, or the Texas pen, by election time." He let out a loud guffaw. "Here's a good one for you. Drake manages to buy enough votes with that extra four hundred K, and steals this election. But before he can get sworn in, he's in the Texas pen down in Huntsville. Could he run the government from a prison cell?" He laughed. "I don't know. I hope it doesn't come down to that. Let's just win this thing and not have to worry about that. Maybe they'll let ole Ron take his painting with him, hang it in his cell."

# Chapter 27

**Crystal walked into** Jim Bob Wilson's campaign headquarters in Tyler. The gubernatorial candidate had a large ranch not far from Tyler, the Rose Capital of the World. So much of his campaign work was based out of this office. Fortunately, one could reach Wilson's headquarters in a twenty minute drive from Wooden Nickel.

When Crystal finally found who was in charge, a middle aged man named Lester Principal, she asked that they discontinue comments about Ron Drake likely being in jail. She pointed out no charges had been filed, nor were any likely to be filed. But since it was Mr. Drake's painting, and since the victim was found in Mr. Drake's house, it was not unusual for him to be consulted frequently on the case. Crystal could tell she was making no impression on the man. "Jim Bob said he wanted a fair race," she reminded him.

"And we're getting one - now. Wasn't too fair when Drake had seventy percent of the vote and was overwhelming the public with publicity. But now, well, this is turning into a real dogfight. And I think Jim Bob always wins in a dogfight."

Crystal wondered if political races should be dogfights, but decided it best to ignore that statement. "He said no mud-slinging. Putting out stories that are not true is mud-slinging. Suggesting Mr.

Drake might be in prison by election time, when he hasn't been charged, and won't be charged, is hardly playing fair. All I'm asking is that you put out only the truth. Not innuendo. Not shocking statements that have no basis in truth."

"Well, Ms. Moore, you can rest assured Jim Bob Wilson will continue to wage a tough, but true, campaign. No mud will come from this side." Crystal started to speak, but Les kept right on. "However, the public has a right to know what's going on with the candidates. I guarantee Jim Bob has not said Drake is guilty. And he won't, unless the courts announce it. Jim Bob will just report what he hears—just like he's been doing. Then the voters can decide how likely it is that a rich man like Drake can escape prison or not. This is an important case. We don't want any secret deals, anything swept under the carpet. Let's get everything out in the open. Let the people decide."

When it was clear Principal wasn't about to consider her arguments, Crystal turned without saying goodbye, dejected. Every mention of Drake and jail was a clear example of mud-slinging.

As she turned to leave, she found herself looking at a woman she had seen before. But where? Her mind raced through all the people she had come in contact with lately. None matched this young woman. The tingle she felt down the back of her neck made her believe it was important. But her mind was a blank. She started toward the door again when the picture popped into her brain.

The young brunette in the District Attorney's office.

The woman was talking with a man when Crystal approached her. "You're Fran ...."

"Summers. And you are?"

"Crystal Moore. You work in the DA's office."

"That's right." Fran's voice and manner became cautious.

"But you're here, in Jim Bob Wilson's campaign office."

The cautious attitude morphed into aggressive. "So? I'm free to support any candidate I choose. What's your problem with that?"

"I don't care whom you support. But private information from the DA's office has been leaked to the media."

Summers now looked angry. "Are you accusing me of leaking information?"

"Not accusing you. But I do find it interesting you are here and information from the DA's office, which was not to be made available to the media, has been leaked."

Now the Assistant DA was almost screaming. "How dare you come in here and make accusations."

"Did you leak that information?"

To Crystal, it looked like Summers might become physical. Her hands formed tight balls, the muscles in her arms tensed. Crystal felt like retreating a few steps, but she refused to back down from this excitable, out-of-control woman.

The man Fran had been talking with stepped in closer. "Ladies, ladies. Let's not let this get out of hand. Ms. Moore, Fran said she didn't leak any information. Maybe we should just drop this discussion."

"She didn't actually say that."

Fran's face was angry and filled with hate. "I didn't. Now, get out."

"You didn't what? Didn't say it, or didn't leak it?"

Summers's face had become red, puffy, and looked ready to explode. Her fists drew back slightly and she leaned toward Crystal. The man stepped directly in front of Summers, blocking her from moving any closer to Crystal or striking out at her. But Summers's voice carried throughout the building. "Get out of here."

Crystal made her way to the door. Just before she reached it, she saw a young woman watching her, obviously embarrassed by the screaming coming from Summers.

"Sorry to have stirred things up," said Crystal. "Thank goodness that man saved me. Would you tell him thank you for me? What's his name?"

The woman nodded. "That's George Weeks. Nice man. I'll tell him you said thanks."

Crystal left. *George Weeks may be a nice man, or he may be trying to defuse a situation he and Summers are both involved in. And clearly, I touched a nerve for Summers.*

As soon as Crystal walked in to Eula's house, she headed for the telephone. It took her only thirty seconds to find the number in the directory. When a woman answered, Crystal simply stated it was important and confidential. Seven minutes later, Abbott finally came on the line. Crystal wasted no time.

"My name is Crystal Moore and I think I've found who is leaking your information to the media. I believe it is Fran Summers."

The District Attorney hesitated only a moment before responding. "I find that hard to believe. She's been a trusted employee for nearly a year. She isn't here right now or I would ask her. Why do you think that, Ms. Moore? Do you have any proof?"

"I know she's not there. She's at Jim Bob's campaign headquarters."

There was silence for a minute. Finally Abbott said, "That does not mean she has leaked any information. She is free to support any candidate she chooses. But I will ask her about it. I don't tolerate anyone giving out information from my office unless I have okayed it. Thank you for your call."

Crystal placed the phone back in its cradle.

"Who'd you call before you even speak to your Nana?" Eula asked.

"The district attorney. I think I found who's leaking the information. Abbott said she'd put a stop to it."

"Good work," said Eula. "But a mite too late, I'm thinking. I just heard a report on the radio. Ron's down to a seven point lead."

"But he's still ahead, even with all this bad publicity."

"Yeah. But he's going down and Jim Bob's going up. Ain't good for Ron."

## Chapter 28

**Crystal spent an** hour scanning the Internet for anything on Fran Summers. Nothing of help showed up. No political connections listed. No mention of political involvement when she was in school. Crystal sighed and logged off. She started to get up, but settled back in her chair, looking down, not really seeing anything. Her mind was focused on George Weeks. Something about him kept niggling at her. But she couldn't put her finger on it. She concentrated on her mental picture of him, and let his image fill her brain. And then she remembered the description of the man who rented the unit under Ron Drake's name - the one given by the young woman who handled the rental. She logged back onto the Internet and began searching.

Within minutes, she found two pieces linking a George B. Weeks to political dirty tricks. He was not charged with anything, but the articles presented a strong case that Weeks had orchestrated the release of information that likely had an impact on the outcome of two elections. One of the stories suggested Weeks had been involved in other dirty tricks but there was less incriminating evidence.

Crystal closed her eyes and put her head in her hands. Leaking information like that would certainly qualify as a dirty trick. But often, the information leaked was true. Perhaps not relevant, and certainly something the candidate didn't want presented to the public. With the information on Ron, it was slanted, given as truth when it was only conjecture. Certainly Jim Bob's campaign was presenting it as true. And it was damaging.

If Summers provided the information, Weeks could leak it to the media. Whatever the process, it was working. Clearly, it was only the bad, negative, unfair stories that were dragging Ron's numbers down, destroying his lead. Before this disinformation had been widely released in the media, Ron's numbers were soaring. Now they were sinking. Fast.

Of course, Weeks didn't need to do anything, if Summers was leaking the information from the DA's office. Maybe he wasn't involved at all. The mere fact he had engaged in political dirty tricks in the past didn't mean he was doing it in this race. But he had a track record. And what about Summers? Would she go so far as to call the media? That would really be putting her job on the line. She could pass the information on to Weeks, just a little friendly gossip, and let him contact the media.

What to do?

Crystal walked out on to the veranda where Eula was rocking and watching the birds and squirrels playing in the yard.

"Nana, who do you know that might be working in Jim Bob's campaign headquarters in Tyler?"

Eula still rocked, but now her eyes were not focused on anything. After a minute, she looked at her granddaughter. "I reckon Terrie Portal would be a good bet. She's always gettin' involved in politickin'. And she thinks old Jim Bob number one is the second coming. So she's probably backing Jim Bob number two. Why? What you got in mind?"

"I'm pretty sure Fran Summers is leaking the information from the DA's office. Surely she wouldn't be foolish enough to pass it on to the media. So, who's the middleman?"

"What'cha gonna do? Erase 'em?"

"No. But I would confront them and see if I couldn't get it stopped. As you pointed out, the current trend is not good for Ron. We've got to find a way to reverse it. And quickly."

"Be careful there. Terrie wouldn't hurt you, but somebody killed Nat Owens. And I'm thinking that whole theft thing's got more to do with the election than with some paint on a piece of canvas."

* * *

After a few pleasantries, Crystal got down to the point of her visit. "Sounds like you do a lot for Jim Bob's campaign."

"Oh yes. I know his father, known him for years. And I'm sure Jim Bob will do a good job," said Terrie.

"You might know a man I met the other day. I think his name is Weeks, maybe. Something like that."

"Oh that would be George. George Weeks. He's such a nice man. Always ready to help me. He won't let me carry anything that weighs more than two pounds. And he almost always has a smile on his face. Where did you meet him?"

Crystal was not prepared for that question. She did not want to say it was at the campaign office. "Ah, I saw him at Jim Bob's office." There, she didn't say campaign headquarters.

"Are you working on the election, too?"

Crystal smiled. She could honestly say, "Yes, I am. This is an important election."

"Indeed it is. And George is a big help. He makes things happen."

Crystal looked at her watch. "Oh my gosh. I'm late to pick up Eula. I'll tell her I got to meet you. Thanks, and try to stay out of this hot weather."

*Makes things happen. That's what I'm afraid of.*

# Chapter 29

**Saturday, October 20**

**"Listen to me**." George Weeks had pulled Ginnie aside and led her out the door. The sun was beating down, but that wasn't what made George so hot. "She came into headquarters yesterday and accused Fran of leaking the information from the DA's office to the media. They almost got into a fight. I had to keep Fran from attacking her."

"That's Fran's problem, not mine." Ginnie was more concerned with getting back into the air conditioning.

"Then I find out she's asking questions about *me*."

"What on earth would she be asking about you? There's no way she can know anything about us."

"I don't know. I don't know how she knows Fran was feeding me all that good stuff on Drake." He shook his head. "I don't know how she knows, but she does. It was clear. She knows. And Fran, she may be a lawyer, but sometimes she acts like she doesn't know what day it is. She lost her cool. I'm listening to it and thinking she practically admitted it. She flew into a rage. Guilty was how it came across. And that Moore woman knew she had nailed her."

"So, what's she going to do?"

"First, I'll lay odds she's already talked to the DA. We probably won't be getting any more great tips from that office. But why is she asking questions about me?"

Ginnie shrugged. "Haven't a clue."

"I don't either. But it's not a good thing for her to be snooping around. She'll probably find out I've been into Podirts before." Ginnie started to speak but George stopped her. "The information's out there. She'll find it, if she's looking. And I think she is."

"So? That's history."

"But it will tell her she's on the right track. It will encourage her to keep snooping, keep digging. I'm telling you this because you have more to lose than I do."

"Wait a minute. We're in this together."

George was shaking his head before she finished. "I told you this after you — after that guy died. I'm in for falsifying that rental agreement. I'm not in on the … other."

Ginnie's face turned hard and her voice was sharp. "Don't you dump me just to save your ass."

George took a deep breath and let it out slowly. "I won't give you up. They won't get anything out of me. But I didn't agree to any violence. None. I'll protect you as much as I possibly can. But you need to understand how serious this is. Why is she poking around? What is her motive? What is she looking for?"

"She's just mad because Jim Bob is catching Drake."

"Maybe. But we don't know she works for Drake. Maybe she does. Maybe not. Problem is, she's scratching around where she might find stuff on us. We need to be *very* careful. Remember, you have the most to lose."

Ginnie started to speak but George held his hand up. "I said I wouldn't give you up, and I won't. But if it all comes down around us, if they find out what's happened, you have more problems than I do. Watch your step. This woman could be trouble."

"What's her name?"

"Crystal Moore."

Ginnie turned and marched back to the cool air inside. Her jaw was set and she ignored the greetings several called to her. As angry as she was at George, she knew he was right. She had more to lose. A lot more. More than even George knew. And she didn't intend to let that nosy, highfaluting Crystal bitch stir things up. Time to find her.

# Chapter 30

**Fran Summers did** not return to the campaign headquarters. But she did call that afternoon and talk with George, telling him the leaks were over. The Moore woman was causing trouble for her and George had better be careful, too.

George passed this message to Ginnie.

It didn't take Ginnie long to find information on Crystal Moore. *The Wooden Nickel Gazette* had several stories on her. It appeared she really lived in Dallas, but had been raised in Nickel and had a grandmother here. And she was in Wooden Nickel helping Ron Drake in his effort to beat Jim Bob Wilson. A cold smile creased Ginnie's face. "That's a big mistake on her part," she muttered to herself.

It only took an hour to find where the grandmother lived. *Not good*, she thought as she looked at the long drive curving around, across a small bridge, and disappearing over a hill. In the middle of a large piece of forest, it would be almost impossible to smash the crystal there. A crystal is fragile. Hit it and it will shatter. She smirked at the allusion. She would crush this Crystal.

A gun would be best. But Ginnie didn't have one. If she bought one now and Crystal was shot a few days later, it might point the police in her direction. Of course today, anyone could get one illegally, no paperwork, no trail. But she didn't know how, or who to contact. She'd ask George.

*No. If push comes to shove, George might give me up.*

Maybe she should just leave. Go to another state. This was fun, but she would not go down for murder. Move three states away and who would find her?

She drew her lips into a thin, straight line. What good would that do? The police could trace her wherever she went. She'd have to have a new driver's license, new credit cards. a new identity. How would she even do that? She mulled this over in her mind. And what about her job? She could do her work from another state, but the police would find out who she worked for and then demand the company reveal her address. George might not tell the police anything. He said he wouldn't. She pursed her lips. If they put enough pressure on him, he might. *Yeah, he would.* But the company she worked for wouldn't hesitate to provide her new location.

She had disposed of Littlefellow and left no trail. That might be the best way to eliminate this current threat. One last loose end to snip off. She tried to think of any other "loose ends" that might show up. From what Fran had said, the DA wasn't looking at anybody but Drake. Fran herself knew nothing of the Podirt. No one at Jim Bob's headquarters had mentioned, even in passing, anything about Littlefellow's death. And Fran had never mentioned anything about the DA looking into the hit-and-run. No one cared about another accident. Certainly not during a heated campaign for the governor's office.

For a moment, Ginnie thought about taking another person's life. She closed her eyes and shook her head, trying to dispel the idea. It was clearly another case of self-defense, just as surely as Littlefellow was. She wasn't taking a life. She was saving a life—hers.

Now that she knew where the grandmother lived, she had a good place to pick Crystal up and follow her. She found a small road that ducked into the trees. Little more than a path, weeds grew in the two tracks. No one would bother her here. She backed in and turned off the engine. From here, she had a good view of the drive into the grandmother's place.

*Patience is the key. The perfect opportunity will present itself. Patience.*

* * *

That evening, Crystal and Brandi drove over to Melva Larson's house. Melva, one of Eula's long-time friends, had invited them to join her and Eula for pizza.

They were hardly in the door when Melva asked Brandi, "How'd you get that card? Didn't they ask for ID?"

An impish grin appeared on Brandi's face. "Simple. It's all in how much confidence you show."

"And we all know how much confidence Brandi has," Crystal said.

"All compliments accepted." Brandi grinned. "I picked a shift when I thought the least confident person was on duty. Then, I just bluffed my way, said I'd forgotten my driver's license. Told her I could hurry home and get it, but I really needed to get it rented today so I could unload my stuff before I left on a trip tonight. I'd run get it and come back. Just wait. It won't take me but a few minutes. Of course, I had picked closing time. I could see she already had her purse on the counter and was ready to leave. She did *not* want to wait. So she caved in and let me sign it with no ID."

Melva persisted. "But what if she wouldn't? You'd already said you were leaving that night. What were you gonna do?"

Brandi smiled. "I still had my trump card: the competitor. I say, 'Forget it. I'll go to Nickel Storage. And this is a cash deal.' They like cash."

"Okay, but how did that lawyer guy get a copy of the card?"

"You've met Nuchols," said Eula. "He could get you to give him a classified document if he wanted it. But right now, it's time to go get the pizza, Crystal."

Crystal hopped up. "I'm on my way. Nana, will you move your car up about ten feet? Then I can park behind you. I don't like to park on the street, particularly after dark. Thanks. I'll be back before you know I'm gone." She dashed for the door.

* * *

As the screen door banged shut, Melva tugged on Brandi's arm. "Go with her and make sure she doesn't get any little dead fish on the pizza."

Brandi jumped up. "No dead fish. Got it."

"Better get an extra pepperoni," called Eula. "Bill said he's coming by."

Brandi popped open the door and started toward the road.

Crystal was crossing the street to get in her car. Brandi heard a noise and looked down the road. A car with no lights on was coming down the dark street. It was headed for Crystal. As Brandi's eyes adjusted to the light, her heart skipped a beat.

The car was rapidly gaining speed.

"Crystal! Watch out!"

By now the car was closing in on Crystal, accelerating, and aiming right for her. She turned her head, saw the car, and instantly dove for the side of the road. In less than a second, the car raced past, missing her by two feet, forced to turn slightly to avoid crashing into Crystal's car.

Brandi rushed across the street, yelling at the speeding car. "Stupid asshole." She reached Crystal, still lying in the weeds next to the road. She wasn't moving. Brandi knelt beside her friend. "Are you okay?"

Crystal slowly rolled over, moaning as she did. For a moment, she lay there, breathing deeply. She wiggled her hands, then her feet. "I don't think I broke anything. But I'm going to be sore for awhile. Give me a hand."

Brandi stood up, grabbed Crystal's hand and pulled her to her feet. "Stupid fool. Driving with no lights, speeding, and damn near hit you." She helped brush the dirt and leaves off Crystal.

"Ouch. Careful where you pat me. I really bruised my hip." Crystal carefully picked a number of grass burrs off her jeans. "I don't know what he was thinking. That was dangerous even if I hadn't been in the road."

"You know I always see these things different from you. I think the bastard was *trying* to hit you."

Crystal just stared at her friend. "Trying to hit me? Why would he do that?"

"I don't know the why. Just the what. If your car had not been there, he would have swerved over and taken you out."

For a minute, neither said anything. "If you're trying to make me feel better, you failed," said Crystal.

"Sorry 'bout that. I just call 'em like I see 'em."

Crystal opened the door and got in the car. "You always take a dramatic view. Probably a teenager. Maybe had a few drinks."

Brandi hopped into the passenger's seat. "Yeah. I'd like to believe that, too."

*But, I don't.*

* * *

Twenty minutes later, the two women walked into Melva's carrying pizza boxes. "No fish, alive or dead," said Brandi.

Melva reached for one of the boxes. "Good. Let's dive in. I'm famished."

"What was the hollerin' out there when you left?" Eula asked.

"Some ass—"

Crystal cut Brandi off. "A crazy teenager was racing and almost hit my car. Brandi told him off."

Eula grabbed a slice of pizza. "Thought I heard a car racing by."

"I smell pizza." Bill Glothe was standing at the front door. "Anybody want to invite me in?"

"Come on in, Bill," Eula said. "Got a whole pepperoni one just for you."

The sheriff opened the door and walked into the dining room. "In my line of work, timing is very important. I try to arrive just as the boxes are opened."

"Pull up a chair and dig in," Melva said.

Brandi finished the slice she'd been eating. "I'd say you were a bit late. Some fool racing down the road almost hit Crystal."

Everybody stopped chewing and looked at Brandi.

"Brandi exaggerates sometimes," Crystal said. "But he did almost hit my car."

"I'm not as smart as Crystal when it comes to book learning," Brandi said. "But I got more street smarts. And I think the guy was *trying* to hit Crystal, not her car."

Bill stopped, with the pizza half way to his mouth. Melva let out a small gasp.

"Now, Brandi," Crystal began.

"Let her have her say," said Bill. "I like to hear people with streets smarts."

"Me, too," said Eula.

"It was dark and I'd just come out of the house, so my night vision wasn't too good. But it sure looked to me like he was *aiming* for Crystal, speeding up. And I think if I hadn't yelled at her, and her car wasn't there, the bastard would have nailed her."

"No lights?" asked Bill.

"No. Not until he was way past Crystal's car. He turned at the next corner and that's the last I saw of him"

"Could you tell anything about the car?"

"Naw. It was dark and he was moving fast."

"You're okay?" Glothe asked Crystal.

"Yes. I fell in the dirt beside the road. My hip's a little sore. Otherwise, I'm fine."

For several minutes, nobody said anything. Eula had moved over and put her arm around her granddaughter. Melva and Brandi worked on polishing off the pizza.

Glothe finished his pizza and took a long drink of iced tea. "I've been the sheriff for over ten years. In all that time, we've had only one fatal hit-and-run. Sure glad you weren't number two, Crystal."

"Amen," said Melva.

"That was John Littlefellow, wasn't it? Back in the spring?" Eula asked.

"It was. Nice guy. Taught at the high school. Social studies, I think," Bill said.

Brandi had been listening intently. "Anything unusual about that one, Bill?"

"It *was* a bit unusual. He's gone to the post office. He got hit in the parking lot. At night. We have people getting hit in parking lots ever now and then. But not thrown sixteen feet in the air. The post office parking lot isn't that big. Hard to get up that much speed. 'Course the car didn't stop to render aid." He took another drink of his tea. "We looked for anybody who might have a grievance against him. Couldn't even find an unhappy student or parent. No enemies."

"Ever find out who did it?" Brandi asked.

"Nope."

"Just wondering. Sounds a lot like tonight."

"Wasn't a red car, was it?" he asked.

Brandi sat up a little straighter. "It could have been. As it turned the corner, I caught a glimpse of it. Can't say for sure, but it might have been. Why?"

Bill shrugged. "We were never sure. But the car that hit Littlefellow was likely red. Don't know for certain. But we got red paint off one of the brads on his jeans. Since he doesn't— didn't— have a red car, I expect it came from the car that hit him." He paused. "Probably should of kept my yap shut."

"I'm not way sure tonight's car was red."

"Even if it was, it's just a coincidence," Crystal said.

Glothe nodded. "You're right, Crystal. I just don't like coincidences, particularly in pairs."

Eula jumped in. "What do you mean, 'pairs'?"

Glothe put his hands up. "Nothing."

"What's the other coincidence," said Eula. It was not a question.

"Oh nothing, really. It's just, this week, we pulled Bert Monday in. He had found Drake's painting in the storage unit next to his. He has number seventy-two. That's also the unit Littlefellow had. 'Course, his wife canceled it after he was killed." He paused a moment. "Wasn't anything connecting 'em. It's just we pulled Monday in a couple of days ago and it was on my mind, I guess. I thought, old unit seventy-two is just unlucky."

# Chapter 31

**Monday, October 22**

**Sunday, Crystal put** Brandi on a bus back to Dallas, then returned to Eula's and spent the rest of the day letting her bruised hip rest. She hated to admit it, but her dive into the weeds to avoid the speeding car had made her sore in several places.

Monday she was back trying to come up with some way to stop Ron's slide in the polls. Mark had encouraged her to spend whatever time was needed to help Ron's campaign.

Mid-morning, Brandi called. "My nose has been itching ever since Bill talked about those coincidences."

"Your nose always itches," Crystal said.

"Not true. But for sure I don't think a storage unit is unlucky."

"Coincidences really do occur in real life."

"Maybe. But in pairs? Too much of a coincidence. And another thing. Why does someone steal a painting? To sell it and make big bucks."

"Or because they love that painting and want to keep it for themselves, but can't afford to buy it."

"And neither of those would prompt you to put it in a storage unit." Brandi was on a roll. "Certainly not right there in the same town. I'd have hightailed it out of town, from Drake's house right across the state border. Why take a risk putting it in the warehouse where somebody might see you? And then, you've got to get it out of the warehouse without anybody seeing you. Two chances to get caught."

"But—"

"Nobody knows it's gone right after the thief takes it. Well, the dead guy, but he wasn't telling anybody. How long will it take you to get out of Wooden Nickel?"

"Ten minutes."

"The county?"

"It's a small county. Maybe twenty minutes."

"So the thief and the painting could be out of the county before the EMS people get to Drake's house, before anybody even knew the painting was missing. If he headed east, he could be out of the *state* before anybody thought to ask the police to look for it."

"Maybe he panicked."

"No, no, no. Won't fly. The theft was too perfect. Left no trace, knocked out a guard. Clever as a raccoon. And what is it now, six or seven months and still no clue? Not the kind of guy who panics. So why'd he leave it there, in a storage unit? And then, like a dumb-ass, he leaves the storage vault unlocked. At least that's what the guy told the police."

"Glothe believed him."

"Yes he did. But he didn't like coincidences. And then he had a double coincidence. How would he feel about a triple coincidence? Wait. Wait. Brandi Brewer is going to make up a saying. Are you ready?"

"Ready."

"One coincidence is maybe; two is maybe not; and three is impossible. How's that?"

"I like it. Very good."

"Some of your smarts are rubbing off on me."

Crystal laughed. "You're smart enough. But what's the third coincidence?"

"I'm thinking—a new experience for me—the picture got found right after the insurance company coughed up the money, and right before the election. I'm thinking this smells like the third coincidence. Rotten. And you know what my mother always said. If it smells rotten, it is."

Crystal put the phone back in its cradle and walked out on the veranda. The sky was deep blue with not a cloud to be seen. It was October in Texas. What did she expect? Already the temperature had climbed to near ninety degrees and it wasn't even noon yet.

She sat in one of the old rockers and considered what Brandi had said. Why would the storage unit be unlocked at all? If you took the risk to steal a valuable painting, whatever your reason, you would keep it in a secure place. A locked place. And was it just another coincidence it was suddenly unlocked just after Ron collected insurance money? But before the election.

Eula's warning popped into her mind: "I'm thinking that whole theft thing's got more to do with the election than with some paint on a piece of canvas."

Crystal took a deep breath. Nana's thinking was usually right on the money. And now, Brandi's questions led in the same direction.

Crystal felt she was missing something. What? She needed to revisit everything to see if she had missed any clues. And she needed to start looking on the fringes. She hated the expression, but nonetheless, she needed to start thinking outside the box. Maybe her thinking, and Glothe's, had been too limited.

Shortly after noon, Crystal rang the doorbell at Donna Littlefellow's house. The frame house appeared to be well taken care of. The yard was neat, with well-cut grass and flower beds on either side of a small porch.

"Yes?" Donna Littlefellow stood at the door, clearly in the late stages of pregnancy.

Crystal had a sudden fear she'd made a mistake. "Oh, ah, I'm sorry. I shouldn't have come unannounced. I didn't know.... I mean, I ..."

Donna smiled. "It's okay. You're here. What did you want?"

"I wanted to talk with you about your husband's death. But now I think that was a bad idea." Crystal shook her head. "I apologize for bothering you and bringing up your recent tragedy." She turned to leave.

"Wait."

Crystal turned around.

"I've come to terms with Johnny's death. And I'm not ready to let him out of my life. In fact," she rubbed her tummy, "this is John Junior. And I want him to know his father. That means I must remember a lot about Johnny. Please come in."

Crystal entered the small living room. It was nicely furnished, with flowers on the coffee table, and a large television.

"Can I get you some ice tea?"

"No, I'm fine. But thank you for offering."

Donna sat down in a straight-backed chair. "This is better for my back, which right now, needs all the help it can get." She squirmed around to find a comfortable position. "What did you want to ask about Johnny? Did you know him?"

"No. Bill Glothe, the sheriff, told me John's was the first hit-and-run death in Wooden Nickel in over ten years he's been sheriff. Then, this week, I was almost number two."

Donna let out a small gasp. "You weren't hurt, were you?"

"No. Luckily, my friend yelled a warning and I managed to jump out of the way. If she hadn't, I'd have been hit. And the car was really moving fast."

"Thank goodness." She looked down for a minute. "I wish someone had warned Johnny."

"I'm so sorry to bring all this back to you."

"It's all right. Was your near-miss at night?"

Crystal nodded. "Yes. On a pretty dark road. And the car had no lights on. My friend who warned me, said it looked to her like the car actually moved over to hit me. But I dove off the side of the road and the driver had to turn away or hit my car."

"The police said there were no skid marks or any indication the driver tried to avoid Johnny. It was in the post office parking lot. Who would be racing there? They said it looked deliberate." Donna's eyes were now moist and she brushed the back of her hand across them. "But everybody liked Johnny. His students loved him. He was always bringing something home a student had given him. One student's family had a little truck farm and the son brought him vegetables all the time. A girl's parents raised blueberries they sold at the farmers market. We had free blueberries all season long. Another boy's father was a mechanic. We never got charged when he worked on our car." She paused and again, tears began to form. "Who would want to hurt him?"

Crystal didn't know what to say.

After a minute, Donna said, "I'm sorry. I sometimes ... . What did the police say about your near-miss?"

"Sheriff Glothe said, no hit-and-run fatality for over ten years, then one and almost another within a few months of each other. He doesn't like coincidences." Crystal paused a moment, and then asked, "Did John ever say anything about his storage unit at Wooden Nickel Mini Storage?"

Donna looked at Crystal, her eyes cloudy, her eyebrows pulled together. "His storage unit? I don't think so. He had had it only a few months. I mean, he didn't keep much stuff in it. I just closed it after his ... he passed away. What ... why would ... ."

"He had storage unit seventy-two, right next to unit seventy-three," Crystal prompted.

For fully thirty seconds, Donna bowed her head, eyes closed. "Johnny told me something. I'm trying to remember."

"If it's painful, please forget it. I shouldn't have asked you."

"It's okay. And it's coming back to me. Johnny went down to put a highchair in it. This was just two or three days before he was ... killed. I think I've come to terms with Johnny's death. But I still have trouble saying that. For a long time I couldn't. I'd say he passed away, or something like that. Now, I can say Johnny's death. But I might cry after I do." She stopped to wipe her eyes again.

"I'm so sorry. And I shouldn't have come."

"No. It's all right. Really. I've got to get in better shape, soon." She patted her stomach. "When Johnny Junior comes, I will talk about his father and I can't cry. That has to be happy talk. No tears." She smoothed out her dress and smiled. "The storage unit. What did Johnny say about his visit there? I know it was just a few days before Johnny was ... killed because we'd just bought that high chair and then he was gone."

She paused and Crystal could tell she was trying to compose herself. After a few moments, she continued. "I was just a few months pregnant, but we were excited. We saw it at a yard sale and Johnny bought it. It needed a little work - sanding, painting. But he was so excited over the pregnancy, he was ready to buy anything for a new baby. We'd tried for several years with no luck. Then, suddenly, I knew." She paused, eyes looking down. "Anyway, he said he'd refinish it and have it ready. We didn't know then whether we were having a girl or a boy." A little smile graced her face. "I remember now, he said there was a woman putting a painting in the unit right next to ours. He was surprised anyone else was there that late at night." Suddenly she gasped. "Oh my God. Was that the painting stolen from Mr. Drake? The one causing such a commotion?"

"I believe it was. Just a few weeks ago, the new owner of number seventy-two saw unit seventy-three was unlocked. He looked in and there was the painting. Of course, he had no idea it was a famous painting. You said it was a woman who put the painting in the storage unit?"

"Yes. I distinctly remember him saying it was a woman. I asked him if she was pretty." Again, she smiled a little. "I was feeling kind of puffy and ... well, less pretty right about then. Had just begun to lose my waist."

"Did John say anything about the woman?"

Again, Donna appeared to be searching her memory for details. "Said she was not very friendly. I think that's all. He wisely did *not* say she was pretty." Once more the tiny smile highlighted what a pretty woman this expectant mother was.

"Donna, I really appreciate your help. The DA is trying to put a case together against Mr. Drake, saying he stole his own painting to get the insurance. But I know Ron Drake and he did not steal that painting. He's the most honorable man I know." Crystal stood up, ready to leave. "Here's my card. Please call me if you think of anything else."

"I don't think I was much help. Sorry."

"Oh, yes. You have been a big help. You've told us it was a woman who put the painting in the storage unit."

As they reached the door, Donna said, "I remember he said she had a cute little red car. I don't think he told me what kind of car. If he did, I don't remember. But I do remember it was red."

# Chapter 32

"**Bill, I just** talked with Donna Littlefellow and she said —"

"Whoa." The sheriff cut Crystal off, almost dropping the toothpick that had been stuck in the corner of his mouth. "Donna Littlefellow? That's John Littlefellow's wife?"

"Yes."

"And how were you talking to her?"

"I went to see her. After we had been talking about the coincidences."

They were standing in the sheriff's office. Crystal had started in so quickly, Glothe didn't even have time to offer her a seat. So, he stood up with her. His face revealed his disapproval of Crystal talking to people connected to an investigation.

"Okay. I'm not too happy about you talking to people in an active investigation, but I guess it's done now. What did she have to say? I can see you're excited, so I'm sure she told you something."

"She said her husband, John, had gone to put a highchair they bought into their mini-warehouse. And while he was there, a woman was putting a painting into the unit next to his, into unit seventy-three."

"And he saw this woman do it?"

"Yes. Donna said he spoke to the woman, asked if she needed any help, but she said no. He said she wasn't very friendly."

Glothe was getting more interested. "Did he describe her?"

Crystal laughed. "No. Donna said she asked him if the woman was pretty. Donna's pregnancy had just started to show and she was feeling a little self-conscious. John, wisely, said no."

"Would have been nice to get a little description."

"But, don't you see? A woman put the painting in there. Not a man. Not Ron."

Glothe rubbed his chin and shook his head a little. "Doesn't mean much, though. The DA will just say Ron paid someone else to put it in the mini-storage."

"Who?"

"Besides, Littlefellow isn't here to give the evidence. So, it's hearsay."

"If Donna told what John said, wouldn't that help?"

"Probably not. Just adds a problem for Abbott. But then, I think the whole case is a problem for her. She jumped into this and now she doesn't know how to get out."

"And the leaks from her office have really cost Ron. What a disaster she is. How'd she ever get named the District Attorney for the county?"

Bill thought about it for a minute. "Now don't go jumping on me. You asked and I'm gonna tell you what I think. She got one hundred percent of the women's votes, plus a few of the men who thought she was good looking and hoped they might get a date with her."

"You're kidding, aren't you?"

"Well, of course I don't rightly know. But from talking with a lot of people, that seems the best bet. Littlefellow didn't tell his wife anything else did he?"

Crystal slapped her forehead with her hand. "Duh. I almost forgot. John told his wife the woman who was putting the painting into unit seventy-three was driving a red car. How do you feel about that coincidence?"

The sheriff's eyes opened wide and his mouth dropped open. His toothpick hit the floor. "A red car? I don't like that one bit."

"How many red cars are there in Wooden Nickel and the county?" Crystal thought about it and realized if she were at her office, she could find out exactly how many red cars were registered in Wooden Nickel and in the county, thanks to a program she had developed a year ago for her company. Not important right now.

"Red's pretty popular. I'd say probably at least a hundred in Wooden Nickel, maybe two hundred in the county. He did say car, not pickup?"

"Car. He said, 'A cute, little red car.' I think a pickup is out."

"Good. It would be worse if we had to consider pickups too."

Bill reached down and picked up the toothpick and dropped it in the waste basket.

For several minutes neither said anything, letting thoughts run through their minds. Then Crystal looked up and said, "Bill, I want to go through that storage unit, number seventy-three."

The sheriff stared at Crystal, his bushy eyebrows knitting together. "Why? the crime scene guys went over it with a fine-toothed comb. Got a bunch of shoe-prints from the dust, but they were pretty standard. Nothing else there, apart from a slight change in the dust level where the painting sat."

"No fingerprints?"

"None. Well, there was Monday's on the handle used to raise the door up. But only Monday's. Which was odd actually. You'd think there'd a been prints from previous users of the unit. What do you think you'll find?"

"Haven't a clue. Actually, that's what I'm looking for, a clue. But I don't know what. Probably won't find anything. But I want to look anyway."

"Well, I think it's a bad idea. But nothing's stopping you. We've released it. Not even any yellow tape on it now. Check at the office. Some guy could have already rented it, though I doubt it."

"Thanks, Bill. I know your guys did a good job. But it'll make me feel better if I look at it for myself. Just being there may inspire me to do something else."

## Chapter 33

**Crystal stopped at** the Dairy Queen for a quick burger and a Dr Pepper. Thirty minutes later she was in the office for the Wooden Nickel Mini Storage. "I've talked with Sheriff Glothe and he said it would be all right if I looked around in unit seventy-three. Is it locked?"

"No. Not locked."

"Okay. Will it be okay if I leave my car here? I need the exercise."

The woman looked at Crystal's slim figure and shrugged. "Fine with me."

Crystal walked out of the office, turned left and proceeded to the end of the units. She turned left again and walked down past unit fifty, fifty-one, fifty-two, and eventually came to unit seventy-three. Sure enough, there was no lock on it.

She reached down, grabbed the handle and quickly jerked her hand away. "Wow. That is hot." She fished a tissue out of her purse, wrapped that around the handle and pulled. She was surprised at how heavy it was. Maybe they never lubricated the rollers on the doors. She stepped inside. *Bill was right. It's blasted hot in here.*

She scanned the area along the left side, but found nothing. *Should have asked Bill which side the painting was on.* She started on the other side. About halfway down, the dust and dirt near the wall changed. It wasn't like someone had swept it, but it was cleaner than the area on either side. She tried to measure the length of this "different" area. It seemed like it was about the right length for the Mondrian painting.

A noise caught her attention and she looked back at the door. It was coming down. "Hey. There's someone in here."

She started running toward the door. "Hey. Don't close the door. I'm in here," she yelled.

She got to the door when it was only a foot from the ground. "Hold it."

She grabbed the door and tried to pull it up, but whoever was on the other side kept forcing it down. "Open the door. I'm in here," she screamed.

But the door closed and Crystal heard the noise of metal sliding on metal.

"Open the door," she shrieked.

As her voice died down, the sound of a lock being snapped closed assaulted her ears.

She pounded on the metal, yelling. And now she heard very clearly footsteps crunching on the gravel, walking away. After a few moments, a car started and Crystal heard it driving off. She reached into her pocket for her cell phone, only to remember it was sitting on the front seat of her car.

She grabbed the rope and yanked. The door came up maybe half an inch, then hit a definite stop. Was the person deaf? She felt she had yelled loud enough for the woman in the office to hear her, let alone whoever was pushing the door down. Nonetheless, she banged on the door and yelled some more. All she succeeded in doing was hurting her hand. That and raising her temperature. In fact, it was getting hotter inside the mini-warehouse by the minute.

She looked around in the darkness. No light came in from any window, door, or even a crack in a wall. There was no opening of any kind.

When she had first entered, she had checked around all the edges. Now, she played that trip back in her mind, like a video, hoping to remember something that might help. Was there anything she could use to knock a hole in the door, allow her to reach the latch? Or at least make more noise. "People are supposed to leave a lot of stuff in these units when they finish with them. Why were they so neat on this one?"

But her remembrance produced nothing, not a rock, not a piece of wood, nothing.

She sat down on the dusty floor. Her body was wet with perspiration, her blouse plastered to her skin. She tried to think of a plan, but her mind would only think about the heat. What to do? She couldn't just sit here. Instead of a plan to get out, she could only think it was probably ninety degrees outside when she entered. Now, in this metal building closed up tightly, the temperature must have passed a hundred by now.

She heard a car. She jumped up and started kicking the door and yelling. She stopped after several minutes and put her ear to the door.

Nothing.

She wilted back to the floor. It had been just a little exertion, but it zapped her strength. She unbuttoned her blouse, tried to pull the fabric away from her skin. She rubbed her arms, her hand coming across her fitness tracker. She slipped the bracelet off her arm, trying to get anything away from her skin.

She felt the thin device. Maybe only a quarter of an inch thick. She got up and pulled on the door. She could raise it that much. But it wouldn't stay up while she reached down. She placed the tracker on the floor, raised the door as much as possible, then nudged the tracker under the door with her foot as far as she could. *Maybe someone will see it and open this oven.*

She collapsed on the floor again. She slipped her shoes off. She decided to think of this as a trip to the sauna, where you are supposed to sweat and cleanse your pores. That made things a little better, but only for about ten seconds. She had unbuttoned her blouse and she tried fanning herself with the loose material. But it was so wet it didn't work well and every time it touched her skin, it just stuck there. The effort generated more heat than it dissipated.

A few minutes passed, or was it an hour? She couldn't tell. She had lost any concept of time. She reached up under her blouse in the back and undid her bra. For an instant, that gave her a tiny bit of relief. That quickly passed and she was melting again. She tried fanning herself with her hand. It helped a little, but in seconds it exhausted her.

Crystal closed her eyes and tried to imagine herself in a snow bank. She could feel the granules. She could see the ski lift in the distance. A slight wind blew and chilled her. She shivered and almost lost her balance. Her eyes opened. There was no snow and she was shivering, but it wasn't from the cold. She was so hot, she was shaking.

She pulled her shoes up, put her head on them and stretched out. The heat had depleted her strength and she felt like she could hardly move. She closed her eyes. If she was very still, maybe she wouldn't be as hot. She tried to bring up the vision of the snow again, but only a hot desert scene filled her mind. The sun blazed down. She put her hand up to shade her face and when it touched her face, her skin was like a hot skillet. And then she realized, there was no sun shining on her. Only the heat of the sun.

Now she realized how thirsty she was. Her mouth was dry. Her throat was dry. She had no saliva to swallow and relieve the painful dryness. *How can I be sweating so much and be so dry inside my mouth?* She pulled her blouse up and sucked on the wet fabric. It was wet, but salty. It gave her some temporary relief from the dry throat.

The nausea came on quickly. She turned over, ready to be sick. A dry heave shook her body, but nothing came up. Again, her stomach wrenched, the muscles twisting, shooting pain across her weakened body. After a few minutes it passed and was replaced by a fierce headache. She tried to massage her temples to ease the pain, but in less than a minute, her hands were too tired to continue. She didn't care. It wasn't helping and her arms were too heavy to hold up anyway. Once more, her eyelids crept down and she drifted into an uneasy sleep.

Suddenly, her eyes jerked open. The muscles in her legs were cramping and the severe pain jolted her awake. How long had she been asleep? She tried to get up, to walk off the cramps, but she couldn't pull herself up to stand. She got on her hands and knees and slowly managed to stand. It only took a few steps to ease the cramps. She felt dizzy and quickly sat down, afraid she might fall.

*Don't go to sleep again. If a car comes, I've got to be awake to hear it and bang on the door, attract their attention.*

She had no idea how much time had passed but she could tell it was even hotter than before. And now she noticed her blouse was no longer sticking to her. That was a relief. She ran her hand across her brow. Dry. She had stopped sweating. She didn't know what that meant, but decided it might mean there was no more water in her body to sweat. *That can't be a good thing, can it?*

Even thinking made her feel exhausted. *Don't think. Just listen for a car or a person.* She put her head back on her shoes and closed her eyes. She heard nothing.

# Chapter 34

**Five o'clock. Time** to go home, thought Bill Glothe even though he hadn't accomplished much today. He got in his Ford Crown Vic and started for home. He had turned on to Pecan Street when he looked over and saw what he believed was Crystal's car, sitting in front of the Wooden Nickel Mini-Storage office.

"Funny. I thought she was headed over here hours ago." He continued down the road for another block. "Guess something delayed her visit. Might as well go see what she's doing. She's not going to find anything there."

He made a U-turn back to the storage facility and turned into the parking lot. Crystal was not in her car. He studied the office through its front glass windows. She was not in the office. He looped around to look at unit seventy-three. When he got there, he was surprised to find the door down and locked. He was turning the car around, but suddenly stopped. He got out and walked over to the door. Something was sticking out from under it and he reached down and pulled it out. It looked a lot like Crystal's fitness device. He banged on the door. "Crystal. Are you in there?"

He got no answer. He tried again, this time banging harder and yelling louder. "Crystal. Are you in there?"

Still no answer.

He got back in his cruiser and threw gravel as he raced back to the office. He jumped out, leaving the car running.

"Give me some bolt cutters," he demanded of the woman.

She looked shocked, but said nothing.

"I need some bolt cutters. Now."

"Ah, we, ah, don't have any," the woman stammered.

"Yes you do. You have to have those to cut off locks when people quit paying for their unit. I need them right now. Do you want to get them, or shall I come around there and start looking. Whatever, I need them. Now." The last word, almost yelled, was a clear demand.

The woman took a half step back, her mouth gaped, her eyes wide, more frightened than confused. When she didn't move, Bill started around the counter.

"I, ah, I'll ..." She turned, almost stumbling and went through the door behind her. Within thirty seconds, she came back holding a substantial bolt cutter.

"How long has that car been out front?"

The woman cowered but said, "I, ah, I don't know. I didn't pay any attention to what time it was when she came in. Two or three hours, maybe."

"Call 9-1-1 and tell them the sheriff needs an ambulance here. Right now."

With that, he rushed out the door, got in his car and again sprayed gravel heading back to unit seventy-three. He hopped out, grabbed the bolt cutters and attacked the lock. In less than fifteen seconds, he had the lock off and raised the door.

Crystal lay on the floor just inside. Her face was crimson. He bent over her and felt for a pulse. He found one, rapid, but very weak. He picked her up and carried her to the car. He noted she was not sweating. "Not good."

He braced her against the car, trying to keep her standing, while he fumbled inside the front driver's door to unlock the back doors.

Finally he got them opened, and was able to pick Crystal up again and maneuver her inside and on to the back seat.

He jumped back behind the wheel, reached over and cranked up the air conditioning to its highest level. Then he put the car into drive and carefully drove around to the front of the building.

Within minutes, the ambulance arrived. The EMS personnel checked Crystal briefly, put her on a stretcher and loaded her into the ambulance. They inserted an IV into her arm, pumping vital replacement fluids into the dehydrated patient. Then, with lights flashing, they raced to the hospital.

Glothe followed close behind them.

# Chapter 35

**By the time** Glothe got to the emergency room and found Crystal's cubicle, the nurses had removed her clothing and had a sheet draped over her. A nurse was wiping her arms and legs, with a damp towel. Another nurse had applied a damp cloth to her face and was checking the IV.

The doctor looked at the readout on the thermometer. "One oh four," he said. "Get some ice to cool the water you're putting on the towels. And bring some water. Let's see if we can get her to drink some."

Crystal's eyelids began to flutter a little.

"Where's the water?" the doctor called out.

"I'm on my way, already," the nurse answered, with just a touch of irritation. She brought the glass in with a flexible straw.

"Get some pillows under her head." The doctor spoke to Crystal in soft, soothing tones. "Can you hear me?" Crystal made the smallest of nods. "Good. Now, I'm going to give you some cool water to sip. Don't take it in too fast. But do get some of it down your throat. Okay?"

Again, Crystal nodded so slightly Glothe wasn't sure whether he had just imagined it. The doctor gently placed the straw in her mouth. Nothing happened. "Come on, young lady. You can sip a little water. It's cool and it will make your throat feel better." After a few seconds, she sipped a little. After a minute, the doctor offered the straw again and Crystal took it. This time, she took in more water.

"Good girl. Not too fast. Take as much as you want, just slowly."

Over the next five minutes, Crystal managed to drink most of the glass of water. When she stopped, her eyes seemed to focus on the doctor. "Oh. That's. Good. Stuff." Her speech was slow, and her voice was raspy.

The other nurse returned with a bowl of water with ice cubes in it. Then, both nurses resumed wiping Crystal's arms, legs and shoulders with damp towels. Occasionally, one of them would reach under the sheet and wipe Crystal's stomach and breasts.


Forty-five minutes later, the doctor took Glothe outside.

"She's lucky. Just a few more minutes in that heat and she would have had a full-blown heat stroke. As it is, I think we caught her with only a severe case of heat exhaustion. Not that heat exhaustion isn't serious. But a heat stroke is much, much worse. Her heat exhaustion was very severe. But as I said, heat stroke is much worse. Her core temperature was 104. When she stopped sweating, she was headed toward serious organ failure. Her body was no longer able to cool itself. So, from there, it would begin to do damage to her vital organs." The doctor took a deep breath, and wiped his hand across his brow. "You got her here in the nick of time. We've taken a blood sample and it looks good. Well, not good, but not as bad as it could have been. And her urine doesn't show any damage to her kidneys.

"I can't emphasize how close she was to very serious damage to vital organs."

"Is she going to be okay?"

"I think there is an excellent chance she will be just fine in a couple of days. I don't think there's any reason to worry now. However, should she feel *anything* unusual in the next day or two, she should see her doctor immediately and tell him she had severe heat exhaustion.

"She will need to rest and not exert herself for the next day or two. I would suggest she not spend *any* time in the sun for at least four days. Drink plenty of cool liquids." The doctor gave Glothe a stern look. "I think the best thing right now is to keep her here overnight."

The sheriff nodded. "I called her grandmother. She should be here any minute. I'm sure she'll agree to have Crystal stay in the hospital."

"That would really be best."

"What would be best? And for who?" Eula appeared out of nowhere and approached the two men.

"And you are?" asked the doctor.

"I'm Crystal's grandmother. Eula Moore." She squinted at the doctor's name tag clipped on his shirt. "And you're Dr. Good?"

He looked down at his tag. "Oh, I broke it this morning. It should read Goodall."

"I'd like to make fun of that name, but right now I need to know about my granddaughter."

The doctor gave Eula the same talk he gave Bill, including his recommendation Crystal stay in the hospital overnight.

"And you think this hospital can take better care of her than I can?"

The doctor smiled. "Not necessarily better. But we have more monitoring devices that will constantly be checking many things. We can continue the IV drip. While I don't expect any problems, should one occur, we would know immediately and be able to respond immediately. Just a safety precaution. She could go home, but prudence suggests she stay here tonight."

Eula nodded several times. "Okay. Crystal can stay. And I'll stay with her."

"Oh, that's really not necessary, Mrs. Moore. Our staff—"

Eula interrupted the doctor. "It is necessary. For me." She set her jaw.

Bill leaned in toward Goodall. "Doc, it will be easier on you and your staff if you just let Eula stay."

"Fine. I just don't want you keeping her awake, talking to her. She needs lots of rest."

Eula lowered her eyes and said meekly, "I'll be as quiet as a possum. You won't know I'm here."

The sheriff just snickered.

"Okay. It's settled. You'll need to fill out the paperwork to get her admitted. Once she's in a room, have her take a cool shower, then rest. Drink plenty of liquids, but no alcohol or caffeine. I'll give specific instructions to the nurses. If you have any questions, check with one of them. The sooner you get her admitted, the sooner they'll assign her a room."

The doctor shook hands with Eula and Bill and headed back to the emergency room.

# Chapter 36

**Just after nine,** there was a quiet knock at the door. "Come on in," called Eula.

The door opened and in walked Mark. Without a word, he walked over to the bed and gave Crystal a kiss on her forehead.

Crystal's eyes opened and as she recognized who it was, she smiled. "Is that the best you can do? I'm not contagious."

Mark bent down and planted a firm, warm kiss on Crystal's mouth.

"I'm feeling better already." Now furrows formed across her forehead. "But what are you doing here? How did you know I was in the hospital?"

"What a silly question," said Mark with a grin. "You're in the hospital. Of course I'm here."

Eula spoke up. "I called him. Thought he'd like to know if one of his employees was ailing."

"Particularly if it was a very special employee," said Mark. He pulled a chair up close to the bed and took Crystal's hand in his. "I know your current status. I talked with the doctor. But tell me your version of how you got so ... over heated?"

Crystal started to relate her visit to the mini-warehouse and getting locked in.

"I've heard this four times already," interrupted Eula. "I think I'll go to the canteen and get a Dr Pepper. Behave yourselves 'til I get back."

After Eula left, Crystal said, "That was a nice kiss, but I'll bet you can do better."

Mark scooted his chair closer to the bed, leaned his elbows on the bed and proceeded to do just that.

"Wow," gasped Crystal. "That was better. Way better. How about one more try before Nana gets back."

"Sounds good to me."

Several minutes slipped by and Mark had just straightened up when Eula walked back in the room, Dr Pepper in hand. "Did you miss me?" she asked.

"We certainly knew you were gone," Crystal said.

"And knew about making hay while the sun shines, I'll bet," said Eula.

Mark grinned. "I was just noting the flushed look on Crystal's face. It's very becoming. She looks absolutely gorgeous. You have the most beautiful granddaughter, Eula."

"Thank you. I think so, too."

"Will you two stop that? You're embarrassing me."

Mark's visit lasted nearly an hour. Before he left, they made plans for him to come by in the morning and help get Crystal back to Eula's house from the hospital. Though Crystal felt it totally unnecessary, she welcomed the chance for another visit with Mark, and perhaps some private time as well.

* * *

The next morning, the hospital refused to release Crystal until the doctor checked in on her. So, it was nearly twelve by the time Crystal,

Eula and Mark got settled on Eula's veranda. An hour later, Mark said his goodbyes, and left.

Five minutes later, the sheriff walked in. After the usual pleasantries, Bill turned to Crystal. "I passed Mark on the way in. He's a straight shooter. I sure hope you didn't run him off."

"No, no. He came in last night and then helped Eula get me home today. Of course, I'm perfectly well now, but I didn't mind the attention."

Eula snorted. "You are not perfectly well."

"Okay. I'm much better though."

The sheriff pursed his lips. "I told you not to go over there. You wouldn't find anything. And you didn't. But you almost got ..." He stopped, not wanting to worry Eula any more.

"That's where you were wrong," Crystal said.

"How's old Billy Goat wrong?" Eula asked.

"I did learn something, several things, in fact. First, whoever is behind this is here in town, right now. Second, a woman's involved. Third, she's worried, or why stir things up? And fourth, she wears Eight Second Angels."

"And those are?" asked Bill.

"Them's fancy boots," Eula said. She turned to Crystal. "And what do you know about them?"

"I see 'em when I'm at the rodeos," answered Crystal.

"But you don't even like rodeos. Never went to them with me and your granddad, and I know we invited you many times. You always said no."

Crystal might have blushed a little, but the heat exhaustion made it impossible to tell. "Mark has taken me to a few. They were fun."

"Explains it," said Bill. "More fun with Mark than with grandparents."

"Well, hallelujah. Maybe some good'll come out of this yet."

"Back to the boot," the sheriff said. "It's distinctive in some way?"

"There're all kinds of Eight Second Angel boots. But most are easily identified. And they're not cheap. She was wearing the red-fringed, short boot. Maybe two hundred and fifty bucks. Probably not that many sold around here."

"Could be the break we need," said the sheriff. "I just came to see if you wanted to pick up your car. But it looks like that will have to wait 'til the morning. Get me a picture of them boots. I'll scope out all the women's boots around town."

# Chapter 37

**Tuesday, October 23**

**Ron Drake walk**ed into Joan Abbott's office, this time accompanied by his lawyer, Carl Nuchols, a tall rawboned Texan with the swagger and confidence earned over a long and impeccable career.

There were no pleasantries and the District Attorney wasted no time in getting the meeting started. "This is Fran Summers, my assistant who will handle most of the work on this case."

"There is no case, Abbott," said Nuchols.

"I disagree. And I have a bill of indictment ready to present to a grand jury. I'll let them decide."

"Do you have some evidence I am not aware of? Because I don't know of anything right now that will stand up in court. You have some circumstantial evidence that is as weak as a newborn fawn. I wouldn't think you'd want your name attached to such ridiculous charges. I'll have no problem shredding it."

Abbott's assistant stood up. "We have evidence Mr. Drake stole his own painting, and placed it in a storage unit under his name. And for the record, the Wooden Nickel Storage contract contains the standard Texas Self Storage Association suggested limit of $5,000 as the maximum value of items stored in one of their units. So, right off, he violated the contract. Then later he collected $400,000 in insurance. A clear case of insurance fraud. We have a homicide that occurred in Drake's house, where there was no forced entry, no fingerprints except his. We are still working on the motive for the murder, but it looks like Nathanael Owens may have arrived and caught Drake stealing the painting."

Nuchols held up his hand, laughing. "Hold it right there. First, why would Owens think Drake was stealing the painting, since it was his to begin with? So, there would be no reason for Drake to kill Owens. Second, are you saying you found no other fingerprints except Drake's? None for Owens? None for the housekeeper? I'd say your crime scene techs did a lousy job."

Summers looked a little chagrined. "Well, of course there were some for Owens. What I meant was no fingerprints for anybody else."

"Can you imagine how I'll tear that to shreds on the witness stand? Telling a jury Drake's fingerprints were found in his own house will certainly give them a laugh. And by the way, there's nothing wrong with accepting a payment from an insurance company for a loss."

"But, if he stole the painting, then it's fraud," said Summers.

"*If* he stole the painting. But you can't prove that. It didn't happen."

"The painting was put in a storage unit assigned to Drake."

Nuchols looked at Abbott and then Summers. "Are you honestly telling me you are hanging your case—perhaps somebody's career—" he focused on Abbott, "on some flimsy connection to the storage unit?"

For several seconds, no one said anything. Then Nuchols turned to Abbott. "What do you keep in your storage unit, Ms. Abbott?"

The District Attorney tilted her head to the side and looked indignant. "I don't have a storage unit."

Nuchols smiled as he reached in his inside pocket and pulled out a card. "I have a card here from the Wooden Nickels Mini Storage which indicates you own one of its small storage units. Unit number 8 to be exact."

"Well, it isn't mine."

"But this card says it is."

"I don't care what the card says. I don't own a storage unit anywhere." Abbott puffed herself up, trying to be as imposing as she could.

"Funny, that's just what Mr. Drake says." The lawyer tossed the card on Abbott's desk.

She grabbed the card and stared at it. "What are you trying to pull? I've never had a storage unit there. And that isn't my signature."

"How do I know that?"

The District Attorney looked puzzled. "I just told you it wasn't."

"Let's see your signature - see how this one matches."

Now, she looked indignant. "I'm not going to show you my signature. How dare you even ask? I just told you I never rented a storage unit there."

"And yet, when my client says the same thing, you insist he's lying. In point of fact, a signature, your name, is on that card. There wasn't even a signature on the card for unit seventy-three where the painting was stored. In fact, you don't even have a card for seventy-three for that period. Just a notation in the computer."

Abbott's jaw locked so tight a muscle was twitching. Her hands were curled into hard balls. She fixed the lawyer with a look that bordered on hatred.

It did not intimidate Nuchols. "And unless you have tampered with a witness, the woman who rented out unit seventy-three will give a description which does not fit my client in the least."

"How dare you accuse me?" The DA's face turned crimson. "I don't care if you are a high powered lawyer from Dallas, if I find you've done anything illegal, I won't hesitate to indict you."

Nuchols smiled. "I'll look forward to it. It will only be another defeat on your less than impressive record. And as for my client, Mr. Drake is ready for you to bring this to trial immediately. We have no fear of losing this. It will be laughed out of court." He turned to Drake. "Let's go, Ron. I've had enough of this foolishness." He looked back at the District Attorney. "Let me know what path you're going to follow. It's your career." He raised his eyebrows. "You're not up for election this cycle, but then again, that just gives voters more time to think about your record."

* * *

Once again, Ron Drake made the top story on the ten o'clock News.

"With less than two weeks before election day, we have learned the DA in Wooden Nickel has prepared an indictment against gubernatorial candidate Ron Drake and has it ready to present to a Grand Jury. We could not confirm the exact contents of this indictment, but earlier, both insurance fraud and murder were being considered. Drake is still the front-runner, but his lead has dropped from nearly forty points to a mere four points. That's within the margin of error of our polling. Most of this drop has been in the last week, ever since the stories began to emerge about his missing painting turning up in a storage locker listed under his own name and the death of his bookkeeper Nathanael Owens."

# Chapter 38

**Wednesday, October 24**

**Wednesday, Crystal felt** like crying when both the Houston Chronicle and the Austin American-Statesman newspapers came out backing Jim Bob Wilson. Each had different reasons for the choice, but both cited the possibility of an indictment on Ron Drake. The Houston paper noted the rumors about an indictment, but claimed its decision to back Mr. Wilson was based on his platform and his commitment to the people of Texas. It was not influenced by the rumors. It also mentioned the strong support for the people of Houston by Mr. Wilson's father, a man active in and around Houston for decades.

The Austin paper also noted the rumor of an indictment, but quickly pointed out no indictment had actually been issued. The paper had reached out to the District Attorney's office for comment on the rumor, but had received no response. With less than two weeks before the election, the paper felt it time to select a candidate to endorse.

Crystal almost called Abbott to ask why she hadn't responded to the Austin paper. This gave Jim Bob Wilson the backing of two of the most influential newspapers in Texas. Neither of the major newspapers in Dallas or San Antonio, both metropolitan areas important in the race for governor, had named a candidate it would support.

* * *

Two days had passed since Crystal had been locked in the storage unit. She was getting her strength back and today her car was parked outside the entrance to the Jim Bob Wilson Campaign Headquarters in Tyler. It had been there for several hours. Evidence of this could be found in all the drink cups, hamburger wrappers, and other assorted fast food containers littering the floor of her car.

Julie Johnson sat in the passenger's seat, alternately munching on french-fries and spooning out some of her turtle pecan Blizzard. She had come home for a weekend visit, and Crystal had managed to get her to come and look at workers in the political office. Julie had said it had been months since she rented unit seventy-three at Wooden Nickel Mini-Storage. She wasn't at all sure she could recognize the man she had rented the unit to. But, when Crystal said she'd pay her fifteen dollars an hour to watch people come out of the office, plus all the fast food she could eat, Julie agreed to give it a try. If Julie saw someone she thought was the man, great. If not, that was okay. Either way she'd make the same money.

Thus far, many people had departed the building. None was the person Crystal was hoping for. But she gave no indication to Julie whom she was looking for or what he might look like. In fact, she hadn't even said it was a man. Crystal admitted to herself that was extreme. But she wanted to make certain she was not directing Julie in any way whatsoever. Of course, Julie had said she had rented it to a man who claimed he was Ron Drake.

Just then, a man and a woman opened the door and exited the campaign office, heading for their car. Julie sat up straight and studied the man. "Nope. Not that one. I'm sure of that."

Crystal sighed, then immediately regretted it. She didn't want Julie to get bored or give less than her full attention. "That's fine. And the

152

person might not be in there at all. But we'll give it a little more time."

The sun was down and the heat was dissipating, making for a much more pleasant evening. After her encounter with heat exhaustion two days ago, Crystal did not want to get overheated, or even a little hot for that matter. The doctor had warned her about heat and exertion and the dangers she could still face. She had run the air conditioning a good bit, but now Crystal rolled down the windows and a gentle breeze carried the smell of fried potatoes out of the car.

The lights in the parking area had come on. Crystal didn't want to call any attention to her and Julie so she kept the radio volume turned down. But when Andrea Bocelli began singing *Time to Say Goodbye*, she reached over and turned the volume up slightly.

Another man and woman walked out of the campaign office. Julie leaned forward and stopped chewing. She tracked the man carefully and for a few seconds, he looked directly at her, perhaps picking up Bocelli's voice. She turned to Crystal and grabbed her hand. "I think that's him."

It came out louder than Crystal would have liked and she thought the man looked back at her. But again she decided it was probably Bocelli's famous song that attracted his attention. Then he was gone, getting into a car. The car started and left the parking lot.

"I really think that was him," Julie said. "I didn't think I'd recognize him, but I'm pretty sure that was the guy. Of course, his hand has healed, you know, like, he doesn't have the bandage on it. But it looked like the same guy. Same face, you know, only he wasn't smiling tonight. But I think that was him. How 'bout that?" Julie was excited. She grinned as she took another spoonful of her Blizzard.

Crystal could hardly move. The man Julie had identified was George Weeks. And George Weeks had been into political dirty tricks before.

## Chapter 39

**Thursday, October 25**

**"I'm telling you,** it was her."

George was sitting across from Ginnie in the coffee shop just a block from Jim Bob's campaign headquarters. The waitress had brought them coffee plus a cinnamon roll for Ginnie. She looked across at the normally calm man who was her mentor in the political arena.

"How can you be sure? It's been, what, over six months? You saw her for five minutes. Was she that attractive?" Ginnie took a bite of her roll.

"She was a kid, in high school. But it was a special meeting. That wasn't an ordinary day for me. So I remember her."

"Okay, you remember her. What are the chances she would remember you? You're probably old enough to be her father. You're just one of the older generation, the old folks. She probably didn't remember you the next day."

George looked down at his coffee, but didn't drink any. "I get what you're saying. But, how was it she was outside Jim Bob's headquarters. That's a pretty odd coincidence."

"What was she doing? How did you see her?"

"I came out. As you know, the lot is well lit. I angled over toward where my car was parked and I was looking right into this car. It was a nice evening and the windows were open. There sat the girl who rented me the storage unit under Drake's name."

"Did you speak to her?"

"Are you crazy? Of course I didn't speak to her. I hoped she didn't really look at me closely. I did nothing to call attention to myself." He paused for a moment, thinking. "And just as important, guess who was sitting in the driver's seat?"

"I give up. Who?"

"That Moore woman. The one who came into Jim Bob's Headquarters and got into a yelling match with Summers. The one who accused Summers of leaking stuff to the media." George was shaking his head. "This was no accident." Ginnie started to say something but George cut her off. "And it was no coincidence. It was planned."

Ginnie finished another bite of her roll. "What have we got? Two weeks to the election? Less than two weeks actually. Whatever she does will be too late."

"Too late for Drake, maybe. But they can still come after us after the election is over. And keep in mind, you've got more to lose here than I do."

"But Jim Bob will be governor." She stuffed the last of the roll into her mouth.

George gave a short, mirthless laugh. "Don't think that's going to help you. Jim Bob will distance himself from this as fast and as far as possible. He knew nothing about it. And you can bet your britches he will not want to hear about it. Anybody tries to tell him about it, he will shut his ears."

Ginnie shook her head. "I thought I put an end to that woman. Left her in an oven for hours. She should be dead. Or at least out of commission for a few months. How the hell did she get out?"

"I don't know, but she did."

"I parked out away from there, but where I could see the unit. I stayed there for over an hour. It was hotter 'n hell in my car. With the windows open. She's in a closed storage unit. No windows. No circulation. It had to be a hundred and forty, probably more. She should have had a heat stroke, at the least."

"Well, she's not out of commission. She's on our trail. I don't know how. I don't know why. But she is. From what you've said, she ought to be in the hospital. Well, she's not. She's moving closer, faster. I'm worried." He sipped his now-cold coffee and frowned. "It was bad enough she was on to Fran. Now she's got that girl who handled the storage rental. And she was looking for me, at me."

"I like you, George. But you are not that memorable. I mean, not to a young kid anyway. You were just some old guy."

"I hope you're right. But it worries me." He looked Ginnie in the eye. "And you should be worried much more than I am. My getting that place under a false name is no big deal. Maybe a slap on the wrist. Except, it ties into the stolen painting. And that ties into the guy's death. But I knew nothing about the guy getting killed."

"We were in this together. We planned it together. Don't think you can weasel out of it."

"Together on the painting. Not on the homicide."

Through clenched teeth, Ginnie said, "It was an accident."

"I know that. You know that. The police and the DA don't. And they won't accept that for a moment." He shook his head. "I told you this at the time. I didn't sign on for violence." Ginnie started to speak, but George held up his hand and kept talking. "I know you didn't mean to. And I can testify to that if we get to that point. But, Ginnie, I'm not part of the murder. "

"What was I supposed to do?"

"I don't know what I would have done if I had been in your place. But I wasn't." He nodded slightly. "What I *do* know is, if I were you, I'd be gone. I'd be in another state."

For several minutes, neither said anything. Ginnie picked up her purse and scooted to the edge of the booth. "I'm not running. Not yet. I'll be packed and ready, just in case. But I'd like to put that prissy, nosy, Crystal in her place."

"Be careful. Remember the good advice from Kenny Rogers."

"What's that?"

George tried to sing in a soft voice. "Know when to hold 'em. Know when to fold 'em. Know when to walk away. And know when to run."

"I don't run."

"Sometimes that's a mistake."

* * *

"You look beat, Crystal. Have any luck?"

"I think so. But I'm so tired, I'm not even sure."

"Let me get you some dinner and you'll feel better." Eula started toward the kitchen.

Crystal dropped her purse on the hall table. "Don't bother. I've had so much junk food, I think I'll skip dinner tonight."

"I made chicken and dumplings. And apricot fried pies."

Crystal had started toward her bedroom, but she turned back. "Well, maybe just a little bit." She followed her grandmother into the kitchen.

Eula probed for more information as she dished up the food. "Okay, what do you mean you're not sure you had any luck? You did or you didn't."

Crystal slumped into a chair and leaned on the table. "Julie believes she saw the man who rented the storage unit under Drake's name."

"Well, come on, gal. Who was it? Did you recognize him?"

"I did. It was George Weeks."

Eula let out a yell. "Fantastic. 'Course, I don't care who it is, long as it wasn't Ron. But you told me George has a history of tampering in politics. What'd Bill have to say?"

"I haven't told him yet." Crystal straightened up as her Nana put a plate of food in front of her. "I just dropped Julie off at her parents' house and drove straight here. I'm beat. We sat there watching for over four hours."

"Well, I guess you aren't up to snuff after being half baked in that storage unit. Doctor said to take it easy."

"I was just sitting in a car. But I feel exhausted."

"Eat some of my fried pies and you'll be good to go. Let's get Billy Goat over here and let him hear what you got to say."

* * *

Half an hour later, Bill Glothe, Crystal and Eula sat around the kitchen table, all enjoying the warm apricot fried pies. Bill and Eula had vanilla ice cream along with theirs, but based on all the junk food Crystal had eaten earlier, she skipped the ice cream.

"So, how long were you out there?" the sheriff asked.

"Nearly four and a half hours," Crystal said.

"I bet the doctor wouldn't approve of that. He told you to take it easy for a few days."

"I'm okay, Bill. I just sat there. And ate junk." But in fact, she did feel unusually tired and was ready to drop into bed.

"Could Julie have just been tired of the game?" Bill pushed. "Tired and wanted to quit, so she grabbed the next person who came out?"

Crystal was shaking her head before he finished. "No. She didn't seem tired. And I was paying her by the hour, so she was happy to sit and eat French fries and Blizzards and make more money."

"Did you suggest Weeks when he came out?"

"No. In fact, I hadn't really noticed him. I was fooling with the radio. I was aware a couple came out the door, but hadn't looked at them until she grabbed my hand."

"Grabbed your hand?"

"Yes. She was excited. She said 'I think that's him,' and kept studying him."

158

"She *thought* it was him. She wasn't sure?" A slight frown crept up Glothe's face.

"Come on, Bill. It's been over six months. She only saw him that one brief time. The interesting thing is, he looked at her. At first, I thought maybe he had heard the radio and was looking to see where it was coming from. But as I think about it, I believe he might have recognized her as well. She kept her eyes on him and after he was gone, she said she hadn't expected to recognize him. But it was more money than she made working at school so why not give it a try. And when he came into view, she surprised herself. She remembered him."

Bill focused on the remaining bite of the pie, taking time to enjoy it. "Is she going to be in town awhile?"

"She'll go back to Dallas on Monday."

"I wish she'd said she was positive."

Eula had been unusually quiet, but now she jumped in. "Bill, you just want a fish in a barrel. We're talking about an encounter with one of us old people and five or six months ago to boot. She's in college. I'm amazed she feels like she really picked out the guy. Do a lineup, or whatever you call them things. See how she does with that. Watch and listen to her and you'll have a good idea how strong her identification is. You want me to come watch her? I'll be able to tell right off."

Bill drummed his fingers on the table and thought for a minute. "Got an idea. Is Ron in town?"

"He's got rallies in Tyler and Longview Sunday," Crystal said. "He's here today. So, I expect he'll be here tomorrow, maybe Monday morning as well. What do you have in mind?"

"Unless this Julie's identification is rock solid, I can imagine Abbot giving it no credibility at all. She'll dismiss it. I'm thinking I could put Weeks and Ron both in the lineup, and others, of course. So, she'll have a chance to pick out Ron, too. If she ignores him and selects Weeks, Abbott won't be able to write that off."

"I like that," Eula said. "Ought to put a hole in the DA's balloon."

"Great idea, Bill," Crystal added.

"'Course Weeks isn't under arrest. So he doesn't have to do a lineup."

"Well, shoot," Eula said. "Sounded like a good idea."

"Let me think on a way around that." The sheriff shifted his focus to Crystal. "There is a risk for Ron. This Julie girl might pick him out. That would send Abbott running to the Grand Jury with her indictment clutched in her hot little hand."

Crystal shook her head. "I don't think she'd pick Ron, though. Not with Weeks right there, too."

Bill shrugged. "It could happen. She's probably seen Ron on TV in the last few months. Maybe even at her school. He might look awfully familiar to her. She could get mixed up, even if she's trying to help."

For a moment, the seriousness of the possibility silenced them. Finally Crystal spoke. "I bet Ron is willing to take that chance. He knows he's innocent and he trusts our legal system. But, you'll just have to ask him - and warn him about the risk."

"Got another one of them pies?" Bill asked Eula.

"I do. But you're putting on a little weight."

"This case is working it off. I think I'm losing weight."

"Yeah. Like I'm getting younger." But Eula reached around behind her, snagged another fried pie and put it on the sheriff's plate.

# Chapter 40

**Saturday, October 27**

**Saturday morning had** gloom written all over it. Clouds had rolled in from the west and a light mist fell across Wooden Nickel. After the heat of the last three weeks, the cooler weather, even if damp, was welcome. Still, Crystal didn't like the atmosphere. Dreary. Murky. Depressing. She was hoping for a bright, sunny, happy day with a lot of good news.

She picked up Julie at her parents' house and took her to the police station. Julie had never been in a police station before and she kept up a steady stream of questions about everything. Crystal and the officer ushering them to the lineup viewing room answered most of them. On a few, the officer suggested Julie ask Sheriff Glothe once the lineup was finished.

They entered a small, rectangular room, painted an institutional shade of ugly. One of the long walls contained a window which ran the length of the room. Four plastic chairs faced the window. Only Crystal chose to sit. They had been in the viewing room no more than a minute when the sheriff walked in, introduced himself to Julie, and then explained what they would do.

"We're going to bring in eight men. They cannot see or hear you. You can ask them to do anything, like turn to the left or right, or even say some words you specify. The man who rented the storage unit under the name of Ron Drake may not even be in this group. But, if you are confident you see the man who rented the unit, then you should tell us which one it is. We are only interested in the man who you rented unit seventy-three to on March 18 of this year, paid cash, and said his name was Ron Drake. As I said, he may *not* be in this group. But if you are sure he is, point him out to us. Do you have any questions?"

Julie had kept her eyes on Glothe and appeared to absorb every word. "They can't see or hear me?"

"No. If you have a request, for example, to turn to the right, you just tell me and I'll tell them. And all the men will do the same thing at the same time."

This time, she just nodded.

At that moment, Fran Summers entered, followed by Carl Nuchols. Before Bill could say anything, Summers demanded to know why Nuchols was there.

"He has every right to be," said Bill.

"Drake hasn't been charged yet. His attorney shouldn't be in here."

"The law clearly states anyone appearing in the lineup can have a lawyer present. Drake is in the lineup and Mr. Nuchols is his lawyer." Bill continued to stare at Summers.

The assistant DA's mouth opened and she looked puzzled. "Why is Drake in the lineup? Is this some sort of a trick?"

"On the contrary," the sheriff said. "He's in the lineup for y'all's benefit. Mr. Drake's taking a chance here. If the witness selects him, you get a stronger case. But Mr. Drake is willing to take that chance."

Summers clenched her jaw. "I want it on the record I am objecting to both Nuchols being in here and Drake being in the lineup."

"So noted," said Glothe. "By the way, what is your objection to Mr. Drake being in the lineup?"

Everyone looked at Summers. She started to speak, then stopped. After another moment, she said, "I don't have to explain myself to you."

"Fine," said Glothe. "Then, let's get this rodeo moving." He clicked the switch on the microphone he held. "Slim, bring in the men."

"Wait," Summers shouted. "Did Weeks agree to this?"

"Yes, he did. And I had two other officers there when I asked him."

"If he wasn't under arrest, why would he agree to it?"

Glothe shrugged. "You'll have to ask him. After we're through here."

The door on the right opened and slowly, the eight men paraded into the room. They were all similar in height. Five appeared to be about the age of Weeks, while Drake and one other appeared to be a good bit older. They were all dressed exactly alike.

Summers quickly objected. "You have eight men in the lineup. Six is normal. What are you trying to pull?"

Nuchols laughed. "Are you suggesting having more men will make it easier for her to select the right one?"

"Well, ah," Summers began. "I, ah, I don't know. But it's usually only six."

Bill looked at Julie, then asked the other officer to escort her outside for just a minute. Once they were outside and the door closed, Bill turned to Fran and spoke slowly, as if explaining this to a child. "I wanted six of the same age as Weeks. But, you've accused Drake of renting the storage unit and I want to give the witness a chance to select him, so I added two older men. Let's give the woman who handled the rental a chance to look at him. Shall we proceed?"

When Summers didn't say anything, Glothe opened the door and invited Julie back in. "Sweetheart, take your time and look at each one carefully. As I told you, if you want them to do anything or say anything, you tell me."

Julie nodded.

It was clear she was checking each man carefully. Crystal could see her look at a man for six or seven seconds, then shift her head and focus on the next man. After a minute she turned to the sheriff. "Can you ask them to smile?"

"Just smile?"

Julie nodded.

Bill thumbed the microphone. "Will you please smile?"

Julie studied them thoroughly. "Once more, please."

Again, Bill thumbed the microphone. "Please smile once more."

Again, the young woman looked at each man. Then, she turned to the sheriff. "I am certain number four is the man who rented unit seventy-three last March."

Glothe thumbed the microphone once more. "Will number four please take one step forward? Thank you." He turned the microphone off. "Is that the man you are selecting?"

Julie nodded. "Yes."

"Are you quite certain?"

"Yes, sir. I'm sure."

Summers pushed up beside Julie. "It's been six months. How can you be certain?"

Crystal laid her hand on Julie's shoulder for support.

"It was an unusual thing, ah, rental. He paid cash for eight months, and I had to rent it to him, you know, without getting a signature. I was so worried. I thought I might get fired. But he was so nice and had such a great smile, and his hand was all bandaged up so he couldn't write. I never had anybody pay cash for eight months. And that was the only time I didn't get a signature. It was, like, you know, kinda different."

"How about number seven?" Summers asked.

Glothe took a step toward Summers. "Hold it right there. You are trying to influence the witness. I won't have it. And I'll bet Abbott won't be happy about it either." He moved the mike to his mouth. "Thank you gentlemen. That will be all."

The men in the lineup turned and walked out the door they had entered.

Julie turned to Summers. "Number seven is too old. And not as, you know, ah, heavy."

Glothe put his hand up toward Summers. "No more." Then he turned to Julie. "You did good." He looked at the other officer. "Take Julie and buy her a soda in the break room and then the two of you wait for me in my office. I'll be there in a minute."

Once they were out and the door closed, Glothe looked directly at Summers. "You were out of line on several occasions. I will--"

Summers interrupted. "I'm the Assistant District Attorney. I am entitled to be here at this somewhat unusual lineup."

"It was unusual. But your conduct was unacceptable. I will discuss it with the DA. And you and I will have a long talk before you enter another lineup of mine. And before you concoct any stories, remember this was all captured on video." For a few seconds, he fixed her with a steely glare. Then, "Crystal, Carl, let's go."

And the three walked out leaving Summers steaming, and alone.

# Chapter 41

**"We're in the** kitchen, Bill. Come on back," yelled Eula when the front door opened and closed. Moments later, the sheriff joined Eula, Crystal and Ron in the kitchen. "Grab a bowl of red. The cornbread's on the table."

Glothe filled a big bowl with the chili and took a chair at Eula's table. "Smells mighty good. Easy to understand why this is the official state food of Texas."

"And Nana's is one of the best."

"You're right there, Crystal," Ron said.

Eula snorted. "Probably the best 'cause you don't have to cook it. But I'll take the compliment anyway."

Crystal pushed her now-empty bowl aside and propped her elbows on the table. "Okay, Bill. How did you get George Weeks to agree to be in a lineup. He wasn't under arrest, so he didn't have to do that, did he?"

The sheriff took another bite of the chili, savored it, swallowed and wiped his mouth. "That's a trade secret. Can't give that out or people would steal it, spread it around and then I couldn't use it anymore."

Everybody laughed. Eula said, "I ain't gonna have any use for it. Was it just your sweet, kindly manner? Or did you threaten to beat his head in if he didn't?"

Bill dipped his cornbread into the rich chili and took a big bite. "Fine, then. We had a little Come to Jesus Meeting. I did talk right sweet and nice to him. Only a little threat here and there. He didn't deny he'd rented the storage unit. Didn't admit it either. But he flatly denied any involvement with the theft and the homicide."

"Did you believe him?" Ron asked.

Bill helped himself to some of the pinto beans served in another bowl. "I'm not dead center certain one way or the other. But based on some of the things he said, and the way he said them, I got an inkling maybe he didn't actually steal the painting. But he knows more'n he's telling."

Ron nodded. "You haven't arrested him, have you?"

"No. Ain't worth arresting him for getting the storage unit under a false name. But 'cause the stolen art was stored there, I've told him not to leave town and I will likely be back to talk to him."

"But Bill," Crystal was almost pleading. "We need something to get in the media, to counteract all the bad publicity Ron has been getting on the stolen painting and all. Stop his slide in the polls. Turn this thing around."

"Hold it." Ron leaned forward. "Crystal, believe me, I'd like to quit losing ground in the governor's race. But the important thing is to find Nat's killer. If I don't win, I won't lose any sleep over it. I'll just have more time to fish. Or travel. But we need to find who killed Nat Owens. He was one of my best friends. He didn't deserve to die. I'd like to see whoever did that behind bars. The way things are looking, he probably got killed because of my running for governor. That will stay with me forever."

"Stop right there." Bill put his spoon down and leaned over the table to get closer to Ron's face. "You did not break the law. You did not encourage anyone to break the law. Someone came into your house and committed three crimes. That person is guilty. Not you."

"But if I hadn't --."

"Don't do that. You cannot take the blame. If I buy a new car and someone steals it, it is not my fault for buying a fancy car. You did not entice them to steal from you. And certainly you did nothing to encourage them to kill Nat. Yes, we want to find and punish that person. But you cannot take any of the blame." Bill paused a few seconds, fixing Ron with a hard look. "Got it?"

Glothe glared at Ron for another minute. No one said a word. No one moved. Finally, Bill leaned back in his chair.

"I got a question for one of you." Eula looked at Bill and then Ron. "How come you was in the lineup? That seems a mite dangerous to me. What if she recognized you from your TV appearances and picked you out? Did Carl talk you into that, Ron?"

"No, he didn't. It was Bill's idea."

Bill nodded. "It was. Figured if she had a chance to pick him out and didn't, Abbott would have to drop that stuff. I did talk with Carl and he admitted there was a slight danger in it. As you just said, Eula, she might have seen him on TV and not realize that's where she saw him. Just that he was familiar. But since she had already seen Weeks the other night with Crystal, we figured she'd get it right."

Ron laughed. "And they both said it was my neck anyway, not theirs."

"Whoa," Eula said.

"Carl told me not to worry. He'd get me off even if the young woman did pick me out."

Eula turned back to Bill. "Okay. You said you don't think Weeks stole the painting and killed Nat. You got any idea who did, then?"

"Not a single lead."

"Well, I do," Crystal said.

All heads turned toward Crystal. Eula spoke first. "Okay. You got the floor. Let's hear what you got."

"It's a woman, with a red car, who wears Eight Second Angel, red-fringed short boots."

"How do you know all that?" Eula asked.

"Donna Littlefellow said her husband saw a woman put a painting in unit seventy-three. That had to be your painting, Ron. And Bill doesn't think Weeks stole it and handed it off to her. So, I'd say she stole the painting herself. And whoever stole the painting killed Mr. Owens."

Eula started to speak, but Crystal kept right on talking.

"And, it was a woman who locked me in the storage unit and came close to putting me out of commission. And that woman wore red-fringed, Eight Second Angel short boots. Plus, Bill said the technicians suggested it was most likely a red car that killed Mr. Littlefellow."

Ron nodded. "Littlefellow sees her put the painting in the storage unit, so she kills him to keep him from telling the police, possibly even identifying her?"

"That'd be my guess," Bill said.

Crystal looked encouraged. "So, we have some things to go on."

"Only, we've checked every body shop here and as far as Tyler. No job matching what we were looking for. Everybody in my department has kept an eye out for a car with the kind of damage we expect it caused. I haven't found a single car with that kind of damage, regardless of color."

Eula looked disgusted. "'Course she got it repaired and painted."

"Where? And how quick?" asked Bill.

"If'n it's me, mighty quick. And not around here." Eula looked at Bill. "I'd drive up to Oklahoma or into Arkansas and get it fixed up and painted. Or sell it."

Crystal grinned. "Why not Louisiana? It's as close as Oklahoma and Arkansas."

"I don't like Louisiana. I'd head north."

Bill threw a hand up. "Sorry, but I just don't have the man-power to check all the body shops in four states."

Ron cut in. "Bill, you said you thought Weeks knew more about it. And he did rent the storage unit. So, it makes sense he knows who stole the painting."

"He said he just got an anonymous note with five hundred dollars in it. Asked him to rent unit seventy-three for eight months under the name of Ron Drake, pay cash and he could keep the remainder."

"Does he —"

"Surprise, surprise. He no longer has the note. And no, I don't believe it."

"Had to give the key to somebody," Eula said.

"No," Bill answered. "They don't give you a lock and key. You put your own lock on it. And before you ask, whoever sent the note could just go look and see which ones were available, the ones without locks. I don't believe him. But it's possible."

Crystal jumped back in. "Let's just say this woman probably knew Weeks. There's a very good chance she worked at Jim Bob's campaign headquarters. Why can't we go find out who works there, maybe someone who doesn't show up anymore, or even which ones drive a red car?"

For a moment, everyone seemed to be considering this tactic. Finally, Bill said, "Well, I don't think we can demand that kind of information. Even who works there. But we could ask. See if they want to play nice."

"I could go in and look at all the shoes, see if there are any Eight Second Angels," offered Crystal.

Eula laughed. "After your last screaming visit there, I reckon they won't even let you in the door."

"Then you go, Nana."

Eula gave a short nod. "I could do that."

Bill looked at Eula. "Just be careful. We know one person, and probably two, have been killed over this. I'll see if I can scrape up any info on the people who work there. Don't expect I'll get much."

"And look for red cars. Littlefellow's wife said Johnny called it a cute little red car. So no red Caddies or big SUVs." Crystal looked around the group. "And everybody look for Eight Second Angel. Short boots. Red fringed."

# Chapter 42

**Monday, October 29**

**Ginnie grabbed a** cup and filled it with ice, then Coke. She carried it over to the booth where George Weeks sat and slipped in across from him. Ginnie had suggested this cafe because at this time of the day, there wouldn't be many people here. Only one other table was occupied and it was at the other end of the room. Music was playing softly, a Willie Nelson song about a whiskey river.

"I'm amazed you're still here," George said.

"No need to run. They don't have a shred of evidence that puts me in Drake's house. Without that, they can't say I stole the painting or killed that man."

Weeks shook his head. "Yeah, and they didn't have any against me for renting the self-storage either. But that Moore woman managed to get them to haul me in."

"What'd you say to them?"

"Not much. I didn't admit I'd rented it, but I'd bet that girl ID'd me. 'Course, I couldn't see who was in the viewing room. And they didn't tell me anything after the lineup - not who they picked out, or who was doing the picking. But they did ask me to step out. So, I was certainly being considered."

Ginnie sat back. "I'd say they didn't get a good ID. Otherwise, I'm sure they'd have grilled you a lot more, maybe even locked you up."

"Not for falsifying a rental form."

"So, you think all of this was caused by that Crystal Moore woman?"

George gave several short nods. "Had to be. I mean, the sheriff could have found the girl on his own and brought her in, I guess. But Moore was sitting in the car with her when I came out of the campaign headquarters. And the next day, I'm hauled in." He slammed his hand down on the table, almost tipping Ginnie's cup over. "I said, just like you have, no evidence tied me to the rental. I didn't sign anything. I didn't even touch the form. My fingerprints were on the money I paid for the unit, that's all. You can bet that was long gone six months ago. I even opened the door using mostly the heel of my hand. No shred of evidence."

"Except if the girl ID's you."

"And Littlefellow saw you put the painting in the warehouse."

"He's not going to tell anybody now."

George studied the woman across from him. She had been uncertain about doing the podirt because it might be illegal and she didn't want to do anything illegal. But once she got in, and things went south, she changed. When her neck was on the line, she forgot about illegal. Now she had killed a man. Probably an accident. But he wondered about Littlefellow. A hit-and-run. He didn't know for sure, but Ginnie talked about a man seeing her put the painting in the storage unit. Might not have been Littlefellow. But, a couple of days later, Ginnie had disappeared for a few days. And never said where she was or what she was doing.

"Sheriff's told me not to leave town, or I'd already be gone. What's keeping you here?"

"The Moore bitch. I want to put her in her place." She smiled. "Maybe a grave."

* * *

The sheriff had been waiting for fifteen minutes. He had arrived precisely on time for his appointment with District Attorney Joan Abbott, and she had selected the time. He looked at his watch again. Sixteen minutes now. *I'll give her four more minutes and then I'm leaving.*

Five minutes later, he got up. "Tell Abbott I was here for our appointment. But I've got some important things to take care of. She can call —." Just then the intercom on the secretary's desk buzzed.

"Would you bring the sheriff in now?"

The secretary got up and led Glothe into Abbott's office. The secretary closed the door behind him. He sat down without being asked and wasted no time.

"Have you filed the indictment on Drake?" He looked at the DA and could tell she was not happy to see him.

Abbott just stared at him for a moment. "No."

"I'm sure Fran has talked to you."

"She has, and I'm wondering what you were doing calling a lineup. There's been no arrest. Has there?"

"No. Try thinking of it as saving your job."

A look of indignation cascaded across the DA's face. "That's rather presumptuous of you. I don't need you to save my job."

"Well, as I said, I'm sure Summers has talked with you. We put George Weeks, Ron Drake, and six other men in the lineup. The witness had no problem picking out Weeks. And she confirmed she was certain of her identification. Even when your assistant tried to influence the witness."

"What do you mean, 'influence the witness'?" She put her hands on her desk and set her eyes with laser-focus on the sheriff.

Glothe leaned forward and met her glare. "After the witness had identified Weeks, Summers asked her to reconsider and look at Drake. In all my years here, I've never had a member of the DA's office try to influence a witness during a lineup."

"I can't believe Fran would do that. You must be —.""

"It's on videotape."

Abbott just stared at the sheriff, her mouth still open. Nearly a minute passed. "Who was this witness?"

"Her name's Julie Johnson. She's the person who actually handled the rental of unit seventy-three under Drake's name."

"Why did she rent it without identification or a signature?"

"She was young. The man was very nice, smiled a lot, she said. And his hand was bandaged and he claimed he couldn't write or even hold a pen. He was paying cash for eight months." Glothe shrugged. "Who knows why? Those are the things she told us."

When Abbott said nothing, Glothe continued. "Since your main reason for indicting Drake was your thinking he rented that storage unit, the indictment makes no sense now. We put Drake in the lineup to give you every chance to have him identified. As for killing Nat because he caught Drake stealing his own painting, that won't fly. It was Drake's painting in Drake's house. Why would Nat think he was stealing his own painting? I think it's time to drop the indictment."

"What about … insurance fraud?" The last two words came out a little loud, as if she was grasping for something, anything.

"The insurance investigator confirms Drake never asked for payment, other than filing the original claim when the painting was stolen. It was strictly the insurance company's decision to pay the claim when they did. I've spoken to the head investigator. He says the company will not support an insurance fraud charge."

The DA sat a little straighter and raised her chin. "So you think you've got everything all sewed up?"

"Not at all. I still don't have any suspects for the murder of Nat Owens. I don't believe it was Weeks, but we've got very few clues."

"Have you dismissed Drake completely?"

"I have. No motive. People kill their friends when there is a clear motive. We have none here, not even a fuzzy or shaky motive. Nothing at all. Unless I find at least one bit of evidence Drake killed his friend, I'm gonna be looking for someone else."

The DA looked at Glothe in silence. The sheriff said nothing else; just waited. "You said 'few clues.' Few indicates some, though. Can you let me in on some of those, or what possible suspects you have?" Her voice had lost its hostile tone.

Glothe looked down at his hands for a moment. "I can tell you this. I'm looking for a person of interest. A woman."

"Why a woman?"

"I'd rather not say until I find something more concrete. But there have been two incidents that point to a woman being involved."

"And you won't tell me?"

"One was hearsay evidence. So you wouldn't like it. But someone saw a woman put a painting in storage unit seventy-three, probably on the day Drake's painting was stolen."

"Hearsay? Can't you get the person in to make a definitive statement?"

"He's dead."

"How'd he die?"

"Hit-and-run. Shortly after the theft. Shortly after seeing a woman put a painting into seventy-three.

"You think there's a connection?"

"Well, I'm not much on coincidences. He sees a painting tucked in this unit. What are the chances it's not Drake's? Then shortly after that he's killed." Glothe leaned forward and put his hands on his knees. "He was in the post office parking lot. You think that was a simple traffic accident?"

"No witnesses?"

"'Course not. And yes, we looked for any car with appropriate damage. Nothing."

Neither said anything for a minute. Glothe got up. "So, you going to drop that indictment?"

Abbott focused on her desk for a moment. Then she looked back up at Glothe. "Yes."

"Are you going to..." He almost said "leak" but decided not to irritate the woman. "Release that to the press?"

"We'll take care of it." It was almost a dismissal.

# Chapter 43

**Tuesday, October 30**

**Crystal surfed the** Internet, looking for any scrap of good news. What she found only moved her mood further down the scale. Newspapers in Fort Worth, Waco, and Beaumont each threw their support behind Jim Bob Wilson. The swirl of accusations and possible indictments of Ron Drake were listed as the main reasons for not backing Mr. Drake. Each listed the positive qualities of Jim Bob Wilson, and the important work his father had done for Harris county and the surrounding area. None of the three mentioned a single program that Jim Bob proposed as a reason for giving their support to the man.

# Chapter 44

**Wednesday, October 31**

**Crystal heard Eula's** car pull up. Anxious to hear what she found at Jim Bob's Headquarters, she met her grandmother at the front door.

"How'd it go, Nana?"

"Let me get these shoes off and something to drink. I'm dry as a horned toad." She discarded her "formal" shoes, as she called them, and headed barefoot to the kitchen, Crystal trailing behind.

Eula opened the refrigerator. "Want some peach tea?"

Crystal said yes and retrieved two glasses from the cupboard. "What'd you find out?"

Eula pulled a pitcher out, filled the two glasses, and slumped into a chair at the table. She drained a third of her glass. "Ah, that hits the spot." She put the glass down. "Well, I just moseyed into that office of theirs. My gosh, people were running all around the place. You'd think they were at a fire sale."

"Any of them wearing short boots with a red fringe?"

"Not that I saw. I wandered around, picked up a few pieces of junk. All had Jim Bob's good looking face on it. If I just voted on looks, I'd check his box."

"How about the parking lot? Any cute little red cars in the parking lot?"

"Didn't see any. Then some woman comes up and asks if she can help me. Well, what she really said was, 'Kin I hep ya?' Thought maybe she was playing a role on TV or something. I said she couldn't. I was just looking at some of the literature. We visited a minute and I left. Had trouble understanding the woman."

Crystal frowned. "Maybe this Eight Second Angel has flown away."

"Could be. No threats on your life lately?"

Crystal ignored that.

"Where's Mark? Ain't seen him around for a good time. Not since the day you almost got heat stroke."

Crystal looked at her grandmother warily. Where was this going? "He's at work. We aren't all retired like you."

"But you're not working. At least not on your paying job."

"Mark gave me time off to help Ron. After all the bad publicity started coming out, he told me to see if I could help turn things around. I told you that. He believes Texas really needs Ron, and thinks Jim Bob would be a real mistake."

"You and Mark cooling off?"

Crystal frowned. "There's not a me and Mark, Nana. He's my boss. I'm a good worker."

"Yeah. And I'm a clay pigeon. Your Nana knows you and Mark got a thing going. I just wanted an update."

Refusing to look into her grandmother's eyes, Crystal said, "We're good friends. And that hasn't changed just because I'm down here helping Ron."

"What you gotta know is, I can tell. And you ain't fooling me. Neither is Mark. But, I'll try to be patient. I know you'll tell me before the ceremony." She finished her tea and set the glass in the sink. "I checked the Tyler paper. No mention of the indictment being dropped."

"Bill said Abbott was going to take care of it. Maybe I need to nudge things along."

"Get on it. Election's less than a week. And right now, they show Ron and Jim Bob neck and neck, within their margin of error, whatever that means."

Crystal called the *Tyler Morning Telegraph* and got put through to the reporter who had written the recent stories on the election race.

"I'm calling on behalf of the sheriff's department in Pine County." She made a mental note to let Bill know she had used his office for validation. "A press release was sent out which stated that the District Attorney had no more interest in Ron Drake in connection with the art theft and the murder of Nathanael Owens. No indictments were filed, or would be filed, with Ron Drake's name included. But apparently some of those have been lost. If you haven't received one and wish to verify that information, please call the Pine County District Attorney's office, at 903-555-0966."

"When was that P.R. sent out? And how was it addressed?" asked the reporter.

"You should have received it today. But, I don't have the information on how it was addressed. It should have had your name on it. But it might have just been addressed to the news department."

The reporter said she would confirm it and try to get it in the next edition.

Crystal made similar calls to the Longview paper, each of the three TV stations in Tyler and several radio stations.

Next she called Drake's P.R. firm and suggested they get something out to the major newspapers plus TV and radio outlets. She gave them the telephone number for Abbott's office, suggesting they call and get a quote from the district attorney.

The news of the indictment being dropped didn't do much good if the public didn't know about it.

Clearly, bad news traveled faster than good news.

* * *

The cute little red car was sitting at station 18 at the local Sonic drive-in. The passenger door opened and George slipped in and closed it. Ginnie handed him a cherry limeade.

He took a quick sip. "This should be our last contact. At least in person. Things are getting heavy."

"Jim Bob's pulling closer to a win."

"And things are pulling closer to us. I've got to meet with the sheriff again tomorrow. And today, a woman comes into Jim Bob's and starts nosing around."

"So?"

"So, her name was Eula Moore. That's gotta be a relative of Crystal."

"The bitch's grandmother."

"Anyway, why's she poking around in Jim Bob's campaign office?"

Ginnie shrugged. "Who knows? Maybe she's figured out Jim Bob's the best candidate. And the polls are showing it."

George drained his drink. "Ginnie, don't mistake this. Jim Bob is not the better candidate. He got on the ticket by a fluke. I was already committed to the campaign, so I stayed. You just wanted to get in on the election excitement.

"We - you and I - are why his poll numbers are up. Or more accurately, why Drake's numbers are going down. We've done our job. Now, it's time to get out while we still can. If you've got any brains, you'll drive out of town right now and keep going. As soon as I get out from under the sheriff's thumb, I'll see this town in my rear view mirror."

"I'm packed. Won't take me five minutes to load it in the car. I got one little chore to do and then I'm just a memory here. They got nothing on me. Not a clue. And don't tell me somebody saw me put the painting in the building. He's not going to testify, that's for sure."

George looked Ginnie in the eye. "A lucky break?"

"Yeah, lucky. Nothing ties back to me." She studied her friend for a few seconds. "Unless you give me up."

"I said I wouldn't. I haven't. And I don't think they can make a case against me for the theft or the dead man. But..." He stopped and looked away.

"But, what?" Ginnie's eyes narrowed and she grabbed his arm. "What were you going to say? You're going to turn on me? Double-cross me? Don't do that George."

"Leave town, Ginnie. I won't name you. I don't know you."

"But?"

George clamped his teeth together and his eyes turned dark. "If it looks like they can pin the murder on me, self-preservation might take over." The big man dropped his cup in the drink holder between the seats. "Leave while you've still got the chance." He opened the door and was gone.

For several moments, Ginnie just stared at the door he had slammed. Her best friend and he might give her up. All because of that bitch. *I swear, I'm going to crush Crystal. Break her into a thousand bits of glass.*

Ginnie took a drink of her cherry limeade. It wasn't George's fault. He had to protect himself. And she had to protect herself. Crystal wanted to put her on death... . No, she wouldn't even say that. But just like George said, self preservation. *Even my mother understands self defense. It's Crystal or me. And the sooner I take care of her, the better.*

# Chapter 45

**Thursday, November 1**

**The P.R. firm** had sent out releases to all major papers in the state, and all radio and TV stations stating that all charges had been dropped against Ron Drake. They had not been able to get a quote from Abbott. The DA's office would only confirm the indictment had been dropped, which they included in the release.

The ten o'clock news carried the story, but not as the lead.

The lead covered a student walk out in protest over gun violence. The story which could have a large impact on the election came buried after six straight commercials. And it was short.

"The indictment Pine County District Attorney Joan Abbott had prepared against Ron Drake for art theft, insurance fraud, and murder has been put aside. 'The current evidence does not warrant continuing at this time' she said."

After another commercial, the Dallas and Houston stations ran a seven-minute piece on the improved Dallas Cowboys who, without giving up a single touchdown in the last three games, had crushed their opponents.

Newspapers ran a similar story on Drake, buried on the back page of section 2. The Cowboys got the prime position on the front page of the newspaper plus the sports section.

And Ron Drake's numbers continued to inch down.

* * *

"Most of the readers and listeners are gonna fall in two groups." Eula skinned sweet potatoes while she talked to her granddaughter. "One, those who believe the DA just couldn't quite get enough evidence to get a conviction and didn't want to lose. Two, the group that thinks Drake paid her off. I hate to say this, but the lousy stories they're putting out now ain't gonna help Ron much."

"Come on, Nana. Ron was losing voters because they thought he was going to be indicted. Now, he's not. His numbers will come up."

"Tell you what, I'll make you a bet Ron is going to lose."

"Okay. What do you want to bet?"

"If I win, you tell me the full and true story about you and Mark. If I lose, I'll tell you how your grandfather and I got together."

Crystal laughed. "Not a fair bet. I already know how you two met and started going together." She sliced off a bite of the still warm potato and stuck it in her mouth. "How about the full and true story of you and Bill?"

"Not much to tell there. But you're on." Eula cut the sweet potatoes into small cubes and put them in a baking dish. "So, what are you going to do for these last couple of days? You've got the bad news stopped. What good news are you getting out to the voters? Stuff that P.R. bunch put out ain't gonna help much."

"Not much I can do."

"So you're puttin' your saddle in the barn and callin' it a day?"

"I wish there was something I could do, Nana."

"Wishin' is waitin'. If you really want it, you gotta make it happen."

Thirty minutes later, Crystal came back into the kitchen.

"Well, whatcha got?"

"I've got Ron set up for interviews on television stations in Dallas, Houston and San Antonio. None of them would promise to give it a prime spot, but we can hope. At least Ron can put his message out."

"I hope he'll work on the DA's statement. What I heard on the radio sounded like she ain't given up the idea. Just bidin' her time."

"I'm going to talk with Ron in the morning and make some suggestions of things he might work in. He'll just want to talk about his platform, but I think he needs to get in the mud just a little. Counter Jim Bob's attack about being accused of murder and insurance fraud. Make it clear that was all a big mistake."

* * *

"Glad you called. I've been thinking about you today." Crystal was getting ready for bed when the call came in.

"That's good," said Mark. "What were you thinking?"

Crystal giggled a little. "Hmmm. What was I thinking? That I wished you were here with me."

"Right now?"

"That would be okay."

"Okay?"

"Well, maybe great. No, definitely great."

"I'm missing you. Remember, I'm used to seeing you every day. This is a long time without you."

"Only four more days until the election." Crystal's voice lost the excitement she felt when she heard Mark's voice. "I guess you've seen the polls. Ron is down and Jim Bob is up. And the papers that were so happy to put in big stories about the possible indictment, now hardly give any space to the 'no indictment' story."

"Bad news sells papers. Good news takes up space. You think Ron can turn this around?"

"I'm working on it. I've got TV interviews in Dallas, Houston, and San Antonio set up for tomorrow and Saturday. I'm trying to get him to dispell all the negative publicity. He, of course, just wants to talk about his platform. "

"That's Ron. But you're right. At this point, he needs to shift his focus." Mark paused a moment. "What *I'm* worried about is you. Anything unusual happen since I left?"

"The only bad thing since you left is — you left. I miss you. In fact, I have a great idea. Why don't you come to Nickel on election day, after you vote of course? You can help us celebrate Ron's victory. Stay a day, before we head back to Dallas. Then I can start earning my paycheck again."

"Tuesday? I could do that."

"That's the best news I've had all day."

"It was pretty easy to beat the other news. But thanks. I'll be there Tuesday. I love you, Crystal."

She felt like she might cry. Whenever he said he loved her, her heart fluttered and she tingled all over. "I love you too."

# Chapter 46

**Friday, November 2**

**Friday morning brought** more bad news. *The San Antonio Express-News* ran an editorial endorsing Jim Bob Wilson for the governor's office. They cited questions about the charges considered against Ron Drake. "Though we believe in 'innocent until proven guilty,' we cannot throw our support behind Mr. Drake. We are in no way suggesting he is guilty of anything. But we expect Jim Bob Wilson will bring some of the energy to this office that his father showed the people of Houston and Harris county. Therefore, we endorse Jim Bob Wilson for the office of governor of the State of Texas."

But that wasn't the worst news. The latest poll showed Jim Bob pulling ahead of Ron Drake. It was the first time in the entire campaign Ron was not in the lead.

Crystal bounced out Eula's front door and headed for her Buick. With several good interviews lined up for Ron, maybe they could stop the slide in the polls. It was now or never. Only ninety-four hours until the polls opened.

Why didn't the DA give a more definitive statement? Crystal hated to admit it, but Nana was right. Abbott sounded like she was equivocating. Ron needed to make it clear there was no case against him and would not be one. She'd hammer that home with Ron this morning. One last reinforcement before his TV appearances. Stay on message. No indictment. Never was one. Never any cause. If the storage unit comes up, he needs to say flat out the police now know who rented it, illegally using Ron's name. Ron had no knowledge, no connection whatsoever with that storage unit, or the man who rented it.

She settled into the driver's seat, her mind on the interviews for Ron, when out of the corner of her eye she saw a figure rushing toward her. She turned to look fully at the woman.

But all she saw was the knife.

# Chapter 47

**Crystal jerked her** hand to the door and tried to yank it shut but not before the knife found her arm, cutting a long gash nearly to her elbow. The woman stepped closer and raised the knife for another slash. Crystal grabbed the door handle and jerked the door closed. It caught the intruder's arm, smashing it against the frame of the car. The woman let out a scream, but the knife stayed firmly in her hand. Crystal could see hate and determination in the woman's eyes. The woman pulled on her arm, trying to get it out from between the door and the car body.

Crystal eased the pressure and the woman yanked her arm out. But before Crystal could get the door closed, the woman reached in for another strike. Crystal was ready and managed to get her arm out of the way. Again she slammed the door against the attacker's arm. The woman screamed in pain.

Crystal's right hand grabbed the steering wheel to steady herself, landing on the horn, sending a loud blast into the quiet woods. She released the pressure on the door slightly, then tried to yank it closed again.

Now the woman had her leg inside the door. She would not let her arm get smashed again. Crystal pulled. The door dug into the woman's leg. But Crystal could not close the door.

The woman let out a stream of curses. There wasn't enough room to get a good swing with the knife. Crystal tried to keep the door from opening wider, but blood now covered her hand and she could barely hold the door. Slowly the attacker pushed her weight against the door, opening it wider. She was getting enough room for a more deadly attack.

Crystal desperately tried to scramble across the seat, away from her attacker, but the center console held her in easy reach. Managing to take her eyes off the knife, she quickly looked for anything to deflect the knife or otherwise stop the attack.

She found nothing.

The roar of a shotgun blast stopped the woman, her knife raised over Crystal's leg.

Eula stood outside her back door, shotgun leveled on the scene. But, the car was between her and her target. She had fired a warning high over the car. Eula edged to her right angling for a better shot at the woman trying to kill her granddaughter.

The woman looked at the shotgun and instantly turned and ran in among the trees.

In just a few seconds, Eula was around the car, but the woman had vanished into the woods. Eula pointed the ancient shotgun in the direction the attacker had run and fired another round.

"Probably didn't hit her, but it ought to keep her running." She walked over to the driver's side and looked at her granddaughter. "What's going on?" Then she spotted the blood. "Oh my God. What happened?"

Crystal had straightened herself up and was inserting the key, ready to start the car.

"What are you doing?" Eula yelled.

"She's got to have a car down the drive some place. I'm going after her."

"No you're not. You've got blood all over yourself and more blood pouring out."

"She'll get away."

"Let her go. She's still got a knife and you don't. Let's go take care of your arm and call Bill." Eula reached in and pulled the keys out of the ignition. "Come on."

Crystal eased out of the car. Blood covered her left arm, and splotches of red decorated the left side of her blouse and part of her pants. "That crazy woman tried to stab me."

"Didn't just try. Let's get you in the house and see the damage."

By the time they got inside, Crystal's adrenaline had slowed, and she began to shake. Eula wrapped her arms around her granddaughter.

"I couldn't move. She just kept stabbing."

Eula drew her closer. "Sorry I didn't get off a better shot."

The two stood in the kitchen, Eula holding her only family. Slowly, Crystal's breathing returned to normal and her muscles relaxed a little. "I guess we ought to clean off the blood and take a look."


Ten minutes later, Eula had washed the blood off Crystal's arm, painted the cut with New Skin and was wrapping some gauze around Crystal's arm.

"Looks like you're luckier than a three-legged chicken. That's a long cut, but fortunately it's shallow. Better let Doctor Kim have a look at it. See if it needs a stitch or two. You get a good look at the woman?"

"Not really. I could tell you more about what the knife looked like than what she looked like. But she was wearing Eight Second Angel, red-fringed short boots."

"Same kind you saw when you got locked in the storage unit?"

"I'd bet money they were the exact same pair."

"Well, first thing, get out of that shirt and pants and run some cold water on them 'fore that blood dries. I'll give old Billy Goat a call."

Thirty minutes later, the sheriff was seated at the kitchen table, a glass of sweet tea in one hand. Crystal had related the details of her encounter with the knife-wielding woman.

"You didn't hear or see a car?" he asked.

"No. I wanted to drive down the road and see if I could find it, but Nana demanded I come in and let her look at my arm."

"Eula does have a good idea ever once in awhile," Bill said.

"Except, I might have seen what kind of car she had, what she looked like." Crystal raised her shoulders and shook her head. "I'd have had the doors locked."

"She had a knife with her. Maybe she had a gun in the car. No point in chasing a bear with a switch. We'll find her." He reached over with a finger and lifted the short sleeve on Crystal's left arm. "And I think Eula is right again."

"Wow," said Eula. "Twice in one day."

Bill ignored her comment. "I think you ought to have the doc look at it."

"It's not deep," Crystal protested.

"Just saying, don't want it getting infected. Or could be some damage we don't see. And she'll know if some stitches will make it heal prettier. Don't want an ugly scar on such a pretty arm."

"I've got to get over to Ron's house and help prep him for those interviews," Crystal protested.

"Ron can handle himself," Eula said. "'Sides, you prepped him yesterday. If you can get in to see Doc Kim, it probably won't take ten minutes." Crystal started to object again, but Eula pushed on. "I'll call Ron and tell him you'll be a few minutes late. And I'll call the doctor and tell her you're on your way."

Bill stood up. "Okay, it's settled. You go see the doc first. And I'll go looking for a knife-wielding maniac. Oh, and wearing Eight Second Angel red-fringed short boots. Did I get that right?"

# Chapter 48

**I'm packed and** ready to go, but I'll be damned if I'm going to let that bitch run me out of town.

Ginnie sat in the Sonic, guzzling her cherry limeade.

*If I had time, I'd take out her grandmother, too. Had to be her grandmother. Looked older than dirt. Blasting away at me with a shotgun. If she'd been a minute later, I'd have shattered her dear little Crystal.*

She thought about calling George. He was on her side and almost always made her feel better about ... about the political dirty trick. And he knew what was happening, how the race was shaping up. She pulled her phone out of her purse. She scratched that idea. He'd just rag on her some more about getting out of town. She was leaving. He didn't need to bug her any more. But it was Crystal who had caused her problems. Crystal was the reason she needed to get moving. Crystal was, if she really wanted to pin it down, the source of *all* her problems. If it weren't for Crystal, life would be good.

She looked at her cell phone. She could get the latest on the governor's race online. She quickly pulled up the state news, looking for information on the election. *Hot Damn! Jim Bob has pulled ahead of old Drake.* She read the story. "Jim Bob Wilson, at one point nearly forty points behind Ron Drake in the polls, has pulled ahead. While still within the margin of error, the reversal has been dramatic. Just a month ago, it seemed like this was a 'Ho hum' affair. Now, a few votes one way or the other will determine the outcome."

She started the car and backed out of her slot. What to do next? *I'd like to get her in front of my car. I'd run her down and keep going out of town, out of state.* She eased the car out into the traffic.

She had moved out of her apartment, packed up everything. Even if the police searched it they would find no hint of who she was, what she did, or where she might have gone. She really was ready to leave this town. If the old bitch hadn't come out with the shotgun, she'd have finished off Crystal and by now be in Louisiana.

*Maybe I should just go ahead and leave.*

*No. Crystal is the only one who has even a clue about me. She's seen me, knows I was trying to knife her. She's smart enough to know I'm the one who locked her in the storage unit. No one else has any idea who I am, or what connection I might have to any of this. She's got to go.*

Out of nowhere, Ginnie's mother was speaking to her. "Don't do anything wrong, Gin Girl. Follow the rules."

The voice seemed so real that Ginnie actually looked around the car. "It's okay, mom. This is self-defense. It's her life or mine. Surely you approve of self-defense."

But no answer came.

# Chapter 49


**Doctor Kim began** by cleaning the wound.

"How did you get this cut?"

"Some crazy woman attacked me with a big knife. I was lucky I didn't lose an arm." Crystal grimaced as the doctor put some antiseptic on the cut.

"Sorry. Unfortunately, the best germ killer does sting a little. It shouldn't last over a minute or two." She continued to work on the long cut. "Actually, it's not a bad cut. The problem is, you don't know where that knife had been, what was on it. Could have been as clean as a surgeon's scalpel. Or, it could have been used on someone with AIDS. So, we'll try to kill any germs it might have introduced. If you have the knife, we can test it."

"We don't have it." *And I don't want to see it again.* "You think it will leave a scar?"

"Most likely a thin one. I don't think it will be very noticeable."

"I could work a tattoo around it, make the scar part of the design."

"Do *not* do any tattooing around that scar. At least not for six months. You don't want to do anything around the scar tissues."

"I was just joking. I can't see myself ever getting a tattoo."

"Good. If the wound bothers you, take an acetaminophen, like Tylenol, or something similar, something over-the-counter. Not aspirin, since you've been bleeding a lot. But I doubt it will be much of a problem. From what you tell me about the woman I'd say you were lucky. Any idea why she attacked you? And did you call the sheriff?"

"I have ... in truth, I have no idea why she did it. But it's the second time she's tried to ... incapacitate me. I did talk to Sheriff Glothe."

The doctor stared at Crystal with a disbelieving look. "The second time? And you don't know why?"

Crystal shook her head. "Not really. The sheriff and I have talked about it, speculated. But nothing concrete, or even reasonable."

"If I were you, I'd work on that. Once might be a fluke. Twice suggests to me there'll be a third time."

*  *  *

Crystal and Ron worked for an hour. Crystal played the part of the interviewer, firing questions at Ron and trying to twist his answers away from his intention. She also hammered away at him to keep the message out front. That he was not under investigation, that the DA had dropped even any speculation he might have been involved, and in fact, that he was the victim. She reminded him the sheriff now knew who had actually rented the unit, illegally under Ron's name. "Make it clear you had no connection with the storage unit, or the man who rented it."

Ron objected several times saying that Nat was his friend, Nat was the victim. While Crystal agreed, she kept reminding him of the importance of dispelling any hint that he, Ron, had been at fault. He was still the person seventy percent of the people had backed before these rumors started circulating.

"I think you're ready." Crystal stood up and stretched her arms, trying to get her blood circulating again. "Just don't let them lead you off your message. Whenever they start down one of those alleys, get 'em back on the main road."

"I'll do my best. And thank you for being such a nasty interviewer. I ought to be ready for whatever they throw at me." Ron Drake walked with her to the front door. "Any new thoughts on your attacker?"

"No. But between Bill and Nana, I'm sure I'll be okay. I'll tune in and listen to your interviews. Good luck." Crystal didn't share her private thought, that the attack was connected to the art theft, and by extension, the campaign. Ron already felt enough guilt over Nat's death. She would not burden him with the possibility her problems were related.

* * *

Crystal stopped at the grocery store before heading back to Eula's. She had just entered the door when she saw him. Struggling to remember his name, nonetheless she walked over to him and said hello.

A startled look descended over George's face. "Excuse me," he said, moving past her and out the door.

Crystal followed, and his name came to her. "George. Have you got a minute?"

She hurried to get in front of him. He looked like he might walk away again, but he didn't. "Yes? Do I know you?"

"We met once at Jim Bob's campaign headquarters in Tyler. You were gracious enough to stop a catfight between myself and Fran Summers."

"Oh, yes. Now I remember."

The lie was too glib, and Crystal was certain he had remembered her immediately, when she first spoke to him in the store. "I'm having a problem and wondering if you could help me once more."

"Ah, I've, ah, got to get home. This isn't a good time."

"It will only take a minute and it's important to me." When he didn't walk away, she quickly said, "Someone is trying to kill me."

She watched his reaction closely. That statement would have brought a surprised look or one of dismay to most people's faces, but George just stared. Then, almost as an afterthought, "I'm sorry to hear that."

"I have a strong feeling it has something to do with the campaign."

She could see George was giving that some real, fast thought. "I know Fran was angry, but I can't imagine she would do anything like that."

"Truthfully, George, I think it's connected in some way with the art theft from Ron Drake's house. Since you —"

His hand shot up and George interrupted her. "I have not tried to kill you. I have not had any contact with you in the least. And I do not believe in violence. I'm sorry you are having problems, but I can't help you." He turned to go.

Crystal hurried to get beside him as he walked down the sidewalk. "I'm not accusing you in the least, George. I just thought, since you spend a lot of time at the campaign headquarters, you might know if there was anyone there who had a temper that might make them want to kill me. Please think about it. I've had two, and maybe three, attacks on my life. Once I had to go to the hospital and the doctor told me I was very lucky to be alive." She held her arm out and pushed her sleeve up. "If my grandmother hadn't come to my aid, this small cut would have been stabs into my chest." Crystal realized she was exaggerating a bit, but she needed to get him to pay attention. And help.

He looked at the long area covered with a bandage. Crystal could see he was unnerved, maybe by what she said, or by her arm, hard evidence staring him in the face.

George kept his focus on the scar for several long moments, then shook his head, but did not look at Crystal. "I don't know who did such things to you. As I said, I don't approve of violence. So, people wouldn't tell me about it. I'm sorry I can't help you. And I truly hope there are no more incidents. I really mean that."

Crystal watched him go, still shaking his head. She wondered if that was because he found her story incredible, or because he didn't. Maybe someone he knew was doing something he couldn't condone.

# Chapter 50

**After half a** block, George glanced back. She wasn't following him, wasn't watching him. She'd probably gone back into the store. He pulled out his cell phone and hit a number on the speed dial.

"Hello, George. "What's up?"

"I've just been talking with that Moore woman. She was asking me about attacks on her. Says someone has tried to kill her twice."

Ginnie let out a sinister laugh. "I told you she was dumb. It's been three times. She doesn't even know when someone is trying to kill her."

"She's smart enough to figure it has something to do with the art theft," George said, leaving out the fact Crystal *had* mentioned the possibility of a third attack.

He heard a sharp intake of breath. "You didn't tell her anything did you? You promised."

"I didn't tell her anything. I said I couldn't imagine anyone trying to kill her, and that's the truth. I don't understand why you are doing this. You know I don't approve of violence." He let out a sigh. "Ginnie, just get out of town."

"I'm all packed. Everything in the car. Ready to leave. Where'd you see her?"

"I was coming out of Brookshire's and she was going in. I tried to get away but she chased me down. I hope you're on the highway right this minute."

She laughed. "Soon. You're sure you didn't give her any info about me?"

"I didn't.

"Let's catch up with each other once we're both out of state."

"Sure, Ginnie," he said.

*No way*, he thought.

***

Ginnie didn't like the way that ended. George was her best friend, her only friend in Wooden Nickel. Maybe George was her only friend—anywhere. Could she call her boss a friend?

She sat in her car, drumming her fingers on the steering wheel. Damn that Crystal. Now she was onto George. He said he wouldn't give up any information. But he left himself an out. If they tried to pin the murder on him ... she didn't know what he might do. Any way she looked at it, it was her life or Crystal's. Ginnie slammed her hand on the steering wheel. Why couldn't that bitch leave it alone.

Ginnie couldn't figure out how, but they seemed to be closing in on her. *Got to get out of town.*

She started her car. George had said she'd been at the grocery store. *Maybe one last chance. Catch her in a deserted aisle and end it right there.* She headed in the direction of the store. When she got there, she saw no baby blue Buick.

She turned her car toward the highway, cussing all the way. "I'm just so frustrated. She ought to be dead already."

She banged her hand on the steering wheel. Everything seemed to be against her. Even George. He seemed to be getting more distant. She hated to leave with unfinished business. But, George was right. Time to get rolling.

She had driven only three blocks when she looked ahead and saw the baby blue Buick Verano approaching the road Ginnie was on. *That's her car. She's going to cross in front of me.* Ginnie mashed her foot down on the gas. Her Fiesta leaped ahead. In three seconds, it reached the fifty miles per hour mark. She braced herself and leaned back away from the steering wheel as far as possible.

She closed her eyes and T-boned the Buick squarely in the side with such force it moved the heavy car sideways down the road.

## Chapter 51

**The shoulder belt** held her back but Ginnie's head jerked forward and the airbag slammed into her face. She almost passed out. She took several deep breaths. Her eyes were clouded and she blinked several times, trying to regain her eyesight. Slowly her vision began to clear and things came into focus but all she could see was a grey bag. There was a fine dust in the air and she had difficulty breathing. She groped around with her hands until she found her purse. Quickly she reached inside, pulled out the knife and began slashing at the bag. In seconds she had it out of her face. The engine had stopped. She reached forward and turned the key. The motor caught and she pushed the gear into reverse and mashed her foot on the accelerator.

The car moved only a few inches, dragging the Buick with it. Her bumper was caught in the ripped metal of the Buick's side. The engine died. Ginnie tried to start it again but now it would not catch. And in the distance, she heard the siren. She tried the ignition again.

Nothing.

*Damn. I can't just leave my car.* The siren's wail focused her attention. She grabbed the door handle and tried to open it, but the door was jammed. The siren grew louder. She pulled the handle again and this time threw her shoulder against it. The door swung open. She almost fell out, but she caught herself. She grabbed her purse. Blood ran down her left leg. She stood and tested her legs. They were not broken. She took three steps and when that felt okay, broke into a full run.

Her mind was moving as fast as her feet and after only a few steps, she cut a sharp left and raced away from the accident. She slowed for a couple of steps. She really wanted to check on Crystal. Was she injured, unconscious, dead? It would only take a minute. She'd love to see this crystal shattered. But the siren was getting closer. She took a quick glance back at the Buick. There was no movement.

Ginnie headed away from the crash, increasing her speed with each step. Time to get out of sight.

Maybe I finally took Crystal out.

## Chapter 52

**Gradually, Crystal's eyes** opened. She was hemmed in on three sides by airbags. The seat felt like it had been knocked off its track, but it was still behind her. Even the smallest movement she made unleashed pain. Her face burned where she had been hit by the exploding airbag. Slowly, she began to wiggle fingers and toes. Nothing seemed to be broken. *Thank you, Lord — and all you airbags.*

Her mind raced to recall what had happened. She'd been at a four-way stop. She had stopped and then proceeded. A car was coming on the street to her right, approaching the stop sign. And then, out of the corner of her eye, she saw it was not going to stop. It was accelerating. She'd slammed on the brakes, trying to give the driver as much room as possible to go around her.

And in the instant before it hit her, Crystal realized it was a little red car.

Could it have been that crazy woman? Bill said there were lots of red cars in Wooden Nickel. Still, this red car wasn't slowing down.

A chill ran down her back and her mind recoiled. *Did she deliberately ram my car? Was she trying to kill me?* Crystal's stomach cramped and for a few moments she thought she might throw up. *She might really have tried to kill me.* Her mind held that thought until it was pushed out by another. *What do you think she was trying to do with the knife, dummy?*

Slowly, the front airbag deflated. She carefully reached up and felt her face. She thought her nose might be broken but as her shaking hands examined it, she decided it was just bruised. Smoke, or a fine powder, floated in the air. The smell was nasty and breathing it made Crystal want to gag. A siren blared in the distance.

The center front airbag was still inflated but she could see under it a little. The passenger door was pushed in and the seat was badly deformed. Even the floor on the car's right side looked crumpled.

The smell of gasoline registered in her brain and panic seized her. Her muscles cramped. Her heart, already pumping rapidly, began to race. And for an instant, she couldn't breathe. A massive crash, gasoline. Fire was sure to follow. In her mind flashed a movie of her car completely engulfed in flames and she was trapped inside.

Like she was right now.

She fumbled around for the door handle under the airbag. A moment of hope eased her fear as she pushed the door handle to open. She found it and pushed but it moved less than an inch and then stopped. Firmly. As if hitting a brick wall. She pushed harder. No movement.

Now her breathing accelerated, trying to keep up with her heart.

"Open. Come on. Open up." It was not a scream, but said softly through gritted teeth. At that moment, she heard a noise, the same *Whoosh* she heard when she tossed a match into charcoal briquettes soaked in fire starter. Something was burning and she was locked in.

She tried to twist around so she could kick the door with both feet, but she couldn't move. "Stupid. Unsnap the seat belt." She found the trigger but now she was shaking so hard it took her three tries to release the constraint. She managed to scoot around and kicked the door with both feet.

It didn't move.

She tried again.

Still, it did not move.

"Come on, open up." Her voice desperate, now an octave higher.

She moved back to try to kick the door again. This time, she felt heat. The center airbag was still inflated. She couldn't see the fire.

But she could feel the heat.

She kicked. The door didn't move. And suddenly, she could smell smoke. Fire to the right. A frozen door to the left.

Her breathing was coming faster and fear threatened to paralyze her. Beads of sweat popped out on her forehead, and her stomach cramped. She felt like crying, but no tears came.

Now she heard voices outside and saw the flashing lights of emergency vehicles. "Hey! I'm trapped in here. Help," she yelled as loud as she could.

No one responded. The smoke was getting thicker. She could *hear* the fire burning ... something. Crackling. Closer.

She turned her head and she saw the fire through the center airbag, not the actual flames, but the image they cast on the bag, dancing closer each second. And the heat was rising rapidly.

She tried to yell but it came out more as a whimper. "I'm trapped in here. Please help me."

"We're going to help you, ma'am. Stay calm."

Crystal felt someone outside pulling on the door, the car rocking just a tad. But it didn't open. Once again she was aware of the heat from the fire. She looked around. Now she could see flames beginning to burn through the nylon.

A man was yelling. "Bud! Need the jaws. Now."

"Spreaders?" another man yelled back.

"Yeah."

"Thirty seconds. Johnnie, get some foam on that fire."

The inside of the car was getting hotter and Crystal tried to move closer to the door, away from the heat. The sidewall airbag was deflating, but slowly, and the flames were growing.

She still could not see out. She heard another vehicle skid to a stop and a door open and then slam shut.

She looked back, toward the passenger side. Flames were beginning to burn the airbag more rapidly. Panic surged. "Please hurry." The fire was getting closer by the second.

She could feel the car move slightly on its springs, as if someone were pushing on it. And now a whirring sound, like a small electric motor. There was nothing to see, but her head swiveled from watching the door that wouldn't open to the fire closing in on her.

The sound of compressed air escaping came from the other side of the car and Crystal looked in time to see the flames make a last flash and then die.

A loud pop sounded on her side and then hands were pushing the airbag aside and reaching for her. In seconds, she was lifted out of the car.

"Thank you, thank you," she said to the firemen holding her. "I think I'm all right." She started to move out of their grasp and her legs buckled.

"No, no. Take it easy. Just wait a minute and then move very slowly. With this severe a crash, you need to have the medics check you over."

"I'm okay. You guys got me out. I'm okay."

"No, Crystal. Joe Don's right." Bill Glothe walked up behind the fireman. "We got to have you checked out. There could be some internal injury you aren't feeling right now. Happens all the time in these kinds of accidents. No arguments. An ambulance is on its way."

Crystal stepped around Joe Don and put her hands around the sheriff's neck. "I was so scared, Bill. When the fire started, I ..."

And now the tears came.

Glothe wrapped his arms around the woman who was the closest thing he had to a daughter. "And rightly so. Anybody would be. Let me help you to my cruiser and you can sit there until the ambulance gets here."

In the distance, the shrill whine of an ambulance could be heard.

# Chapter 53

**Glothe followed the** ambulance to the hospital and made certain Crystal got immediate attention. Within five minutes, she was in an examining room. "I need to go back to the accident scene. But, I'll be back. Even if they release you, wait here until I get back. That is not a request; that's an order."

Forty minutes later, the doctors pronounced Crystal to be free of any major injuries. Nonetheless, they wanted her to stay in the hospital for at least another half-hour to see if anything developed.

Bill had just returned when the doctor came back. "How are you feeling now?"

"My heart has settled down and I think I'm getting back to normal."

"You will have some bruising and soreness around the hips and the chest area, where the seat belt held you. And the airbags smashed into you. You're lucky the front airbag didn't do more damage to you. And having that center front airbag probably saved you from much more serious whiplash injuries. Probably an aspirin should handle that. But if you feel anything at all unusual, see your doctor, or come back here. In this kind of trauma, there can always be something internal we don't find the first time. Do not pass it off. Have it checked out. Okay?"

Crystal promised to do that, and then followed Bill out to his cruiser.

"Bill, it was a little red car."

"Yeah. I saw it embedded in the side of your car."

"That's the car we've been looking for — the one that killed Littlefellow."

"Well, it is a red car. But then there're lots of red cars in the county."

"But this little red car deliberately ran into me. I saw it speeding up just before it rammed me."

Glothe nodded. "There weren't any skid marks."

"It's the same woman."

"Did you get a good look at her?"

"No. But it was a woman."

"Well, she doesn't have a car now. We'll find her soon enough. With her car, we got her name and address."

"She could rent a car and get away." Crystal was sounding desperate.

"She won't go far. Don't worry. We'll get her. While you were in the hospital I notified the car rental agency to call us if a Sally Leverett, or anyone matching the description you gave us this morning, tries to rent a car."

Crystal closed her eyes as Bill slowly drove through town. They were just about to hit the highway, heading for Eula's, when Crystal's eyes popped open. She looked at her watch and jerked up straight. "Turn right. Here! Right."

Glothe looked at her. "What on earth are you wanting to do?"

"It's two minutes after one."

"So?"

"So, the bus leaves at one ten. She doesn't need a car. She can just take a bus right out of town."

Bill sped up a bit. "And how do you know when the bus leaves?"

"I just do, hurry."

Bill grumbled.

"I've picked up and dropped off Brandi a number of times. Just hurry, please."

Six minutes later, they pulled into the large travel station that also served as the bus stop for Greyhound. Before the car had even stopped, Crystal had the door open.

"Crystal, just wait," Bill yelled, too late.

She was gone.

She raced over to the bus. The driver was just getting on. She followed him into the bus.

"Ma'am, do you have a ticket?"

"Just looking for someone."

"You can't ..."

But she was already walking down the aisle. Half-way down she stopped. She was staring down at Eight Second Angel, red-tasseled, short boots. Crystal looked up at the woman who she believed had tried to kill her—probably four times now. She was attractive and appeared to be just a little older than Crystal. She didn't look like a killer.

The woman glanced up. Slowly, shock and disbelief registered on her face. Her expression left no doubt in Crystal's mind. This was her nemesis.

The bus driver was now right behind Crystal. "Ma'am, you must get off the bus right now, or I'm calling the police."

Crystal's attention remained on the woman in the seat, but she said to the driver, "Please do. He's right outside the door."

And before the woman in the red boots had a chance to move, Crystal swung her hand around and punched Ginnie in the face.

The blow wasn't strong, but Ginnie was pushed over against the woman next to her. She turned her head, mouth slightly open, and eyebrows hunched down over her eyes.

Crystal's wallop was weak, but the shock of seeing her stunned Ginnie as much as a kick in the teeth. She stared at Crystal, hatred invading her face. But it was tinged with fear. She was no longer the attacker. She had been attacked.

As she straightened up, she pulled her purse into her lap and ripped it open. In one second, she found her knife and yanked it out.

This time, Crystal used her entire body and caught Ginnie with a roundhouse punch to the jaw. The owner of the Eight Second Angel, red-tasseled short boots, fell back in the seat, knocked out.

The knife clattered to the floor.

## Chapter 54


**Bill Glothe walked** into the District Attorney's office, hoping she had not left for the day. She hadn't.

"Joan, I've called a press conference for ten a.m. tomorrow. If you'd like to take it, I'll let you have the spotlight."

"What are you talking about, Bill?"

"We have in the county jail right now a 'person of interest,' as we say."

"Interest for what?" Joan Abbott's tone was surly as usual, but the sheriff clearly had her attention.

"Ginnie Leverett T-boned Crystal Moore's vehicle this afternoon. And I believe we have the knife she used to attack and stab Ms. Moore earlier in the day. It's already been sent for a DNA test."

"And I'm interested in a press conference on this because...?"

"We have reason to believe she also locked Ms. Moore in a storage unit where the temperature reached 140 degrees and almost caused severe heat stroke." He paused just a moment to add a little suspense. "That happened to be Wooden Nickel Mini-Storage unit number seventy-three. And a report that a woman was seen putting a painting in that unit the night it was stolen from Mr. Drake's house."

"And that was the report from a man who is now dead, so probably not usable," Abbott pointed out.

"That's right. And I'm not charging her, at this point, with anything other than assault with a deadly weapon and maybe attempted murder. But the point is, we have a likely suspect for both the art theft and the murder of Nathanael Owens."

"But no evidence on those crimes."

"Correct." Glothe placed his hands on Abbott's desk, leaned closer to her and spoke as if he were instructing a rookie cop. "But as you know, once we have a good suspect, so we know better what we're looking for, evidence will come forward. I've already got a court order to get her phone records. We'll find something there once we get the records."

"And why are you having a press conference so quickly?"

He straightened up. "Information, apparently leaked from this office, has damaged the reputation of an innocent man and practically ruined his campaign for the governor's office. I think we owe it to him—and the people of Texas—to try to correct the misinformation regarding Ron Drake and the painting and the murder of his friend. Voting is only a few days away."

For several seconds, neither said anything. Finally, Abbott said, "As I said before, you have no evidence she was connected with those crimes."

"And she just decided to attack Crystal Moore? The truth is, Ms. Moore has been working on finding out who stole the painting and killed Nat Owens. I think this woman felt Ms. Moore was getting too close."

Joan Abbott stared at her desk. Glothe let the silence continue. Finally, she said, "I think you can handle the press conference."

"Yes, I can. I should tell you I will start out by issuing an apology to Ron Drake for the misinformation that has been released, leaked that is, about the art theft and the murder. Then I'll say that at last, we have a viable person of interest in those cases. And while I am not ready to release a name, I will say it is a woman."

"You still have no evidence. You should make that clear."

"I have as much evidence as you had when you wanted to, in fact, almost *did*, indict Ron Drake for those crimes. And the statement you did release sounded like you were biding your time, that you might pull Drake in again. Should I mention to the press the main evidence against Ron was Nat *might, conceivably,* have seen Ron holding his own painting in his own house?"

Abbott sat up straighter and gave the impression of indignation. "That's not true. We had the lease card from the mini-storage company showing Ron had rented that unit."

Glothe almost laughed. But didn't. "Sort of like the card from the same company about the storage unit you rented."

Abbott's face turned beet red and for a moment, Bill thought she might lose her temper.

A minute passed as she composed herself. Bill studied her desk, wondering how she kept it so neat. Without moving his head, he cut his eyes to the left so he could look out the window. He could see clouds forming. *We really need rain, but please, not until after the press conference.*

Abbott also had her focus firmly fixed on the top of her desk, obviously deciding what to do. Would she let him have total control over the press tomorrow? Bill was in no hurry. The press conference was sixteen hours away and he knew what he was going to say. Frankly, he didn't care if she came or not. This was just a courtesy.

Finally, the District Attorney looked up from her desk, but she didn't look Bill in the eye. "Would you like for me to come and tell the press we have no further interest in Ron Drake with regards to the art theft or the murder of Nathanael Owens?"

Bill nodded. "I think that would be appropriate and the press would appreciate it." He glanced at his watch. "It will start promptly at ten o'clock. On the steps of the courthouse. See you there."

# Chapter 55

**"So you got** the gal." Eula sat on the large veranda that faced her lake some hundred yards down a slight slope. The promise of rain earlier had drifted away, but it had dropped the temperature by ten degrees and that was welcome. Now, the gentle breeze made it feel like the autumn evening it was.

"That we did." Crystal wiggled in the large rocking chair, trying to get comfortable. The crash had left her sore in more than one place. The doctor was right. More sore spots were making themselves known by the hour. Or maybe she was just coming down from the high of capturing the Eight Second Angel woman. Now, she had the luxury of cataloging how much of her body was in pain.

"What's ol' Billy Goat charging her with?"

"Right now, he's got her on assault with a deadly weapon and leaving the scene of an accident."

"The deadly weapon was a car?"

"Yep. A cute, little, red car. Not so cute now."

Eula frowned. "That don't sound like enough to me. How about stealing Ron's painting and killing Nat?"

"They're working on it."

"Well, don't take much work to include attacking you with a knife."

"He's got a witness on that—me."

"And me."

"Did you actually see the knife, Nana?"

"Saw the cut on your arm. 'Ought a be good enough."

"It'll help. And they're hoping to get my DNA off the knife she had. Bill's already sent it in. Said a guy owed him a favor, so he might get the results back in a few days, instead of a few weeks."

"Bet she wiped it off."

"She did. It looked clean when we got it on the bus. But that won't prevent them from getting DNA, unless she scrubbed it with bleach, or something."

"Sounds like sticky stuff. Don't know much about DNA, but seems like it's usually good enough to prove something."

"Tomorrow I've got to see about getting my car fixed."

"From what I'm hearing, you'll be looking for a new car."

Crystal pursed her lips and wiggled her head from side to side. "Yeah. Probably right. Most likely that frame won't ever be lined up again. Need to talk to my insurance agent first."

"So you got her on those charges. Still ain't gonna help Ron much. Tuesday's the big day. And Ron's behind."

"I'm hoping Ron's interviews will help. I heard one this evening, live. Sounded good. Helpful. Two more air tomorrow and one on Sunday. Plus Bill said he was having a press conference in the morning. He's going to announce he has in custody a 'person of interest' for the art theft and Nat's murder. He won't give a name, but he'll say the person is a woman." Crystal's face lit up. "And, Abbott said she'd state clearly her office had no further interest in Ron." Crystal stretched her lips and tilted her head. "Don't know why she couldn't have done that a week ago."

"Well, a woman suspect surely leaves Ron out." Eula rocked for a minute. "'Course, might be too little, too late. I'm stickin' with my statement. Jim Bob's gonna win."

* * *

An officer led Ginnie to a phone in a small room. "I'll be right beside you, so don't ask anybody to destroy evidence or do anything illegal."

"I thought I got some privacy," Ginnie said, trying not to sound as angry as she was.

"No ma'am. So, if it's something you don't want me to hear, don't say it."

Ginnie glared at the officer. She picked up the phone and dialed, putting her body between the phone and the policewoman. "Hi. It's me."

"Where are you? Out of town, I hope." George was shocked to hear Ginnie's voice. He hadn't recognized the phone number that appeared on his cell phone screen, almost didn't answer it. "And you shouldn't be calling me anymore." When he first heard her voice, he was surprised. Now, he was unhappy.

"I was going out of town and had an accident. I'm in jail right now. I need a lawyer."

"In jail? For an accident?"

"I ran into another car. In fact, I'd really like to know if I hurt the woman in the other car. I think someone said her name was Crystal."

"Oh my God, Ginnie. What have you done? No. No. Don't tell me."

"Can you get me a lawyer? That's all I'm asking."

For several seconds, George said nothing. "Is anybody listening? Can anybody hear what we're saying?"

"Only me."

"Okay. I'll get a lawyer I know to call you. I'll try to contact the lawyer today." He looked at his watch. "It's after six, so I may not get him tonight. Tomorrow's Saturday. Might be hard to get him on the weekend. I'll do my best."

"Don't leave me in here too long, G——." She caught herself.

"I will get you a lawyer. Could be Monday." Ginnie heard him take a deep breath. "But that's it. Don't call me again. Remember, they've already talked to me about the storage unit. You do *not* want them to connect me to you."

"That'll be great."

But George had already disconnected.

# Chapter 56

**Saturday, November 3**

**The press conference** had gone well. Glothe corrected himself. *Very well.* The reporters seemed interested, asked a good number of questions, and really sat forward when the District Attorney made her statement that Ron Drake was no longer being considered for any crime.

Bill smiled. Now, if that will only result in some good press.

He thought about what he had on Ginnie. Not much. The assault on Crystal was solid, even without the DNA results. Positive DNA results would make it as certain as grass growing in cracks. But his gut told him Ginnie was also in the middle of the art theft. And that put her right there when Owens was killed. *And if Verizon ever gets me those phone records, who knows what'll turn up*

The sheriff walked back to the cell holding Sally Virginia Leverett. "Slim said you were complaining about the accommodations, Ms. Leverett. Anything in particular?"

Ginnie got up from the bunk and looked at the sheriff. "Yeah. Can I order in a pizza and a cherry limeade?"

Bill laughed. "Nope. We don't really allow that here. I read where some jail in Chicago let prisoners order pizza in. We don't." Bill looked down at Ginnie's feet. "We might be able to get you some more comfortable shoes, though."

"That'd help."

"Got any in your stuff?"

"Yeah. There's a pair of canvas shoes. Should be in the trunk of my car."

"I'll see if we can find them." He turned to go. "If I see a pizza man outside, I'll stop him."


Bill sauntered back to his office. The shoes were right there on his desk. They'd already made impressions and pictures of the soles, and one of his deputies had started the tedious task of checking those against the hundreds of shoeprints they had taken from the dust in storage unit seventy-three. Finding a match had only a small chance of success. Glothe wouldn't pass up any chance, no matter how tiny.

After fifteen minutes, Glothe returned to Ginnie's cell. He held up the shoes. "Are these yours?"

She reached a hand through the bars and took the shoes. "Yeah. They'll be more comfortable."

"One of our deputies had ordered a pepperoni. I managed to snag one slice. If you want it." He held up a paper plate with a thin slice of pizza.

"I'll take it."

The sheriff handed her the pizza and turned to leave.

"Hey, when do I get to see a judge and get out of here?"

Without turning, Bill answered her. "Tomorrow. Don't know what time we can get the magistrate in, though, being it's Sunday. I'll let you know."


Glothe walked back to his office, picked up a pen, and wrote, *Defendant acknowledged the canvas shoes were hers.*

Now, if they could only find a match to some of the prints from the storage unit. And get the DNA results from the knife. And the phone records. Then, hopefully, things would fall into place.

## Chapter 57

**Sunday, November 4**

**"And why are** we here on a Sunday afternoon?" asked Magistrate Rogers.

"Ms. Sally Virginia Leverett was arrested Friday afternoon, so the forty-eight hour rule compels us to be here," said Assistant DA Fran Summers.

"And why weren't we here yesterday?"

"There were extenuating circumstances, sir."

"This says assault with a deadly weapon. What was the weapon?"

"a car," answered Summers.

"I hit the gas when I meant to hit the brake," said Ginnie.

"Young lady, please refrain from addressing the court unless asked to." Rogers turned to the sheriff, obviously not happy. "And you threw her in jail for a car accident?"

"No, sir," said Glothe. "First, it appeared to be a deliberate assault. Our belief was first based on the evidence at the accident scene. Then, we discovered the defendant had attacked the same woman injured in the car accident just a few hours earlier. On that occasion, she used a knife. We have two witnesses. And the knife has been sent off for DNA verification."

"So, multiple attacks in a limited time frame?"

"Yes, sir."

"Okay. What does the state suggest for bail?"

The magistrate had addressed the question to Summers but Glothe stepped forward. "We oppose any bail." When the magistrate raised his eyebrows, Bill continued. "There are two reasons, sir. First, we are following several other investigations that may cause us to add other crimes to the indictment. Perhaps more important on the bail, Ms. Leverett is a definite flight risk. When we captured her, she was on a bus, headed out of state. Her car was packed and her dwelling was cleaned out."

"Judge—" Ginnie started.

"Stop." Rogers held up his hand. If I want you to speak, I'll ask." He turned back to the sheriff. "Her car was packed but she was on a bus?"

"Yes, sir. It appears she was headed out of town when she saw the victim and T-boned her car. One of the results was that Ms. Leverett's car was damaged to the extent it isn't drivable. You'll note she is also charged with leaving the scene of an accident. She fled on foot and later boarded a bus with a ticket for North Carolina."

"Do you care to share where these other investigations might lead?" asked Rogers.

Summers spoke before Glothe could answer. "No, sir. While some progress has already been made, we choose not to share those lines of investigation at this time. But I assure you, they are solid and we expect to expand the indictment within a few days."

Rogers steepled his fingers and rested his chin on them. After a few moments, he raised his head. "Ms. Leverett, do you have an attorney? If you cannot afford one, the state will provide one for you."

"I have an attorney," said Ginnie. "But, he hasn't contacted me yet. I expect to talk with him tomorrow."

"Good. Bail is denied at this time. But once you meet with your attorney, he can apply for a bail reduction hearing." He turned to

Glothe. "The defendant is remanded back to the county. This court session is finished."

* * *

Ron got a little bit of good news Sunday. *The Dallas Morning News* came out with a strong article endorsing him. They explained they had supported Drake and the policies that made up his platform for many months. Then, the accusations he might have been involved in insurance fraud and possibly murder caused the paper to hold off on its endorsement until further information became available.

"Now, both the Pine County District Attorney and the Sheriff in Wooden Nickel have announced in a public press conference that neither has any interest in Drake in connection with those crimes.

"With that out of the way, we can whole-heartedly back this man. Drake has shown uncommon good judgment during his time in Dallas on the Board of Education, on the Police Civilian Board, and then as the Mayor of Dallas. He has, in our opinion, always kept the law and his constituents paramount in his actions and decisions. And he has exhibited a tireless work ethic. Texas cannot do better than to vote Ron Drake in as the next governor.

"*The Dallas Morning News* gives a strong endorsement for Ron Drake in this gubernatorial election."

# Chapter 58

**Monday, November 5**

**Slim burst into** the sheriff's office. "Got it."

Bill Glothe looked up from the new procedural manual he was reading. "Got what? And didn't your mama teach you to knock before entering someone's office?"

"Sorry, boss. But I was excited. I've checked at least a thousand pictures of prints we took in storage unit seventy-three. And—"

"A thousand?"

Slim grinned. "Well, maybe a few less. But, I found a match."

Bill held up his hand. "Slow down. Now tell me exactly what you've found."

"I found one of our pictures of the shoe prints in unit seventy-three matches one of Leverett's shoes."

"How well does it match?"

"Pert near perfect. Her shoe had a little nick on the outside edge. The print from seventy-three had the same nick in the same place."

Bill was shaking his head. "And how many prints matched her shoe?"

The big smile vanished from Slim's face. "Well, ah, just this one. But I wanted to come tell you we can put her in the storage unit."

"So, she just hopped in there on one foot and hopped out without making another print in the dust?"

"Aw, Sheriff. I was excited to get *one*. Ah, the first one. But I wanted to let you know about this one. I'll go find some more."

"I hope you can find a series, where she walked from the door to the spot where we believe the painting sat, and back out. That would make me— and the DA— very happy."

Slim turned and headed back out the door. "I'm on it."

"Good work, Slim. I was just yanking your chain."

# Chapter 59

**Tuesday, November 6**
**Election Day**

**Election day started** bright and warm. By eleven, it was already eighty degrees and climbing. Eula and Crystal got to the precinct polling place a little after eleven-thirty. Crystal was moving in slow motion. Dressing and breakfast had taken twice as long as usual. Even putting on lipstick forced a groan from her.

The lines weren't too long. Eula seemed to know everybody there. Many greeted her with a smile and a friendly hello. But quite a few tried to avoid eye contact and responded minimally when Eula spoke to them.

"Not a good sign," Eula whispered to Crystal. "I'll bet every one of these avoiding me are voting for Jim Bob. They know Ron is a friend of mine. They're embarrassed to look at me and then go vote against him."

A deputy from Glothe's office fell in line behind them.

"Hi, Slim," said Eula. "Glad to see Bill gave you time off to vote."

"Yeah. But he wanted to know who I was going to vote for. Said it might determine if he gave me time off or not."

Crystal's face fell and her mouth gaped open. "He can't do that."

"Just kiddin' ma'am," said Slim. "He did run off a guy who came by soliciting votes for Jim Bob. The man was saying, and I'm quoting, 'Get out and vote early, and often.'"

"I hope you're still kidding," Crystal said.

"No ma'am. I'm not. Maybe he was."


By noon the two women slid into a booth at the Kountry Kafe for lunch. Willie and Waylon were warning mamas not to let their babies grow up to be cowboys. The music was a little loud for Eula and she asked the waitress if it could be turned down a mite. The young woman said yes, handed them menus and left. Eula and Crystal were studying the menus when Bill Glothe sidled up.

"Got room for one more?"

Eula scooted over. "Sure do. Take a load off."

"Glad to. What're you two ladies having?"

Crystal handed him her menu. "Don't know about Nana, but I'm having the pulled pork sandwich."

Glothe folded the menu and put it down. "Sounds good to me."

"Never was one to follow the lead donkey," Eula said. "I'm having liver and onions."

A young, college-aged waitress came to their booth, put down three glasses of water, took their orders and left.

"Voted yet?" Bill asked.

"Yep," Eula said. "Saw Slim there, too. Said you had one of Jim Bob's men soliciting votes."

"Ran him off. Thought maybe I should lock him up, but figured he'd already voted." Bill turned to acknowledge a couple of patrons who had waved at him.

"Have you found out anything more on ... Ginnie Leverett?" Crystal asked.

"Not much. She's really Sally Virginia Leverett. But she refuses to answer to anything but Ginnie."

Eula let out a humph. "Name's not important. Why was she attacking Crystal?"

"We still don't know. I've questioned her. I got Sam—he's usually the best one at getting answers—to grill her. He spent forty minutes and got zip."

"So you got nothing," grumbled Eula. "Are you doing anything else or just waiting for her to confess like they do on TV shows?"

"Now Eula, you know nothing about police work, so don't get your ... don't get upset. We've got several things going. We've sent the knife off for testing. I think we'll be able to get Crystal's DNA off it, if it's the same one she used to attack Crystal. And I'm guessing it is."

"What's that gonna do for you?" asked Eula with a hint of disgust in her tone. "You've already got her for assault with a car."

"That's too iffy," said Bill. "Lawyer'll say it was just an accident. She fell asleep, or blacked out for a minute. Or she stomped on the gas when she meant to slam on the brakes. We need something more to really nail her."

"She tries to kill my granddaughter and you're saying she can get off with, 'Oh my. I didn't mean to.'"

"Nana, give Bill a break. It's only been a few days."

"'S all right, Crystal," said Bill. "We've also had to get a warrant to look into her cell phone records. 'Til a couple a years ago, in Texas at least, if we arrested someone we could look into their cell phone. Now, we gotta get a court order. And as it's been seven months since this all started, we need her phone records from the phone company. We sent the request—with the court order—to Verizon. Now, we just have to wait to get the results. We'll get the information; it just might take awhile."

"What do you expect to get from that?" Crystal asked.

"Haven't a clue." Bill shrugged. "But chances are, it will lead us somewhere."

Eula muttered something about Barney Fife, but both Crystal and Bill ignored her as the food arrived. Pulled pork, and liver and onions took over the conversation.

* * *

"Hi, my name is Randal Goforth. I got a call from George Weeks saying you needed a lawyer."

Ginnie had been led into a small room with a table and two chairs. A well-dressed man, probably in his late thirties, sat in a chair when Ginnie arrived.

"I thought you'd be here yesterday. At the latest," Ginnie said.

"I was out of town. Just got back late last night. Now, why are you in here, and what do you want me to do?"

Ginnie was not impressed with this man. But he was her only hope right now, so she didn't tell him what she really thought. "I had an accident. I hit the car of one of the sheriff's friends, so he throws me in jail. And I know he's trying to find something else to hang on me. He told the magistrate he was looking for something else."

The lawyer started to speak, but Ginnie cut him off. "And what I want you to do is get me out of here, and then make the sheriff leave me alone."

Goforth nodded a few times. "The report says you had attacked the same woman whose car you hit with a knife earlier in the day. Said you actually cut her. You and this woman have something going on?"

"She'd really been bugging me. I just wanted her to back off. If I'd really wanted to hurt her, it would have been more than just a scratch. Then, I hit the gas instead of the brake and it was just my bad luck it was the sheriff's friend I hit."

Again, the lawyer nodded for several seconds. "Ms. Leverett, I'm sure you know anything you tell me is privileged information between a lawyer and his client. So you can be very honest and tell me what's really going on here. It will help me help you if I know everything related to these cases."

"Cases? There's only one case, a car accident. I've got insurance. She can get her money and I can get out of here."

This time, the attorney was shaking his head. "No. I think there is more. The judge wouldn't refuse bail for just an accident with no one seriously injured." He studied his client for a minute, but she said nothing. "I'm pretty sure I can get you out on bail, maybe even on your own recognizance. Are you a flight risk?"

"If the judge says I have to stay in this hick town, I'll stay. But of course, I'd like to get as far away as possible." Ginnie tried to look compliant, but she wasn't thinking that way. *Give me a chance and I'll disappear. Ginnie the shadow. Gone.*

"I'll ask for a bail reduction hearing. With luck, we can get it tomorrow." He stood up to leave. "And if we go much further, Ms. Leverett, you will need to be honest and open with me." He fixed her with a piercing look. "I can not defend you well with blinders on."

# Chapter 60

**Crystal, Eula, Brandi**, Mark and Bill sat on Eula's large veranda. The sun had settled down below the horizon and the cicadas were singing. A gentle breeze wafted up from the lake. A small TV sat on a table made out of a pine log, now lacquered to maintain its rich brown tones and the historical record of its growth. The TV was tuned to a Tyler station that periodically posted updates on the gubernatorial voting. Eula held the remote, ready to click the sound up whenever a new election report came on.

"Sure glad you two made it out here to help us try and pull Ron across the finish line first," Eula said.

"Thanks for the invite. I've been wanting to come back for a visit ever since I was out here renting a storage unit," said Brandi.

"Ah, yes." Mark had been watching a raccoon trying to get into a bird feeder, but Brandi's comment brought his attention back to the group on the deck. "I never did get the details on that. Just heard it shot the DA out of the saddle. Care to share?"

"Not much to it. You know how persuasive I can be." Brandi shook her head and aimed a big smile at Mark. "I dazzled the clerk with my five-thousand watt smile."

"I'm sure that would have been sufficient—if the clerk were a man. But I understand it was a woman."

"True. So, with the woman, I just threatened to keep her there beyond closing time or take my business to a competitor if I couldn't get it without all the hassle."

"I'm sure there was more to it, but —"

"Hold it," yelled Eula. "Here's an update."

The announcer stood in front of a map of Texas. "Another county has completed the tally on the gubernatorial race. Camp County in northeast Texas." He pointed to a spot on the map which was now colored. "Camp County has reported the following results. Ron Drake, 843 votes. Jim Bob Wilson, 671. This county is near Mr. Drake's home base and he was expected to carry this county. Overall, based on just 17 of the 254 Texas counties, the numbers as we have compiled them— that is, not official— are as follows. Ron Drake, 188,598. Jim Bob Wilson, 189,371." He stepped back to reveal more of the map. "All of these come from smaller counties. It will take the larger counties longer to get all the numbers tallied. But stay tuned and we will bring you the numbers as they are released. Now, back to our regularly scheduled programming."

Eula clicked the sound off. No one said a word for several seconds. Mark broke the silence. "That leaves Ron 773 votes behind. Not too big a hill to climb. I'm sure Dallas county will wipe that out and give him a big lead."

"And Harris County will snatch it right back," Eula said.

Brandi asked, "Where's Harris county."

"Mostly, it's Houston," Bill answered.

"And I'm bettin' it goes for Jim Bob," said Eula. "His father, Jim Bob number one, 'sgot a strong backing there. Always has."

"Ron had a big lead in Houston a couple of months ago," Crystal said.

"Yeah, but that was before all the foolishness about Nat and the picture. I 'magine Jim Bob number one and two made sure that got plastered all over Houston. I surely hope Ron doesn't need Houston to win."

After the ten o'clock news, Mark stood up. "It doesn't look like this race is going to be called tonight. So, I think I'll run into Nickel and grab some sleep at the Good Night Inn. But I'll be back for breakfast."

Eula held her hand up. "Just hold it right there. You're staying here. We got three bedrooms."

"But Brandi is here," Mark said.

Brandi popped up. "I can bunk in with Crystal. Right, Crystal?"

"Certainly. No need to go into Nickel when we've got a bed right here."

Mark started to say something, but Eula was louder and more forceful. "Good. It's settled. Mark gets the blue room and Brandi bunks in Crystal's room. I get the presidential suite. And Bill can grab a cot in the jail."

Bill stood up. "Thanks, Eula. 'Preciate it. But I gotta run anyway. Got the DNA back and it confirmed the knife from Ginnie's purse was the knife that cut Crystal. But I want to see if we've heard anything on the phone records. I'll check in with you in the morning, but don't count on me for breakfast." He held up a hand. "Now don't get on my case, Eula. I got a murder to solve. See y'all tomorrow, sometime."

Bill left and the other four remained on the veranda, talking about the election, the attacks on Crystal and the Nathanael Owens murder case.

The 11:00 news report had nearly a million votes in and the two candidates were only a few hundred apart. But Ron Drake was still on the short side. Dallas, Houston, and San Antonio had not reported results, and those cities, the three largest in Texas, would cast as many votes as the rest of Texas. The commentator said, "It's going to be a long night of counting, folks."

"Not for me," Eula said as she clicked off the TV. "The morning will be soon enough. We can celebrate over breakfast."

# Chapter 61

**Wednesday, November 7**

**Crystal and Eula** were putting breakfast together. Brandi and Mark
had the TV on in the living room, but with the open design of Eula's
house, the two women in the kitchen could hear what the newsman
was saying.

"We still don't have final counts on this election, and officials are
saying we may not have them for a week or so. Now I know you're
saying, 'How can that be? With electronic voting machines, why don't
we know within hours of the polls closing?'

"Here's the problem. This race is so close, every little bit can make
a big difference. What we do know is this. Out of the more than two
million votes counted so far, the difference between the two front
runners, Jim Bob Wilson and Ron Drake,—and this is not official—
is only a few hundred. That's an approximate difference of just one
vote out of ten thousand."

A woman moved into the picture and picked up the narrative.

"And, Walter, here's where the problem gets tricky, and why we
might not get the results for awhile. Early votes are generally mail-in
paper ballots that must be counted by hand. Most of you think mail-
in ballots must be in early, and that's generally true. But, mail-in

ballots from men or women in the armed forces who are stationed overseas are given an extra five days to arrive. Now, usually this doesn't have much impact, since there aren't that many votes from overseas. But if the difference in votes cast within the state is, say two hundred votes, then those ballots from overseas could change the election."

Mark clicked the sound off and headed into the kitchen. "Well, there you go. Could be days before we know anything."

"If it turns out to be that close, could be a recount," Eula said.

"There are several reasons why there would be a recount," Mark said. "But if there is no voting irregularity identified by an election judge, there is no automatic recount unless there was an exact tie."

"But the loser could ask for one, right?" Crystal asked.

"Yes. It's costly. But should the recount change the outcome, then the money would be refunded." Mark shook his head. "Any way you look at it, this is a wild election."

Eula wiped her hands on her apron and leaned on the counter. "I can tell you right now, Ron won't ask for a recount if the difference is fifteen votes."

"Why not?" asked Brandi. "I would."

Eula nodded. "So would I. But Ron won't. He'll say our voting system is good and he won't try to make it look bad."

"I tend to agree with you," Mark said. "But his campaign treasurer can ask for one on his behalf. For that matter, any group of twenty-five or more voters can request one."

"I'm guessing they'd have to put up the money," Crystal said.

Brandi jerked a thumb up and to the side."Well, count me out. Sounds expensive."

"Politics always are," muttered Eula.

* * *

"Glory be." Glothe stood outside his office with a package in his hands.

Slim walked up. "That sounds like good news. What'cha got?"

"Leverett's phone records. Verizon came through in record time." He stuck the package out toward his deputy. "Start going through these. Catalog everything that looks the least bit suspicious. Any pattern that might be useful. And phone numbers that prove interesting."

"Okay. But are you looking for anything in particular?"

"Start back a week before Owens's death. Make that two weeks. Just look for anything that might lead us somewhere."

"Like what?"

Bill inclined his head to the side, drew his mouth into a straight line and stared at Slim. "If I knew what I was looking for, I wouldn't be asking you to check everything. "

Slim took the bundle. "Yes sir. I'm on it."

* * *


Crystal and Mark were seated at a table for two back in the corner of the Kountry Kafe. "I've got to get back this afternoon," Mark said. "The way things are going, they're not going to name our new governor for another four or five days."

"I know. I hardly slept last night just thinking about the possibility Jim Bob might win."

Mark flipped open his phone and tapped a few times, then read for a minute. "Jim Bob has taken an unofficial 237 vote lead. And I think that's all the major reporting precincts."

Crystal put her head down on the table and pretended to cry.

Mark grimaced. "What a disaster he would be. At any rate, I've got to get back in the office. But you might as well stay here until we get the results. Your project is moving ahead. You've done a great job training your people and directing them from here. But I've got the whole company to oversee."

"I'll miss you. It was really nice having you here, you getting to know Nana better. And Bill. He's such a sweetheart. And he's been a great friend for Nana since Granddad died."

"They do seem to get along well, although a person hearing some of Eula's remarks might not know it. She doesn't cut him any slack, does she?"

Crystal laughed. "Not a bit. But Bill is so solid. All her remarks just bounce off him. They are quite a pair. If Ron wins, Nana has promised to give me the full story on their relationship."

"And if he loses?"

"I have to tell her, as she puts it, the full story of me and you."

"I'd like to hear that one myself. Sort of a consolation prize if Ron loses."

# Chapter 62

**Thursday, November 8**

**Fran Summers, Ginnie** and her lawyer stood in silence as the judge read through some papers. Today, they had a female judge whom Summers did not know.

"What am I missing, Summers?" the judge asked. "I see a traffic accident and one driver arrested. Okay. But then you asked no bail be set. State your reasons."

"We have two witnesses, and now DNA evidence to prove the defendant had tried to stab Ms. Moore just hours before she T-boned Ms. Moore's car. Ms. Leverett had moved out of her apartment. Her car was packed and she was headed out of town. When her car wouldn't start after the accident, she fled the scene. We found her on a bus headed to North Carolina. So, she's definitely a flight risk."

The judge held up her hand. "Ms. Leverett, did you tell anybody you were leaving the state?"

"No, ma'am. I —"

The judge cut her off. "Is there anything else, Ms. Summers?"

Ginnie jumped up. "They don't have a shred of evidence that —"

"Counselor, control your client." The judge's voice echoed through the courtroom. "I will not tolerate such behavior. And most certainly, it does not help your case." For a minute, she glared at the pair. "What is your recommendation, Ms. Summers?"

Fran thought about the things Glothe had said. None of them were in concrete. And giving this dumb broad credit for the art theft was stupid. Besides, Fran was still smarting from the tongue-lashing she had gotten after Glothe had talked to the DA about the line-up.

Ginnie's lawyer took the initiative. "I think a $5,000 bond should eliminate the flight risk, your honor."

"Ms. Summers?"

Fran simply nodded.

"Fine. Bond is set at $5,000. Ms. Leverett, you are remanded to the county jail until bond is posted." She rapped her gavel. "This hearing is concluded. Next case."

* * *

The sheriff knocked and then walked through Eula's back door.

"We're on the veranda," Eula called out.

Bill walked through the living room and out onto the porch. "Morning, Eula, Crystal."

"Hi Bill. If you want a cup, the pot's on the stove," said Eula.

"No, I'm fine. Just wanted to stop by and tell you how the case is progressing."

"Or *not* moving," said Eula. "Whoever thought an old Billy Goat could solve crimes?"

"Nana," Crystal scolded. She turned her attention to Bill. "Thank you. In spite of what my grumpy grandmother says, I think you're doing a great job."

"Thank you, Crystal. You'll also be glad to hear we've matched shoe prints from unit seventy-three with a shoe we found in Ms. Leverett's car, a shoe she claims is hers."

Crystal sucked in air and her face lit up. "Eight second Angel?"

"No," Glothe said. "Just generic Walmart canvas shoes they sell by the millions." Disappointment replaced the hopeful smile that had brightened Crystal's face. "However," Bill continued, "there is a small imperfection on the sole of the left shoe. And it matches perfectly the print found in the storage unit."

"So maybe she's the one who lifted Ron's painting," Eula said.

"Another piece of the puzzle. And we finally got her phone records from Verizon. This is a new record for me with them guys. Never got records this quick before. Anyways, Slim's been poring over them since five minutes after they hit our office."

"What's he looking for?" asked Eula.

"Anything that might help us out. Seems like mostly the only person she called was George Weeks."

Crystal sat up straighter. "That's the guy who rented the storage unit under Ron's name, right?"

Glothe nodded several times. "Right. So that puts those two together. Then on the night John Littlefellow got killed, she called..." Bill looked up and frowned for a few seconds. "Mind's slipping. She called ... Rayville, Louisiana. Slim called that number and talked to a woman there. He's headed there right now. See what he can find." He glanced at his watch. "He should be there in a couple of hours."

"Who's the woman?" asked Crystal.

"She said she was a friend of Ginnie Leverett."

"What's he looking for?" asked Eula.

"Slim looks pretty slow sometimes. Most people don't give him credit. But he's good at his job. He found out—over the phone, mind you—that Leverett had a little car accident. Right there in Rayville. Had to have the car worked on a little."

Crystal's eyes lit up. "So, he's headed for the auto repair shops in Rayville."

"Yep. This could get interesting in a hurry."

# Chapter 63

**Friday, November 9**

**Crystal was putting** on earrings, preparing to go out to breakfast before putting Brandi on a bus back to Dallas. Brandi called out from the living room. "You better get the lead out. They've got big news on the election, coming in thirty seconds."

Crystal walked in, still trying to find the hole in her left ear to put in the stud of a tiny butterfly. "What are they saying?"

"Beats me. They just said—oh wait, here it comes."

A woman dressed in a business suit stepped in front of the camera. "I've just been told, on condition of anonymity, that the final vote tally for governor will not be released for days. My sources are telling me the votes are very close and votes from military personnel stationed overseas could swing the outcome one way or the other. State law in Texas gives these people five extra days for their votes to arrive. So officials must wait those days to give our armed forces a fair chance to vote."

She stepped to the side, revealing a graphic. "In the last election, our current governor had a large enough lead in the voting that even if *all* of those votes coming from overseas had gone to the second-place candidate, it would not have changed the outcome. Those votes *would always be counted,* but it was not necessary to wait for those votes to declare a winner. The election judge knows the number of mail-in ballots requested from service personnel overseas. And he has received a tally of how many of the votes have already arrived and been counted. Unfortunately, the number unaccounted for—ballots requested but not yet returned—could determine the winner in this election."

A man appeared beside the woman. "Can you tell us who is ahead from the votes already counted?"

"We have no official tally. I have heard, and this is very unofficial, Jim Bob Wilson has a lead of just over a hundred fifty votes."

"Wow. Out of maybe four and a half million votes."

Brandi muted the TV. "That's not a whisker apart. They'll have to do a recount."

"Not guaranteed unless it's an actual tie."

Brandi just shook her head. "Hear anything about your friend Ginnie?"

"Nope. Still in jail. Bill managed to get the magistrate to hold her without bail."

"Good. I didn't want to leave you with that maniac on the loose."

"You're sure you have to go back today? I just can't leave before we get the results on the election. But if you wait 'til Monday and I can drive you back."

Brandi laughed. "Yeah you can. You got no wheels. But I've got to work tonight. Got the late shift. No way I can get out of it."

"All things being equal —"

"They never are," interrupted Brandi.

"I'll have to rent one. I need to be back Monday. I've got to catch up on my job, keep the boss happy, and find time to look for a car."

"You keeping your boss happy is like finding sand on the beach."

"Our personal relationship has nothing to do with our work relationship."

Brandi gave a skeptical laugh. "That dog won't hunt."

"Well, don't say anything to Nana. She'll be talking great-grandchildren."

245

"Well, don't say anything to Nana. She'll be talking great-grandchildren."

## Chapter 64


**"Thank you for** coming in, Mr. Weeks." Sheriff Glothe stuck out his large hand, offering a cordial handshake.

George looked at it, shrugged slightly, and shook his adversary's hand. He'd dressed to look dignified in a conservative, brown sport coat over a tan shirt and slacks, pulled together with a maroon tie. "Didn't have much choice."

"Well, we always have choices, but I'll give you that some are more attractive than others. Have a seat."

Both men sat down in front of the sheriff's desk. Bill tried to make the tone of the meeting as casual as possible, hoping to get Weeks at ease and talkative. "Nice looking outfit."

"I came directly from my office. Why did you call me in, Sheriff?"

"As you probably know, we have your friend Ginnie Leverett in custody. We're holding her because of two attacks she made on Crystal Moore's life, once with a knife and once with her car."

George's expression didn't change. He didn't nod, frown, or look shocked. He just stared at the sheriff.

"She is a friend of yours isn't she? Ginnie, I mean."

George took a moment to answer. "I know her."

"Was that from work?"

"No."

"From Jim Bob's campaign headquarters?"

George's eyes focused on the floor between the two men. Finally, he raised his head and looked at Glothe. "Yes. I saw her there a few times."

"Maybe more than a few times."

"I didn't really keep track. It wasn't important to me."

Bill cocked his head to the side and furrowed his brow. "And yet, you were the main person she called on her cell phone. And, she called you when we arrested her."

George looked indignant. "I thought those were private calls."

Glothe let out a small laugh. "Not much is private in jail."

"She just asked me to call her lawyer."

"She's going to need one."

For a full minute, neither man said anything. Finally, Bill spoke. "Here's the thing, George. We know you rented the storage unit under Ron Drake's name. And—"

"I told you I got this letter with money in it, asking me to do that. And they paid me a lot to do it."

"I remember you saying that. Fact remains, it was *you* who rented the place. Now, we've got some convincing evidence that shows Ginnie put the painting stolen from Ron Drake in that mini-warehouse." He paused and stared at Weeks, waiting for some sort of reaction. But except for a slight tightening of his jaw, George's expression didn't change and he said nothing.

"You suppose Ginnie sent the letter and money to you?"

"I have no way of knowing."

"And if she did, I guess that sorta implies she was already planning on stealing the painting. I mean, why else have you rent the unit under Drake's name? See what I mean?"

Weeks brushed a drop of sweat off his forehead, but said nothing.

"Now, here's the thing. If she stole the painting ... Well, the thinking here is whoever stole the painting, killed Owens."

Again, the sheriff let the silence hang in the air. "Got any thoughts on that?"

George clamped his teeth together and shook his head. "No."

After a few seconds, Bill stood up. "Well, George, we just thought you might have some insight we were missing. All we have you on is falsifying a rental agreement. Not much. Thanks for coming in."

George got up and turned to leave.

"Unless we charge Ginnie for Owens's death. Then, you could be an accessory to murder."

Weeks stopped as if he'd hit a stone wall.

"See, here's my dilemma, George. I've got you renting the storage unit. I've got Ginnie putting the painting in that same storage unit. And in between, the painting was stolen and Nat Owens was killed. Where did the switch take place? Where did your part stop and Ginnie's start? See my problem?"

George kept his gaze on the floor. More beads of sweat formed on his forehead. Still he said nothing.

"'Fore these attacks on Ms. Moore, Ginnie had a clean record. Not even a parking ticket." Glothe cleared his throat. "But you… heard you've been involved in political dirty tricks in the past."

Bill could see George react to that. His entire body stiffened for a moment. Without turning around, he said, "I don't believe in violence."

"Now, I know I could just put both of you up for the theft and the murder. Let the jury decide. Saves me having to figure it out. I could go fishing. Let the DA pitch it to a jury and the jury could pick one of you. Which one of you looks innocent and which one looks guilty. Or maybe just take both of you for both crimes." Bill reached in his pocket, pulled out a toothpick and stuck it in his mouth. "That's probably the thing to do. Takes it out of my hands. Takes that worry off my mind."

When the sheriff didn't say anything further, George started out the door.

"If you think of anything, call me, George. We can talk about it."

# Chapter 65

**Slim knocked once** and entered Glothe's office. Without saying a word, he placed a clean evidence bag with a piece of red metal in it on the sheriff's desk.

"What we got here?" Bill picked up the bag with the slightly bent oval of metal.

"That's a piece of trim from around the right headlight of Ginnie Leverett's car. Look closely, you're gonna find a small, round indentation. I'm bettin' it'll match perfectly to one of them brads on John Littlefellow's jeans."

"Maybe the one with the red paint on it?"

"I reckon."

"Run that over to the Smith County lab and see if they can determine if this red paint is the same as what we found on Littlefellow's jeans. And that the indentation could have been made by that brad. I'll call Willie and tell him you're coming and what we need. Don't forget to take the jeans with you. And be sure to sign everything in and out so there's no question about chain of custody."

Slim nodded and started to leave.

"'Fore you go, how'd they happen to have that piece of her car? Can they guarantee it's from her car?"

Slim reached behind and pulled a bag out of his back pocket. "They said they'd testify this came from her car. They'd kept it in this bag, with the car's VIN number written on it." He handed the bag to Glothe. "That VIN number is Ginnie's car."

"And why'd they keep this piece?"

"They said it was still in good shape and a piece they'd need sooner or later. It's from a Ford Fiesta and they do a lot of body work on Fiestas. Said we was lucky they hadn't used it already."

"I'm not opposed to a bit of luck now and then."

"They thought it was a bit strange. She said she hit a tree just outside of Rayville, where you leave the interstate and head into town. But the head body man said she'd hit something else, before the tree. Whatever that was, that's what got the light. I ask him if he'd guess what she might'a hit. He didn't wanna say, but I finally got through to him. He said it could have been a person.

"The guy took me out and showed me the tree. Sure 'nough, you could see where it'd been hit. 'Course, how anybody'd hit the tree at that spot's hard to figure. And it's not likely it would've damaged the headlight if they did. And the airbags had not deployed. So, she didn't hit it hard enough to do the damage she got."

"Well, see what Willie can tell us. And if he's gonna look at it today, you might just wait around and see what he gets. Good work, Slim."

Glothe watched his deputy leave, then picked up the phone. "Hi. Bring Ms. Leverett down to room 3."

For a moment, Bill's mouth opened and his eyebrows crowded together. "What do you mean she's not here? Where is she?"

He listened for two seconds. "Bail? I haven't heard anything about another bail hearing."

The sheriff smashed his hat on his head and marched out the door.

At the district attorney's office, the secretary tried to stop Glothe, but he stormed right into Abbott's office. "What the hell's going on over here?"

Abbott jumped up and glared at the sheriff. "What do you mean barging into my office and yelling at me? What's your problem?"

"My problem is, somebody had a bail hearing on one of *my* prisoners without telling me about it."

"You're talking about Leverett? Fran told me she *did* notify your office—before the hearing."

"Where is she? Who'd she notify?"

Abbott picked up the phone and punched a button. After a few seconds she said, "You'd better come to my office right now."

In less than a minute, Fran Summers rushed in. "What—." She saw the sheriff and stopped, her mouth open. Her left eye developed a nervous tic.

"Who'd you tell about the bail hearing? And when?" Bill demanded.

Summers was clearly shaken by the intensity of his questions. "Ah, I, ah, don't remember who it was. Just whoever answered the phone. I called about half an hour before the hearing."

"Whoever answered the phone. That's a non-answer. What happened at the hearing? I thought I'd laid out a solid case for no bail. Who was the judge?"

"Judge Hershal."

"What did you say about Leverett?" Glothe's tone remained at high danger level.

"What you said at the first hearing."

"About flight risk? And possibly other, more serious charges?"

"I told her Leverett was a flight risk, but she had a lawyer this time and he convinced the judge a bond would reduce the risk of flight."

"And the other charges?"

Summers was slowly getting her composure back. "I didn't bring those up. I don't know of any evidence you have or even what those charges might be."

"So, you didn't think having her held without bail might have suggested there was something more serious than a traffic accident?" He turned to Abbott. "I'm once again disappointed with this office. Your office leaked information which possibly will change an election. And now, a viable suspect involved in that, plus art theft and murder—most likely *two* murders—is released from jail." His face was red and his breathing heavy. He turned to Summers. "How much was the bail?"

"Five thousand dollars."

"Five thousand. And you didn't object to that?"

Summers barely shook her head.

"She ponies up maybe ten percent. So, for five hundred dollars she's free to disappear, or go out and kill again."

Glothe stomped out of the office.

# Chapter 66


**"Thanks Nana. I'll** be back at the house as soon as I get a rental car," Crystal said as Eula dropped her off at the rental agency.

"You'll probably git there 'fore I do. I gotta run a couple of errands. See ya there."


It took Crystal only a few minutes to secure a car, which she would return in Dallas Monday or Tuesday. She clicked on the radio as she headed for Nana's. The first thing she heard was Jim Bob's east Texas drawl. "Election's been over three days. I'm the leading vote-getter. So why don't we just get this wagon train moving and name me our next governor. The people of Texas have spoken. Jim Bob Wilson is the new governor of this great state."

Another man, apparently the interviewer, said, "They still need to wait for any votes from service personnel stationed overseas."

"Why wait? I've got the most votes. Those other votes, if any more come in, probably won't make any difference. Let's quit dragging this out."

Crystal cringed as she listened. Did Texans really want this man to lead them? She thought of how the race had looked back in July. Ron had about seventy percent of the votes, according to the polls. That represented what the people wanted. All the publicity unfairly suggesting Ron was involved in insurance fraud and had murdered his friend had swayed a lot of voters. Now, Jim Bob was claiming victory even before all the votes were tallied. *At least, I certainly hope there are more votes coming. And they vote for Ron.*

She pulled the rental car in next to Eula's storage shed and went into the house. Just thinking about Jim Bob as governor made her head hurt. She put ice in a glass and filled it with Dr Pepper. Maybe a little quiet time on the veranda would improve her head and her spirits.

She settled in a lounge chair and gazed out over the lake. Already she was feeling better. Birds were flitting around the feeders. A slight breeze sent a flurry of brightly colored leaves floating down to settle on the grass, still a rich green. The sun had turned the lake into a field of star bursts. Crystal closed her eyes and relaxed completely.

A few minutes later, she heard a car driving in. The car door slammed and a few seconds later, she heard the back door open and close. "I'm on the veranda, Nana," she called. "Grab a drink and come on out."

Thirty seconds later, she heard the telephone ring and the screen door open. She turned to speak to her grandmother and froze.

Ginnie was creeping across the porch, a large hunting knife in her hand.

# Chapter 67

**For an instant**, Crystal was stunned. Ginnie was supposed to be in jail. What was she doing here?

The knife answered that question.

She jumped up just as Ginnie slashed down. The knife caught her arm, the same one she had cut before, ripping through the bandages and stitches and reopening the wound. At that moment, the advice Juan Grande had given to her when they were dealing with drug lords in Mexico flashed in her mind. "Often, cause of death is hesitation."

In one motion, Crystal leaped up and slammed her chair into Ginnie. Then she jumped off the porch and ran toward the corner of the house, headed for her car. As she turned, she saw her attacker go back into the house. And at the same instant, she realized her purse with the car keys was in the living room.

Blood was running down her arm, but she ignored it. She took a step toward the lake. *I'll get in the boat and paddle out into the middle. Let her swim out there and I'll hit her over the head with a paddle.* But her next step was back around the house, as she remembered her cell phone was also in her purse. She'd have no way to contact Nana or Bill. So Nana would come back and unexpectedly run into a crazy woman intending to kill somebody.

Crystal rounded the corner of the house and ran into the small shed next to the cars. Surely she could find something there to defend herself. Sunlight drifted only a few feet into the building, leaving most of it in semi-darkness. It took precious moments for her vision to adjust to the dark interior. She looked for a pitchfork, a machete, Nana's shotgun. At that thought, Crystal almost froze. What if Ginnie found Nana's old shotgun? Eula never hid it. It was generally in easy reach.

Crystal said a quick prayer the old shotgun wasn't loaded.

Just then, she heard the screen door slam. Ginnie was coming out.

Crystal grabbed the only thing she could find, just as Ginnie appeared in the bright entrance. It was hard for her to see into the dark interior, but slowly, her eyes adjusted. "There you are. Time for us to settle this."

Crystal's eyes opened in surprise. "Settle what? You've been attacking me."

"You're trying to get me convicted and get the death penalty. It's you or me. This is strictly self-defense."

Crystal started to answer. Keep her talking. But the woman started in, knife held high in front of her.

Crystal threw one of the pieces of firewood she'd picked up. Ginnie slashed at it, catching the tip of her knife in it. The second piece of firewood, Crystal hurled at Ginnie's knee. It connected and Ginnie went down.

But, she kept the hunting knife firmly in her hand and she had dislodged it from the wood.

As she started to get up, Crystal dashed past her, knocking her down as she ran out the door. She thought of the shotgun. She didn't know exactly where it was. And then, could she really shoot this woman? She thought of the knife and decided she could. But where was the gun? Where was the ammunition? And while she was looking for it, Ginnie would be stabbing her.

Crystal turned away from the house and ran into the woods.

She always felt safe in her private tree house.

# Chapter 68

**As she ran**, she remembered how far her tree house seemed from the house when she was a child, or even a teenager. Now, she came upon it fast. It might have been closer, but it definitely took more effort to climb now than when she was a kid. She scrambled up slats nailed to the trunk of the tree and pulled herself into her safe haven.

Sounds from below said Ginnie was not far behind.

Once again, Crystal looked for a weapon, something to hold off her attacker. A kite with holes from the nibbles of animals. A waterlogged scrapbook. A beanbag chair suffering from years of neglect.

She'd often thought there should be a door or hatch to close the tree house from any visitors. As it was positioned, if a hatch covered the hole she just came through, there would be no way to get into her house. But, they had never done it.

She glanced over at the entrance in the floor. Ginnie's left hand had snaked up and grabbed the floor.

Crystal's first thought was to stomp on the hand. But she didn't. Ginnie was yelling crazy stuff and then the knife made its appearance, held firmly in Ginnie's right hand.

This time, Crystal stepped over and planted her foot down on Ginnie's right hand. More important, her shoe pressed down on the knife. Ginnie screamed as the steel ground her fingers into the wooden floor. She tried to pull the knife out, but as the pressure increased on her fingers, she yanked her hand out.

The knife stayed on the tree house floor. Crystal kicked it away.

Quickly, Ginnie had both hands on the floor, pulling herself up, leaning into the house, grabbing at Crystal's feet.

Crystal backed out of reach. With a maniacal roar, Ginnie jerked herself the rest of the way up into the house.

"No place to run now, is there, Miss Nosey?" She lunged at Crystal.

Crystal dodged to the side, connected a good right punch to Ginnie's stomach, and moved to the other side of the small room. Ginnie let out a grunt. The punch had knocked a little wind out of her, but she wasn't hurt. Instead, it made her even madder. "You've got blood on your arm," she said. "Why don't we just add a bit more — from your stomach?" She raised her hand, but she didn't have the knife now.

Crystal's arm ached and Ginnie's venomous tone was unnerving. But Ginnie didn't have her knife. As she started moving closer, Crystal kicked the beanbag in between them.

There, hidden under the bag was the knife.

Crystal and Ginnie saw it at the same time. Screaming, Ginnie lunged toward the beanbag and the knife. Crystal was closer but leaning away from it. She shot out her foot and kicked the knife. As it slid across the floor, Ginnie dove for it, sliding over the beanbag, grabbing at the knife as it dropped out the hole in the floor. She followed the knife out the hole.

A terrified gasp came from both women.

Ginnie managed to grab one of the steps nailed to the tree, and hooked one leg over the floor of the tree house. She stopped her fall. Upside down. But she couldn't pull herself back up. "Help me."

Crystal looked at her nemesis hanging precariously twenty feet about the ground, unable to pull herself up. A fall from there will probably kill her. I don't have to do anything. And I'll get rid of the person trying to kill me. Who's made my life hell for the last three weeks. And probably the person who killed Littlefellow and Ron's friend. Would serve her right. She got herself in that position.

"Help me. I'm losing my grip. I can't hold on much longer."

And she might pull me down with her.

Crystal carefully moved to the opening. With her right arm, she braced herself at the edge of the hole, and reached her left arm down. Ginnie clutched it and began to pull herself up.

Slowly, her hand began to slip down, unable to hold onto the bloody, slippery arm extended to her.

"I can't hold on. Too slippery. Give me your other arm." When Crystal didn't move quickly enough, Ginnie shouted, "Hurry up."

"My arm is bloody because you stabbed me. It's your own fault you can't hold on."

"Just give me your other arm. Hurry. My hand is cramping."

Crystal shifted her position and reached down with her right arm. Ginnie grabbed it and almost pulled Crystal down with her. But slowly, she managed to pull herself up through the entrance and collapsed on the floor.

After a minute of heavy breathing, she slowly got to her feet. "I won't stab you." She leaped toward Crystal. "I don't have my knife."

She slashed out, raking her nails across Crystal's injured arm, reopening the wound, sending a searing pain up her arm and into the shoulder.

Crystal punched her and jerked away. "I just saved you."

Ginnie ignored that. "You're the cause of all my problems," she yelled and lunged, knocking Crystal back. She fell over the beanbag, on her back, half on the floor, her feet on the beanbag.

As Ginnie jumped, Crystal raised her knee up and caught Ginnie squarely in the stomach, knocking the breath out of her, and shoving her to the side. Crystal scrambled up and hit Ginnie in the jaw with a roundhouse blow. Without hesitating a moment, she locked her hands together and caught her tormentor on the other side of her head.

Ginnie was dazed, but not knocked out. Crystal grabbed the ball of string still attached to the kite and began wrapping it round and round Ginnie hands. After a dozen circles, Crystal took the string up and began wrapping it around the woman's neck.

By the time Ginnie's head cleared, she was tied securely. She screamed and struggled, but could not break the string.

Crystal scooted over and started to climb down the tree.

"Where are you going?" yelled Ginnie. You can't leave me here. I can't climb down with my hands tied."

"I certainly hope not. But remember. This time, *I'll* have the knife."

And Crystal climbed down the tree.

# Chapter 69

**By the time** Crystal got back to the house, her heart was beating at nearly a normal rate. She had stopped shaking. Her breathing had slowed down and her stomach no longer cramped. But blood still seeped out of her arm. Even knowing Ginnie couldn't climb down from the tree house, she still glanced back every few steps to check.

Seeing Eula's car parked near the back door lifted her spirits.

Eula frowned. "You're bleeding again. What happened?"

"Ran into my old friend. She managed to reopen the cut."

"Let me look at it." Eula walked over and peeled back the bandage. "And where did you run into Ginnie. I thought she was in jail."

"So did I. But in fact, she's in my tree house right now."

"Details, gal. Give me the details."

"I will. And I don't think she'll bother us. But to be safe, get your shotgun while I call Bill."

Thirty minutes later, Bill and Slim had managed to get Ginnie down out of the tree house and Slim was taking her back to jail. In handcuffs.

Bill was questioning Crystal. "I think I strained my back getting her down from the tree house. How'd you get her tied up in there?"

Eula broke in. "How 'bout we ask how'd she get here? Your jail can't keep a crazy woman locked up?"

"That's a whole 'nother story. Let's just say I reckon Abbott will be looking for a new assistant."

"You gonna keep her locked up this time, or do I have to keep my shotgun loaded?" Eula asked.

"Oh, we're gonna keep her in jail for a long time. We're charging her with the murder of John Littlefellow, stalking, assault with a deadly weapon— three times, and most likely the murder of Nathanael Owens and art theft."

"Most likely?" said Crystal. "What's that mean?"

"I'm bringing George Weeks in this afternoon. And I'm going to lay out the situation. I'm nearly certain that either Ginnie or George stole the painting and killed Nat. If we can't determine which one, then we'll charge 'em both. One of 'em did it and my money's on Ginnie. George refused to say anything, but if it looks like he's going down, I think he'll roll."

"What about Littlefellow?" Eula said. "His death connected?"

"Got a good case on that one. Crystal, you remember Ms. Littlefellow said her husband saw a woman putting a painting in unit seventy-three, the day before he was killed. I think Ms. Leverett decided he could identify her, so she just eliminated that witness. The forensic guy will testify Littlefellow was killed by Ginnie's little red Fiesta."

"I'm impressed. Who'd think an old Billy Goat could solve this case?"

"Nana. Stop picking on Bill." Crystal turned to the sheriff. "I think you've done a great job."

"Thank you, Crystal. Your grandmother likes to tease me. But that's okay. I like her anyway." He picked up his Stetson and put it on his head. "Right now, I gotta run. I'm gonna see if Mr. Weeks is ready to roll."

"Good idea. But plan on coming Monday for the final election results. Ron will be here, and I think Mark and Brandi are coming out to help celebrate," said Crystal.

"Or comfort the loser," added Eula. "I hate to say it, but I still think old Jim Bob number two is gonna win."

* * *

This time, George Weeks was in an interrogation room. Nothing friendly. Grey metal table bolted to the floor. A straight backed, uncomfortable chair to sit in. The sheriff sat across from him in a padded swivel. One of the deputies stood behind and to the left of Weeks. A voice recorder was on the table.

"Have you had any other thoughts about the theft and murder? asked Bill.

"No," George said flatly.

"Well, I've been thinking about it. Still don't have an answer."

The table had a sketch pad on it and several colored pencils. The sheriff picked up the blue one. "I'm not much of an artist, so just forgive my drawings." On the left side of the paper, he drew a stick man. Under it, he wrote "Into Political Dirty Tricks." in the middle, he drew a frame and made some marks in it, representing a painting. To the right of the painting, he drew another stick man, lying on the floor. And then to the far right of the sheet, he drew a stick figure with a dress on. Under it, he wrote, "No prior record."

He let George study it for a minute. Glothe picked up a red pencil and circled the stickman on the left. "I've got you here, renting the storage unit under Ron Drake's name, a man you didn't know. Right?"

Weeks nodded.

Next Glothe circled the stickwoman on the right. "I've got Ginnie putting the painting in storage unit seventy-three. So, these two red areas are for certain." Bill drew a red line from the figure on the left toward the painting, but stopped short of it. Then he drew a line from the woman back toward the figure lying on the floor, but stopped short of it, also.

"See, I don't know where the exchange took place. Did you get the painting, kill Owens, and then give the painting to Ginnie? Or did you get Ginnie the storage unit and then she stole the painting and killed Owens?"

Bill took the red pencil and extended the line from the man to the left until it covered both the painting and the figure on the floor.

Weeks wiped sweat from his face. "There is no evidence I was ever in Ron Drake's house."

Bill nodded a couple of times. "Funny. Those are the exact same words Ginnie used." He picked up the red pencil again and drew a box around the words "Into Political Dirty Tricks."

"There was never any violence connected with those." George shook his head. "Never."

Glothe circled "No prior record" in red. "Ginnie never even had a parking ticket."

After a minute of silence, Glothe turned to his deputy. "Read him his rights and lock him up, Slim."

George jerked. "What? What for?"

"Material witness. I'm arresting you for conspiracy to commit murder and art theft."

Slim stepped over and put his hand on Weeks's shoulder.

"Wait," George shouted. "What about her attacking that Moore woman? "

"Where'd you hear about that?" asked Bill.

"Ah, ah, you told me. The other day."

"No. I did not. Slim, add conspiracy to commit assault with a deadly weapon." The sheriff got up and started out the door.

Slim pulled the suspect up.

"You can't do this," George yelled at Glothe's back.

Without looking around, Bill said, "'Course I can. Call a lawyer. Or call me when you have something to offer."

# Chapter 70

**Monday, November 12**

**Crystal, Mark, Bill**, Ron and Brandi were all seated in Eula's living room. The TV was turned on and tuned to KLTV. The sound was muted, but Eula held the remote in her hand, ready to bring up the volume on a moment's notice. Last Friday, the office of the state election judge announced the official election results in the governor's race would be disclosed at six p.m. Monday.

"Ron," Bill said. "I'm guessing you're not having a big election results party tonight. I thought that's what candidates did."

Ron laughed. "True. And I did, six nights ago. We had quite a party in Dallas. Lots of people. Lots of drinks. Lots of slapping on the back. Just no results, at least not the one we were there to celebrate. Of course, my campaign wanted to have another tonight, but I said, 'Let's wait.'"

"Bet they were disappointed," said Brandi.

Ron smiled and nodded. "I compromised. Said if I won, then we'd have a big celebration party next Saturday."

"That make 'em happy?" asked Eula.

"Not really. They said there'd be no anticipation, no suspense."

"And no disappointment," added Eula.

"Right. I said then we could just enjoy ourselves and celebrate why we were there."

"Free drinks, naturally" Crystal offered.

"Exactly. Anyway, that's why I'm here."

"For the free drinks?" Eula asked.

"Technically, it's for the apple cobbler. And I don't have to be locked up in a post-election party."

Mark pointed a finger at the sheriff. "Speaking of 'locked up,' Crystal said you had George Weeks in jail. Are you getting a clearer picture of what this was all about?"

"Clear might be overstating it. But slowly the fog is thinning. George lawyered up. Got a guy from Tyler people tell me is tough as a two dollar steak. I got word just 'fore I came over here they'll be ready to negotiate tomorrow."

Eula frowned. "Negotiate? Negotiate what?"

"I think he's ready to turn state's evidence. Give us some stuff so he can get off with a slap on the wrist."

Brandi waved a hand. "State's evidence? What's that even mean?"

Bill laughed. "Technically it means someone who might also be tried in a case agrees to give evidence to help the prosecution, the state."

"And he'd do this because?"

"Not out of any sense of justice. The person agrees to do it only if he gets a good deal from the prosecution, maybe doesn't get put on trial at all, or gets tried for a lesser crime."

"So, there really is some negotiation going on," Eula said.

Bill nodded. "You bet. And if this lawyer is as good as I hear he is, Abbott's in for some tough bargaining."

"Why's the state gonna bargain with a criminal?" asked Brandi.

"Might not have enough evidence. Needs some help. Often a case can't be made without some information this person can provide."

"But, how does he or she know—"

"Hold it," said Eula. "We're about to get some important news." And she turned up the sound.

An older man stood in front of the camera, looking a bit ill at ease. He held several pages in front of him, clutching them so tight they were wrinkled.

"That's the state election judge," said Ron. "Usually, he directs others to do this. That tells you he considers this rather important."

The election judge began by explaining about the Texas law giving overseas members of the military an extra five days to get mail-in ballots to his office. He stressed that those votes were *always* counted, but generally there were not enough to change the outcome.

"Why doesn't he just give us the final count and shut up," snapped Eula. "He's not enjoying this, and we sure ain't."

"Cut him some slack," said Brandi. "Remember, waiting is a virtue."

Eula clicked the sound up another notch.

The man on camera checked his papers. "In total, there were 4,578,247 votes cast in this election. Of that total, 2,109 did not vote for any candidate for the office of governor. That left 4,576,138 votes for governor. There were 923 write-in votes for various persons, animals and things."

"Animals? Other things? What's that mean?" asked Brandi.

Ron laughed. "People will write in votes for Mickey Mouse, Superman, R2-D2, all sorts of things."

The man on television continued talking. "… viable candidates. These numbers have been checked and rechecked. After tallying all votes arriving from overseas military personnel submitting mail-in ballots, the final count for the office of governor of Texas is as follows. The Green Party candidate: 52,554 votes. James Robert Wilson, Jr.: 2,261,231."

Mark started clapping.

"Ronald Drake: 2,261,430. Therefore, as the state election judge, I declare the winner for the office of governor of Texas in the 2018 election to be Ronald Drake."

Cheers, applause, whistles, and yells erupted in Eula's living room. Everybody pushed to get to shake Ron's hand first. The joyful commotion continued for some time. Then Eula called for quiet. The state election judge was gone from the TV screen and the image of a regular anchorman appeared.

"I've just been handed a notice from the Wilson campaign hedquarters which I'll read. 'Due to the closeness of the vote and the fact that Jim Bob Wilson had the most votes cast on election day, and now after waiting for other votes to appear from somewhere, Mr. Wilson's headquarters has announced it will seek a recount. With a difference of less than five-thousandths of one percent, it seems only fair to the people of Texas to make certain all votes were properly accounted for.'"

The newsman lowered his hand holding the note and looked at the camera. "Of course, an official call for a recount has not been registered with the state yet, but it appears the Wilson camp will be demanding one. So, this election isn't over yet, folks. Stay tuned."

# Chapter 71

**Eula had fixed** a beef brisket, baked beans, fried corn on the cob, and potato salad. She took the cornbread out of the oven and called to the crowd in the living room. "Grab your ice tea and come on in to the table."

Crystal and Mark led the way, followed by Ron, Brandi and Bill. When all were seated, Eula tapped her glass with a spoon. "This is a pretty special occasion and I want to say a few words. And you are all special to me, so please let's hold hands."

Eula bowed her head. "Lord, thanks for bringing these good folks together tonight. Thanks for protecting Crystal a bunch of times this last month. I hope You've already welcomed Nat Owens into Your house. And last, thanks for letting the people of Texas get a good governor, even if we don't deserve Ron. Regardless of how they voted, let everybody back Ron. And please guide Ron as he leads our great state. Amen."

When Crystal looked up, her eyes immediately focused on the place setting in front of her. A small, elegant box sat in the middle of her plate. She was sure it hadn't been there when she sat down. She picked it up and turned it around in her hand.

She looked at the box, then at Mark.

Gradually, all conversation at the table stopped as eyes turned to look at Crystal and the box she held.

"Well, open it up, girl." Eula's eyes twinkled.

Brandi held her hand out. "Here, I'll take it, just in case it's a cobra or something."

If Crystal heard Brandi's comment, she didn't react to it at all. Her eyes remained fixed on Mark.

Eula piped up. "I've seen one of those before. Here. Give it to me. I can handle it, cobra or whatever.

"Maybe I should X-ray it first," said Bill. "Just in case there's some explosive in it."

Brandi shook her head. "I'm sure what's in there is explosive enough it'll change lives."

Ron spoke up. "This is a time to be quiet and just observe, politely. In fact, as governor elect, I ask for quiet."

The teasing ceased as everybody complied. No fork clinked against china. No bowl or platter was moved.

Mark gave Crystal a slight smile, his eyes saying things only Crystal understood. Her eyes were glistening.

She bent over and planted a kiss on Mark's cheek.

Brandi couldn't keep quiet. "There's that glow she gets whenever she's around Mark."

Crystal looked over at her housemate, then the rest at the table. "Please ignore us. Go ahead and eat. But I'm very intrigued by this little box. So, I'm going to open it right now, right here, and see what's in it. The rest of you can go ahead with your eating."

"Ha!" said Brandi. "Besides, Mark's already told us what's in there, so we don't care whether you open it or not."

"Open it up," Eula said. "Mark hasn't told us a thing."

Crystal slipped the ribbon off the box and snapped open the lid.

Tears ran down her cheeks and she leaned over and kissed Mark lightly. He pulled her close and whispered, "Can I take that as a 'yes'?"

"Yes. Yes. And yes." She pressed her lips to his ear. "I love you. I have for a long time. And will forever."

Mark brought his lips to hers. Crystal put the box down and wrapped both her arms around him. They were together in their sphere and no one else existed.

Brandi reached over and picked up the box. "My Lord. Is this the biggest engagement ring I've ever seen?"

Bill eyed the ring. "I better check and see if the Hope diamond has been stolen."

Ron shrugged. "I guess getting her to move to Austin to head up my staff is out of the question."

"I may get to be a great-grandmother yet," Eula said.

## Chapter 72

**Crystal and Mark** found the November evening perfect and a chaise lounge on the veranda overlooking the lake provided a private place for the couple. With all the intrigue and anxiety of the last few weeks, there had been little time to just enjoy one another. With Crystal wearing her beautiful engagement ring, the two escaped from the celebration for their own private party. It was after midnight when they said goodnight.

The house was quiet. All the others had either left or gone to bed, but Crystal knew Nana would be awake, most likely reading a mystery novel. She knocked lightly on the door.

"Come on in, Crystal. I'm just reading."

Crystal walked in and sat on the edge of the bed. "Okay, Nana. Time to pay up."

"Pay up? What in thunder are you talking about, girl?"

"You know exactly what I'm talking about. You know I wouldn't forget about it. Give. Let's have the true story of you and Bill."

Eula dropped a card in the book to hold her place and laid it on the bed. "Well, not much to tell. You know we've been friends for - what? Going on fifty years. Your granddad and I started camping with Bill and Elsie, his wife, probably forty years ago." She smiled as she remembered those days. "Continued up until about a year before Dan died. Then Elsie passed close to a year later. I think Bill took that even worse than I did when your Granddad left."

Eula reached over for the glass of water on her bedside table and sipped a little, looking off into space.

"Nana, if this is too — "

"No, it's okay." She put the glass down. "So Bill and I were both alone. I don't know when, but maybe two years after Elsie died, Bill called and asked if I needed a ride to the big Christmas party in town. It was snowing and I guess he thought I ought not be driving. It was a fun night. First time I'd been partying since Dan died."

She smiled. "After that, Bill would call when anything was goin' on and ask if I needed a ride. Mostly, I didn't, but I always said, 'Sure. Come on by.' Then, last year, it was the Autumn Antique Car Rally in Nickel last fall, he called and asked if he could pick me up. I said, 'Is this like a date, Bill?'" She grinned and looked at Crystal. "He said, 'They have been, Eula.' That took me by surprise."

"So, we've been 'dating' since." She looked at her granddaughter. "What are you smirking about?"

"My nana dating. And I'm not smirking. I'm just ... surprised, that's all."

"Think I'm too old?"

"No. Not at all. I mean, I've seen you and Bill together many times, but I never ... Well, I just didn't think ..." She shrugged. "I don't know what I thought. I see him here a lot, but there's always been some 'sheriffy' thing going on. I just didn't ... pay attention enough."

"Okay. What'cha think now? What if we got serious?"

"Sounds like you already have. And I love it. Bill is such a great guy. And Granddad's been gone a long time. I'd be ... I *am* really happy for you. And Bill, too."

"Well, don't go plannin' a wedding or nothing."

"I'm not." Crystal leaned over and put her arms around her grandmother. "I just want you to be happy. Does he ever —"

"That's none of your business, young lady." She grinned. "But I do get lots of police protection."

"I think Bill is a really special guy."

"So do I."

"But you still call him Billy Goat most of the time."

"He'd be disappointed if I didn't. You know— well I guess you don't. But Bill worked for your great-grandfather in his store when Bill was, I don't know, maybe fifteen or so. And we called him Billy. And that made his name Billy Glothe. Back then, no one pronounced the 'e', so it was Billy Gloth, you know, a long 'O.' So, of course I started calling him Billy Goat. He'd miss it if I didn't. Probably think I was mad at him or something."

"Sometimes you're pretty tough on him."

"No more'n I was with your granddad, and you know how close we were. I'm tough on everybody. Bill knows he's a special ... friend to me."

For several minutes, Eula was lost in her thoughts and Crystal didn't want to intrude.

"I've never told anybody this, not even Melva. But sometimes, I'll call him Billy Goat." A grin came over her face. "And he'll say, 'Well, that makes you my Nanny Goat.'" She laughed. "'Course, he'd never say that in front of anybody else."

Crystal got up. "Well, I guess we both won. You got the real story of Mark and me, and now I have, at least some of the real story of you and Bill."

"You do. But don't you tell anybody about the 'Nanny Goat' bit. That's just between ..." She thought for a few seconds. "Between an old couple, the Billy and Nanny Goats."

# Epilog

## One Month Later

**"Glad you could** all make it," said the sheriff. "I really needed to fill Crystal and Ron in on the outcome of everything that happened back in October and November. Well, I guess last March too. Thought I might as well get the rest of you in at the same time."

Bill stood at the end of Eula's long dining table, where Crystal, Mark, Brandi, Eula and Ron sat.

"And what better way to do it," Eula interrupted, "than over some of my homemade pecan pie."

"That will make my speech tolerable."

Brandi stuck up her hand. "Did Jim Bob really pay for a whole recount?"

Ron answered that question. "Yes, he did. Cost his daddy a pretty penny. I actually gained a few dozen votes in it" He grinned. "He's still upset about those late armed forces votes being counted."

"I take it he never served in the military," Mark said.

"No," Bill said. "But, on to my report or Eula might serve the pie 'fore I finish."

Everybody laughed.

"Might anyway. Get on with it."

"Well, George Weeks finally turned state's evidence and filled in a few gaps. It was George who thought up the idea to steal Ron's painting, lock it away, and then later let it be found. His thought was Ron would get a lot of press when it was stolen. Then, when it's found in Ron's own warehouse, all that publicity turns to bad publicity, and consequently, lost votes. But, as happened, Ron collected the insurance and then it's found in his own warehouse. *Really* bad publicity and more lost votes."

Mark stuck up his finger. "Who knew what and when?"

Glothe nodded. "We were certainly interested in that question. But Ginnie and George, each said independently that nobody, not Jim Bob, not anyone else in the campaign headquarters, knew anything about it, either before or after. George said, without any prompting from me, that even Fran Summers, who was leaking all that information from the DA's office, didn't have a clue about the podirt, as he called it."

Brandi looked confused. "Podirt?"

"Stands for political dirty trick. George convinced Ginnie to go along. Said she was such a law abider, she was worried it might be illegal. But he convinced her that they weren't really stealing it, but just putting it away in Ron's own storage locker. So, she agreed to get it. Said when she was young she was good at sneaking around where her father could never see or hear her. But, as she was coming out with the painting, Nat Owens comes in, finds the painting missing and calls Ron. And then he says he'll wait until Ron gets home."

"So, she's gonna get caught," offered Brandi.

"Right. She'd hidden in the pantry and Nat sat down right across the room. She was stuck. So, she grabs a can of tomatoes, steps out and hits Nat on the head. She says she just meant to knock him out for a minute so she could make her escape. Didn't mean to kill him."

"But," Eula interjected, "She'd stepped over the line with the theft. She was on a slippery slope."

"Right," said Bill. "She'd crossed a line. Then she found out that since he was killed while she was committing a crime, she could be tried for capital murder and face the death penalty. The slope is getting steeper and slipperier. Then she remembered John Littlefellow saw her putting the painting in the storage unit and convinced herself he was going to cause her to get the death penalty. Justified that killing him was really self defense."

Crystal nodded. "She used that on me, too. Said her attacks on me were self-defense."

"I think she'd convinced herself to the point she believed it," Bill said. "I don't believe Abbott has decided exactly how she'll handle it. But I can guarantee you Ginnie's lawyer is gonna have trouble if he tries to push self-defense."

"What about George?" Eula asked. "He's the one who got this rodeo started. What's he facing?"

"Not much. With his plea bargain, he did okay for himself. I honestly don't think he foresaw what would happen. He said Ginnie was so reluctant at the onset he couldn't believe what she became. He claims he urged her to leave town immediately after Owens was found dead. That would have saved Littlefellow, a true innocent in all this. And it would have eliminated all the attacks on Crystal."

"Why *was* she hacking away at Crystal? asked Brandi.

"She thought Crystal was the only one who might link her to the murders. 'Course, she was right. But again, if she'd just backed off, even Crystal wouldn't have gotten anywhere." Glothe shrugged.

Crystal nodded. "Absolutely true. Until she locked me in the storage shed, I didn't even know it was a woman. Her Eight Second Angel boots set me on to her."

"Changing the subject, Ron, how's the new job?" Mark asked.

"For another month, I'm still retired, though I can't tell it. Trying to get everything set up is mind numbing. I might get a couple of days off for Christmas. And I will take off three hours to watch Texas in the Sugar bowl. Other than that, it's nose to the grind-stone time. Remind me, why did I want this job?"

Everyone laughed.

Ron spread his hands wide and looked at Eula. "How about some pecan pie to help fortify me for the days ahead? After all, it is the official State Pie of Texas."


## The End


Please read the next page. Thank you.

# From the Author

I hope you enjoyed *Political Dirty Trick*. If you did, it would be a great favor to me if you would leave a brief review on Amazon. It can be as little as two or three sentences - what you thought of the book, any particular character you liked, or any particular scene or situation you found enjoyable or well-done. Reviews are very important to writers. They can make the a big impact on the success of a book.

Click this link https://amzn.to/2pIHMqs (or if not clickable, copy and paste it in your browser). Then, scroll down to reviews and select 'Write a customer review.' Thank you.

If you did not like the book, please email me at: jim@jamesrcallan.com and tell me what didn't work for you. Of course, feel free to write me directly if you liked it.

## The Crystal Moore Suspense Series

*Political Dirty Trick* is the third book in the Crystal Moore Suspense series. The first book is *A Ton of Gold*. Book number two (2) in the series is *A Silver Medallion*.

An excerpt from each of those books is included here, starting on the next page. Please enjoy other adventures of Crystal.

## For Book Clubs or Discussion Groups

Book notes and discussion points are available for each of the Crystal Moore Suspense books. If you would like a copy, please request a set, by book title, in an email to: jim@jamesrcallan.com. I'll rush you a copy.

## Some Readers' Comments on *A Silver Medallion,*

<u>A Silver Medallion</u> is a gripping, action-packed adventure from talented author James Callan. Crystal Moore is a tough and savvy heroine who knows no fear.

**—New York Times Bestselling Author Bobbi Smith**

*A Silver Medallion*, the second title in the Crystal Moore Suspense series, reads like a gold-medal thriller from page one, when Crystal Moore and her grandmother take in a young Hispanic woman who escaped from a drug-dealing, modern-day Texas slaveholder. Crystal emerges as a compelling heroine with a big heart and bold personality, and her fierce independence allows Callan the creative freedom to take his character into the heart of Mexico to rescue two young girls she's never met. ...

**—From BookLife Prize in Fiction, Critic's Report**

A Silver Medallion (A Crystal Moore Suspense Book 2) by James R. Callan is the thrilling sequel to A Ton of Gold. ... Although a sequel, A Silver Medallion is a great stand-alone novel. ... I really enjoyed reading this book! It was interesting and full of action. The page-turning suspense kept me up well into the pre-morning! I look forward to reading future Crystal Moore suspense novels by James R. Callan.

**—Alyssa Elmore for Readers' Favorite ( Barnes & Nobel)**

# A Silver Medallion

**A Crystal Moore Suspense, Book Two**

## Chapter 1

CRYSTAL Moore drove slowly along the sandy road that curved through the property she had roamed as a child. Her grand-parents had christened it "The Park" when they purchased it over fifty years ago. To Crystal, they could have named it Serenity. The tall, stately Southern pines, the oak and hickory trees, the mirror-still lake, the peaceful quiet, all worked to cast a spell of tranquility over her.

Crystal's maroon LeSabre crested the hill. Two hundred feet ahead, her grandmother stood under a maple tree, its autumn foliage creating a golden halo above her grey hair. Eula Moore was staring at the small storage shed about twenty feet behind her cedar-shake house. She aimed a double-barreled shotgun at the door of the building.

Fifty feet from Eula, Crystal switched off the ignition, eased out of the car, and moved forward, careful not to crack a twig or crunch a dried leaf. Now she saw her grandmother's right index finger curled around the trigger. Whatever was going on, she did not want to distract her Nana.

Eula Moore pointed the shotgun at the shed, her wrinkled hands as steady as those of an eye surgeon. "Don't make no sudden moves. I got a nervous trigger finger. I might just blow your head off."

Nothing moved.

"Now, very slowly, come on out in the open, and keep them hands over your head where I can see 'em."

Experience told Crystal her grandmother had heard the car, but Eula's attention never left the shed. The elderly woman stooped down, gaze still fixed on the building, picked up a rock with her left hand and made a sweeping, underhanded throw. As the chunk of limestone arched skyward, Eula pulled the ancient shotgun up and once more trained it on the shed.

The rock struck the tin roof with a satisfying bang. No animal came bolting out the door. The noise echoed and died away. The birds stopped their chirping. All was quiet.

Crystal crept up beside her grandmother. "What's in there, Nana?" she whispered.

"Animal. Person. Beats me. But I didn't git to seventy-five being careless."

Eula Moore, five feet two inches tall, ninety-five pounds with short-cropped grey hair, held a strategic position. No one could leave the shed without coming into her gun's sight. And no one could see her without first revealing himself. Eula looked frail, but her voice was strong, her will stronger. "Better come out 'fore I start shootin'."

A slight breeze wiggled the leaves on a towering oak tree shading the area. A squirrel sat motionless. The scene was as peaceful as a painting of a country lane. Except for the shotgun.

A few moments passed. Then a single finger came into view. Gradually, it turned into a whole hand, waving in a small arc. "*Por favor, no dispare.*" The tiny brown hand fluttered again. The voice quavered slightly. "Please. No shoot. No shoot."

Eula didn't lower the gun or take her gaze off the shed. *"Por favor? Spanish?"* Eula said to Crystal. Then to the tiny hand, *"Manos arriba."*

Now, two hands waved. But no body appeared.

"You need to work on your Spanish, Nana. He may not know what you're saying."

Eula snorted. *"Pardon* me. I didn't go to S.M.U. Or Stanford. Maybe you can do better."

Crystal turned toward the shed. *"Salga con las manos arriba.* Come out with your hands up."

A foot materialized in the opening. "Hands up." Then a body began to emerge. "Hands up."

Was it a child? Little more than five feet tall and slender as broomcorn, she could have been a girl of fourteen. Her uncombed hair, nearly reaching her waist, appeared as black and shiny as obsidian. Pink and blue embroidery decorated the rough-woven, white dress hanging from her shoulders and stopping just short of her scratched knees. Well-worn leather sandals revealed feet accustomed to no shoes at all.

The small hands trembled slightly as the young Mexican edged forward, but she held her head high and her back ramrod straight.

Eula waggled the barrel of the shotgun at the girl. "Far enough. Hold it right there. *Alto."* Eula focused on the girl, but spoke to Crystal. "Okay. So I don't remember my Spanish good enough to find out what I got here. See what you can do. But don't get in my line of fire."

A cloud drifted away, allowing the sun to play fully on the girl's face. This was *not* a child. Those large eyes could not develop such sadness, such pain, in such a short life.

*"¿Como se llama?"* Crystal asked.

The thin young woman maintained her focus on the gun. "Rosa. Rosa Bonita Lopez."

*"¿Habla Ingles?"*

*"Un poco."*

"*Hablo Español un poco. Vamos probando con Ingles.* Let's try English," said Crystal. The young woman's expression did not change, nor did her attention waiver from the shotgun. "Okay. Your name is Rosa Bonita."

"*Si.* Yes."

"And what were you doing in the shed?"

The Mexican woman's forehead wrinkled and she tilted her head slightly to one side. *Is she puzzled by the English or by what kind of an answer to give?* Crystal tried Spanish again. "*¿Que hacias en el cobertizo?*"

After several seconds, Rosa looked at Crystal. "Food."

"You were looking for food?"

"*Si.*"

"Are you hungry?"

Eula made a small grunt. "Dumb question."

"*Si.* Yes."

"When did you eat last? *¿Cuándo comiste por última vez?*"

"*Ayer en la mañana.*"

"Yesterday morning!" Crystal turned to her grandmother. "She's probably starving. Let's take her in and give her something to eat. Then we can find out why she's here."

Eula didn't move or lower the shotgun but Crystal walked over, smiling, took the young woman's hand and led her into the house.

\#

Inside Eula's large country kitchen, Crystal gave Rosa a tall glass of orange juice while Eula put the finishing touches on a chicken and rice meal she'd been preparing for her granddaughter's arrival. Rosa drank the juice without stopping and her dark, wary eyes remained focused on the chicken as Eula moved it from pan to serving dish.

"Why haven't you eaten?" Crystal asked.

"*No dinero.*"

"Where do you live?"

"*No casa. No casa.*"

"No home?" Crystal glanced at Eula, then back at the Mexican girl. "*¿Por qué?*"

"I run away."

"From your husband? *¿Esposo?*"

"No." Her sad eyes closed for a moment, then softly, "No."

"Parents? *¿Padres?*"

"No. From *hombre malo*."

"*¿Quien?* Who is the bad man?"

"*Señor* Blackwood." Rosa scrunched her mouth and eyes as if she had bitten into a piece of spoiled fruit.

"Who is he? What is your relationship to him? A relative? *¿Un familiar?*

The Mexican woman shook her head violently from side to side. "No. *No familiar.* I am ... his ..." She furrowed her brows and cocked her head to one side. "How to say *esclava?*"

Crystal looked down for a moment as she searched her limited Spanish vocabulary for a translation. Finally, she looked up at Rosa. "The only English word I can think of for *esclava* is ... slave."

Rosa's head bobbed up and down. "*Si. Si.* Slave. I am his slave."

# Reader Comments on *A Ton of Gold*

Overcoming obstacles is a theme about which many authors write. Callan has perfected that art in this riveting tale of deceit and disappointment. Throw in a legend and the reader is hooked.
**— Book Editor, Amazon Review**

A Ton of Gold captivates the reader and doesn't let go. Great plot, great characters, great dialogue. I would recommend it to anyone.
**— Paul Paris, Amazon Review**

I had read "Cleansed By Fire" and thought Mr. Callan couldn't write a better book. I was wrong! "*A Ton of Gold*" is one of those books that keep your attention from Prologue to Epilogue
**—sunnyreader, Amazon Review**

The characters are realistic and interwoven into a wild and wicked story. Loved Eula and Chrystal.
**—Amazon Customer**

Loved the characters and the ending is unique and unexpected.
**—G. Powell, Amazon review**

"*A Ton of Gold*" by James R. Callan hooked me on the first page of the Prologue and kept me eagerly turning the pages through the last word of the Epilogue. The plot was beyond intriguing and the characters were so well developed that I felt as if I knew them by the time I finished reading the book.
**—Patricia Gligor, Amazon review**

*A ton of gold* is a story woven to perfection.
**—Ladywordsmith, Amazon review**

# Excerpt from *A Ton of Gold*

## A Crystal Moore Suspense, Book 1
## A Contemporary Suspense

**Crystal** Moore's eyes shot wide open and she sat bolt upright. Disconnected pictures, all bleak, flashed in Crystal's mind, as a chill descended over her. "Tried to kill you!" Her voice almost failed her. Her chest felt like something was crushing it. She could feel her blood pulsing in her veins. "Are you Okay?"

"I'm fine."

"Where are you?"

"Home. Where else would I be?"

*In the hospital.* "What happened?"

"Some fool tried to run me off the road."

Crystal's back relaxed slightly. "Nana, I don't think he was trying to kill you."

"Were you here?"

Crystal reminded herself that this was her grandmother, her only living relative. "Okay. Tell me what happened."

"Well, I was going to town. And some redneck tried to run me off the road. Clear as could be. Meant to kill me!"

Crystal rolled her eyes toward the ceiling. She worried about her grandmother driving, or living alone, for that matter. At seventy-six, reactions slowed. Maybe her grandmother shouldn't be driving at all.

"Every week somebody tries to run me off the road while I'm driving to work. He just wasn't paying attention, that's all."

"That dog won't hunt. *I* was paying attention. I saw him. He looked right at me, then pulled over in my lane. I could see it in his eyes. He intended to run me right off the road—or hit me head-on. He cotton-pickin' meant to kill me."

"Did you call the police?"

"What for? They'd give me the same routine you are."

Crystal took a deep breath and let it out slowly. "What do you want me to do, Nana?"

"Nothing. Nothing you can do."

Crystal struggled to keep her voice as neutral as possible. She dearly loved her grandmother but Nana could be difficult sometimes. She saw the world very clearly, with seldom a doubt on how to interpret it. "Then why did you call me? Just to worry me?"

"No." Crystal detected a trace of hurt feelings in her grandmother's voice. "Because I wanted you to know somebody's trying to kill me. And if I die under questionable circumstances, I want you to tell the police it was *murder*. And make sure they *do* something. You know how old Billy Goat is. If you don't stick his nose in it, he can't find—"

"Nana!" Crystal cut her off. "Bill Glothe's been the sheriff for ten years—and your friend a lot longer than that."

"Ugly truck. One of those, ah, what-cha-ma-callits. Ah, four-by-fours. Big as a dump truck. Puce."

"Puce? They don't make puce-colored cars."

"Well, maybe he painted it, I don't know. Looked puce to me."

"Are you Okay? Is there anything I can do for you?"

"Yes and no. I'm fine and there's nothing you can do. Just remember what I told you. Anything happens, get Billy Goat on it."

# The Father Frank Mystery Series

Callan also has a cozy mystery series, featuring a minister in a small Texas town who gets pulled into arson and murder investigations when they involve members of his church.

Here are some reader comments on this series.

I started Cleansed by Fire this past rainy Sunday afternoon...couldn't put it down, and read it straight thru till I finished it late that night .
**—Bob Hostler, Amazon review**

I really enjoy cozy mysteries when they're this good. And when a writer makes a crime-solving priest as interesting to a Southern Baptist reader as James Callan has done, he's really accomplished something.
**—Roger Bruner, Amazon review**

Move over, father brown, there's another temporal avenging angel in town! when father frank deluca learns through confession that his confessor knew in advance that a church was going to be burned, he is anxious to find this arsonist.
**—ELIZABETH ERIKSE, Amazon Review**

What a delightful mystery! Father Frank is clever and an all around great character. James Callan is a terrific writer who makes all his characters interesting and realistic.
**—Bonnie Engstron, Amazon review**

# About the Author

**James R. Callan** took a degree in English, intent on writing. But when writing didn't support a family, he returned to graduate school in the field of mathematics. He pursued a career in mathematics and computer science. Along the way, he received grants from the National Science Foundation, NASA, and the Data Processing Management Association. He has been listed in Who's Who in Computer Science, and Two Thousand Notable Americans.

But writing was his first love. He has published a dozen books and picked up a number of awards along the way. Political Dirty Trick, the third Crystal Moore Suspense book, is his latest mystery/suspense book.

Callan lives with his wife in east Texas and Puerto Vallarta, Mexico. They have four grown children and six grandchildren. His website is: **www.jamesrcallan.com**. If you enjoyed this book, sign up to receive *occasional* updates on Callan's books at: **www.jamesrcallan.com/news**. *I absolutely promise NOT to spam you, or give, trade or sell your email address.*